DEAD GIRL BLUES

DAVID SODERGREN

Paperbacks and Pugs

ALSO BY DAVID SODERGREN

THE FORGOTTEN ISLAND

"This book read like a blood-drenched love letter to Lovecraft, and didn't hold back on the splatter factor. But what impressed me more was Sodergren's masterful control of dread[...]this book is handled with impressive authority and confidence."

James Fahy, author of *The Changeling* series

"Nothing is going to prepare you for the mayhem Sodergren throws at you once he shows his cards. A novel packed with old movie references, gore, violence, humour, wit and originality."

Gavin Kendall, *Kendall Reviews*

NIGHT SHOOT

"Night Shoot is wildly entertaining. If you're not laughing, you're scared out of your mind. A final girl story people will be talking about for a long time."

Sadie Hartmann, *Mother Horror*

"Sodergren has a gift for storytelling"

Steve Stred, Author of *Ritual* and *The Stranger*

Cover art and illustrations by Connor Leslie
Graphic design by Heather Sodergren

ISBN:9798620351732

To Dario, Mario and Sergio
Thanks for all the good times.

1

At around seven pm on a crisp October evening, Jessica Chalmers stabbed a man twice in the neck and made her escape.

She had her reasons, and now she ran.

She didn't know where she was, or where she was going, but still she ran, using only the moonlight to guide her. They were out there, tracking her, so she avoided the mud, sticking to the grass despite roots that threatened to trip her with every step. Mud meant footprints, and footprints meant they could follow her.

She was surprised at how clearly she was able to think, under the circumstances.

Wizened branches clawed at her naked body. There had been no time to grab her clothes. Just her phone. Thank god she had her phone. Maybe, just maybe, this could all be worthwhile. She realised she still clutched the knife in her bony hand, the man's blood wet and glistening on the serrated blade. She glanced back and saw nothing but the silhouettes of the trees.

But she knew they were following. They couldn't let her live, not now. Not after what she'd seen.

Not after what she'd done.

And so she ran, head down, arms swinging. She needed clothes. Not out of any sense of modesty, but because her pale body would be a beacon in the shattered moonlight that slanted through the branches. Again, the clarity of her thoughts surprised her. If only she had seen things this plainly before. Days ago. Weeks, *months* even. Before it all began, before she got involved.

Oh hindsight, you wretched, useless bastard.

She stopped a moment and leaned against a tree, her breath coming in hitched gasps, heart hammering like an outboard motor, and then she was off again, running for her pitiful life.

She heard a noise, someone shouting. Or did she? She wasn't going to wait and find out. Something caught her foot and she tripped and went sprawling across the grass. The phone and the knife spilled from her hands and she crawled forwards, gasping for breath, sweeping her arms in front of her in a panic. She touched the knife and grabbed it, closing her fingers around the blade, cutting herself, barely noticing.

A light behind her, in the distance. Torchlight. She had to go, *now*, but she couldn't leave the phone. She felt sick, her stomach tightening as she gripped the knife, praying she wouldn't have to use it. Not again. There had been so much blood last time.

So much blood.

A beam of light illuminated a tree twenty feet from her, sweeping through the night. Damn them. Damn them all to hell. Her fingertips scraped the cold metallic sheen of the phone and she almost yelped with joy. She seized it and hurtled through the trees, angling away from her pursuers.

That was too close.

She stole a look over her shoulder, blood pumping furiously through her veins. The torchlight was far away. She had lost them.

For now.

She had to get back to the city, back to Edinburgh.

It was her only chance.

Beyond her the forest ended and became a field that stretched to the dark horizon. She would be out in the open. Exposed. She came to the edge of the trees and knelt, looking for signs of life. The field was huge. There was no way around.

Black clouds swept across the sky like warships, obscuring the glow of the moon. As the field dipped into inky darkness, Jessica took off running again. The torchlight had vanished. Had she really lost them? Could she be that lucky? Too late, she turned and saw the man. She didn't even have time to scream.

Time was in short supply these days.

They collided, crashing to the ground in a tangle of limbs. Without thinking, Jessica raised the knife and brought it down into his chest, once, twice, again and again, blind panic drawing its midnight veil over her eyes.

Oh god what if it's a farmer oh god what have I done...

She stopped, her hand shaking. The blade was covered in straw. She touched the rigid corpse and felt the wooden pole of his spine.

She had just stabbed a scarecrow to death.

Under different circumstances, it would have been funny. The rotten-turnip head leered at her as moonlight edged its way past the clouds, clumps of hay askew within the worn tweed jacket.

'Jesus,' she said, getting to her feet.

She paused. This spooky fucker might yet come in handy. She undid the buttons and stripped the jacket from the scarecrow, stuffing her thin arms through the sleeves. It hung over her shoulders like a sack, several sizes too big. So what? She wasn't strutting down the catwalks of Milan, for fuck's sake. She tried to wrestle the trousers off, inexplicably feeling bad about doing so, but they had been nailed to the post. When she stood, the baggy jacket hung down to her knees like a little girl rummaging through her father's closet. She tucked the phone into a pocket. Ahead, beyond the rolling hills, thousands of lights twinkled dreamily, a distant galaxy, a science-fiction.

The city.

She staggered onwards with renewed vigour. For the first time in a long time, she was filled with a sense of hope.

Home.

It was far away, yes, but she could see it. A train roared past, startling her, and this time she did scream. Blurred faces stared impassively out the window, oblivious to the half-naked girl in the field, the one clutching the bloody knife. Then it was gone and the oppressive silence resumed its chokehold on the countryside, the harsh lights of the train sparkling across the field and disappearing, heading towards the city.

Towards Edinburgh.

Jessica checked her pockets, finding the comforting coldness of the phone. She was tired, her legs throbbing, the soles of her feet bleeding, and yet she kept walking, following the railway line.

Squinting into the night, she thought she could make out a dim light further down the track.

A station.

She choked back a sob and resumed her journey. If she could get on a train, she'd be safe.

She hoped.

2

Willow Zulawski lounged on her bed in a towel, sipping a gin and lemonade and gazing at her phone. From the flat above came the regular monotonous thump of footsteps, as if Frankenstein's Monster himself had moved in. She raised the volume on her laptop to drown out the noise with the sound of Slayer.

'You going to reply or not?' asked Catherine Howards.

'I will,' said Willow, only half-listening. 'Just thinking of what to say.'

'Good. For a moment there, I thought we'd lost you. You've been staring at that thing like you're hypnotised.'

Willow ignored her friend and long-time flatmate, lit a cigarette and re-read Mitch's message.

Looking 4ward to 2nite x

'What do I even say to that?' shrugged Willow, tipping her ash out the window onto the street three storeys below. Cat — she hated the name Catherine, felt it made her sound like a granny — finished her drink and snuggled into the oversized easy-chair in the corner of Willow's room.

'Just say "me too" or something. I dunno, just send a damn text already. I thought you were leaving at eight?'

'I will.'

'Willow, it's quarter-past eight and you're still in a towel.'

'I know, it's just...I mean, who spells forward with a four? We all have predictive text now, there's no excuse.'

Cat rolled her eyes. 'I wouldn't let it bother you. He's probably excited. It is a *he* tonight, yeah?'

Willow nodded grimly. 'Why has he used a number two for tonight, but not instead of to? Who does he think he is, Prince?'

Cat refilled her glass, giving herself a double measure of gin. 'Again, I wouldn't let it bother you.'

Willow tapped at the keyboard and hit send. 'There, done.' She stood, letting the towel fall to the floor, and weaved her way across the bedroom carpet, avoiding the piles of laundry.

Cat looked up from her own phone, then over to the window. 'You know the curtains are open, yeah?'

Willow rummaged through the contents of her underwear drawer. 'What's your point?'

Cat sighed. 'Guess I don't have one. What did you text him?'

'I said "me too", but I spelled "too" as the number three,' said Willow, as she pulled on her underwear.

'That makes no sense.'

'Something for him to ponder. God, maybe I should've put a wee winking face emoji. He might think I'm an idiot.'

'Where'd you meet this one anyway?'

Willow fished out a pair of weathered jeans and held

them up for Cat, seeking approval. Cat nodded her head. 'Perfect.'

'Nah,' said Willow, wrinkling her nose. 'I'm going on a date, not to dispose of a corpse.' She discarded the jeans, digging further into the back of her closet. 'Plenty of Fish.'

'Huh?'

'You asked where I met him. Plenty of Fish.'

Cat sipped her drink. It was reassuringly strong. 'I thought all the kids used Tinder these days.'

'I've exhausted Tinder's supply,' said Willow, holding up a black dress. Once again, Cat nodded, trying to muster some enthusiasm for the charade.

'That's it,' she said. 'That's the one.'

Willow looked unsure. 'I dunno...I'd feel like we're going to a funeral.'

'Why are all your references so morbid?'

Willow had no answer.

'You're so lucky, though,' said Cat. 'Being bi, I mean. You get the best of both worlds.'

'I seem to end up with the *worst* of both worlds,' said Willow from inside the wardrobe. She wrestled a green dress free and held it aloft like a talisman. 'How about this?'

'Good god, Will, you need to go shopping. But I suppose it'll have to do. Jesus, at least iron it first!' she cried, as Willow unzipped the wrinkled garment.

'You're like a nagging wife.'

'Well I know you don't wear clothes at *your* work, but sometimes you have to put in a bit of effort.'

'I wear clothes,' grumbled Willow, her eyes darting around the room, trying to locate the iron.

'Thongs and nipple tassels don't count.' Cat paused. 'You have told him you're a stripper, yeah?'

'Don't be daft. Men are easily confused. If I tell him I'm a stripper he'll hear porn-star and expect a fuck. To be honest, women aren't much better either, so I try to keep that little nugget of info quiet at the start, maybe tell them on the second or third date.'

'You ever been on a third date?'

'Once,' said Willow, watching as Cat laughed. She turned to her friend. 'I fucking hate this. Why do we put ourselves through this humiliation?'

'Shut up and iron your dress. I'm sick of looking at your perfect wee arse.'

'I can't find the iron. Or the board.' She looked at Cat. 'And you're drunk, you lush.'

Cat giggled. Willow made an executive decision and abandoned the ironing. If Mitch — that was his name, right? — was more concerned with a few creases in her dress, then something had gone very, very wrong. She wasn't holding out any hope. She never had much luck with either sex, and sometimes wondered who's fault that really was. She knew people — men in particular — found her intimidating. Tall, beautiful and unafraid to speak her mind. Strong, too, thanks to her ability to work the pole at her job. Her last date, with some wanker named Chris, had ended with a disastrous arm-wrestling match, causing Chris to flip out and upend their table before storming off.

She hadn't been back to that particular bar.

'Willow, stop staring at me like a creep.'

Willow laughed, not realising she had been. 'Sorry, just thinking.'

'Well think and get dressed. I'm almost out of gin.'

'That's not like you.'

Outside, a police car raced by, the siren wailing deep into the night as the first drops of rain fell. Willow crossed the room and stubbed out her cigarette, pausing the music halfway through *Angel of Death*. She listened to the water spattering her window, gradually building in intensity.

'Willow, that guy's staring at you,' said Cat, her voice sharp with agitation.

'Who?'

'The weirdo in flat three.'

Willow peered through the drips that scurried down the glass. He was there all right, binoculars in hand. Her own personal voyeur. He watched, making no effort to hide, his upper body framed by the window.

'I bet he's naked from the waist down,' said Willow.

'God, probably. He's disgusting.'

'Don't worry, he's holding the binoculars with both hands.'

'What do you...oh Will, that's horrible. You shouldn't joke about it. We should call the police.'

'Ah, he's a harmless old perv. I just wish I could figure out how to charge him.' She turned to Cat and smiled. 'You're the only person I give a free show to.'

Cat nodded and stared into her drink. 'A show I never asked for, nor wanted.'

'People pay good money to see me strip. You should count yourself lucky.'

'Put some clothes on,' snapped Cat.

Willow smiled. 'Hey...shall I give him something to stare at?'

Cat raised an admonishing finger. 'Willow, don't. Don't encourage him. I swear to god, keep your knickers on.'

Willow winked at Cat and hooked a finger in the waistband of her underpants. She slowly lowered them, knowing the reaction it would get. She saw it every night at work, could read it in the faces of the men who watched her.

'Willow, I'm serious, stop it! He could be a stalker or

something,' cried Cat, getting out of the chair and storming over to the window, grabbing the curtains and yanking them shut.

Willow pouted at her, then broke into a goofy grin.

'It's not funny,' said Cat. 'There're all sorts of sickos out there. Now stop smiling and get dressed. Honestly, you're a fucking nightmare sometimes.'

3

Jessica crouched by the side of the railway line. Ahead of her sat the lonely station, one of those ridiculous rural ones in the arse-end of nowhere, just a brick shelter and a bench. A solitary crisp wrapper fluttering in the chilly autumn breeze was the only movement.

She wasn't sure if that was a good thing. It meant they weren't here already, waiting for her, but also that she was still alone. A thought hit her; what if the train didn't stop here? Who would need to get on or off in the middle of the countryside?

She had little choice. She snuck alongside the fence until she reached the platform. The station sign had been so heavily graffitied it was illegible, and the timetable was no use, the glass panel broken and the information long gone.

The inside of the shelter was no better, covered from floor to ceiling in spray-painted obscenities. Phone numbers advertising good times, invitations to suck or sit on various appendages — it reminded Jessica of an oversized bathroom cubicle, with the pungent aroma to match. Glass bottles and empty beer cans littered the ground next to used condoms and a sanitary pad. Wary of stepping on any sharp objects, she sidled her way inside as the heavens opened and the rain began to pour.

The memories flooded through her mind like an LSD flashback. It was the smell that triggered her, that cloying, damp, rotten stench. Only then, standing alone in the abandoned shelter, did the tears come. Images flashed before her eyes, glimpses of cold steel penetrating warm bodies and the resulting eruption of fluids.

La petite mort.

She wiped her eyes, ashamed to be crying over something she was partly responsible for. Her moral compass had pointed south for as long as she could remember, but it wasn't too late to change. There was still time to fix things.

Fix.

She shouldn't use that word. Dammit, she needed a fix. How long had it been since her last dose? She scratched at the scabs on her arms, trying to put it out of her mind. She needed to stop thinking about it, or else she would scream and scream and then they would find her and—

Glass cracked beneath her feet and Jessica winced, oddly thankful for the distraction. She hopped over to the wooden bench, brushed away the debris, and sat. A shard of broken bottle protruded from the sole of her foot, big enough to grasp with two fingers, a thin trickle of blood weeping from the wound. She tugged gently on the glass, her gut churning. It made a light sucking sound, the skin parting and sliding until the broken piece was half-in and half-out.

She wanted a fix so bad.

Hey, if you head back, maybe you can get some? Say it was all a misunderstanding, you didn't mean to run away, and can you please have some heroin?

She stopped and shook her head, then let go of the glass, raised her foot and stamped down hard on the concrete.

The impact forced the shard all the way in, scraping off bone. She struck the wall with her fist, pounding until the throbbing in her hand distracted from the piercing agony in her foot.

She deserved this. She knew she did.

After a while, the pain subsided, replaced by the tender kiss of dread, a lover's caress she was intimately familiar with. She sat still, the blood pooling around her foot, waiting for a train that may never come, the withdrawal exacerbating her natural anxiety until she thought she might go mad.

That's when she noticed the figure lurking at the edge of the shelter. She tucked the oversized jacket between her bare thighs, heart thudding in her chest, her hand slipping into her pocket, fingers wrapping around the carved handle of the knife. She licked her lips but her tongue was a dried-up sponge. Nervously, she chewed at the inside of her mouth, her foot throbbing.

The figure stepped out of the shadows into the yellow glow of the station light. A man, well-dressed, a smart suit. His podgy face watched her solemnly, running appraising eyes up her legs. He sat next to her, leaving enough space for someone to sit between them. She tightened her grip on the concealed weapon.

'Some, ugh,' croaked the man. He cringed in embarrassment, cleared his throat, and tried again. 'Some night, huh?'

'Yeah,' said Jessica. Her skin broke out in gooseflesh, and she stared forwards, watching him out the corner of her eye.

A heavy silence descended. Was he one of them? He was smartly attired, but so what? That didn't mean shit. She could hear him breathing, and the smack of his lips.

'You're, uh, not exactly dressed for it,' he said quietly.

'I guess not.' She tried to smile. Her leg twitched and she felt foolish.

'I sometimes come here to think. Get away from it all, y'know?'

Jessica nodded absently.

'It's my wife, you understand. She's never been the same since the children.' He chuckled. 'She's not the woman I married, I'll tell you.' He shuffled an inch closer, waiting for her to speak. When she didn't, he said, 'I've never seen you here before. There's not normally anyone here til about nine.'

The rain was getting heavier, bouncing off the railway and forming small puddles that reflected the distant stars. The man moved closer, so close she could practically taste his cologne. Ironically, after all she had been through, it was the cheap stink of own-brand aftershave that almost made her gag.

Jessica tensed, touching the phone through the jacket pocket. 'I know what you want,' she said. 'And you can't have it.'

'Oh, you like games, do you?' smiled the man. 'So do I.'

'This is no game.'

He's here to kill you. Do something.

'Ah, but it is,' he said. 'What is life if not a game being played by a bored god? It's why only the corrupt succeed.'

'You can't play with people's lives,' said Jessica. 'You have no right.'

Do something! Kill him! Kill him before he kills you!

He moved closer still, his arm brushing her own. He didn't seem to mind that she wore a jacket stolen from a scarecrow. Hell, he probably hadn't noticed.

'No need to be nervous,' he cooed. 'First time?'

In her head, Jessica heard the screams. She saw the bloodshed. She could still feel the weight of the drill in her hands, the warmth of the blood as it showered over her, drenching her, the pliant, tender flesh turning and splitting as the drill-bit rent it asunder.

'I can pay you,' said the man, oblivious to the turmoil in Jessica's head. 'I have lots of money.'

He placed his hand on her thigh, squeezed the bare skin and slid it up to her crotch. Jessica swung her arm towards him, the knife glinting briefly in the moonlight like a shooting star, catching his attention for a fraction of a second before plunging deep into his throat. She withdrew, hobbling on her damaged foot, watching as his eyes widened and bulged and air wheezed from his severed windpipe through the hole in his neck. He stared at her, one hand reaching up to his throat, the other towards her, fingers grasping, faltering, his mouth opening and closing like a goldfish gasping for oxygen.

He was definitely one of them.

But Jessica wasn't finished. The man tried to get to his feet, the blood gushing through his splayed fingers, coming for her, a look of shock and confusion on his fat, stupid face. She stabbed again, and again, and again, bringing the knife down, hacking at his chest. He raised a hand to stop her and she brought it down on the webbing between his thumb and forefinger. He tried to scream but simply gargled blood, his face draining of colour as he collapsed at her feet. She plunged the knife into his stomach, his arms, his face, blood erupting from arteries like a punctured garden hose.

He was dead long before she stopped.

A light in the distance, growing brighter.

Is it morning already, she thought in a dazed stupor. It wasn't.

It was the train.

'Jesus,' she said, reality grabbing her by the scruff of the neck. The train was approaching the station. Slowing.

Stopping.

Panicking, she grabbed one of the man's hands and pulled, dragging his lifeless body across the broken glass. She only had seconds before the train arrived and lit up the crime scene. With a burst of adrenaline, she hauled the man into the shadowy corner, his thumb damn-near tearing off. She reached into his blood-soaked pocket and found his wallet, rifled through it. It was empty.

Bastard.

The train arrived, the brakes screeching tiredly, and she turned, eyes scanning the windows. She couldn't see anyone.

That was good. They were *all* out to get her.

She staggered forwards, pushing the button, letting the doors groan unhurriedly open.

Jessica stepped in and made for the nearest seat. She leaned her forehead against the window. Outside, the rain was already washing away her bloody footprints. The man was nowhere to be seen.

My god, what if he's not dead? What if—

No, wait. She squinted through the glass and saw the soles of his shoes peeking out from the shadows. He wouldn't be found until tomorrow at the earliest, when the sun rose and revealed all. By then she would be long gone.

The automatic doors fizzed shut, the train lurching forwards.

She didn't see the other figure get on the carriage behind her.

As the landscape became an unrecognisable blur, Jessica looked at her reflection in the window and recoiled in horror. Her face was a mask of blood. Her hands, too, were crimson.

Hardly the incognito look she was going for.

She got up and found the nearest toilet. It was vacant, naturally. The whole train was. For a mad moment, she wondered if anyone was driving it. In the cubicle, she hung the scarecrow's jacket on the hook and stood naked before the mirror. She looked like shit, a nightmare version of herself, an evil twin. Lank hair covered her face, and she had cheekbones where once she had none, set beneath grey, hollow eyes. Her ribs protruded through the skin above her chest and she traced her fingers over the visible bones. The soap dispenser was empty, so she scrubbed herself with cold water, the dried blood swirling down the plughole and staining the ceramic.

There was a knock at the door.

A gentle *rat-a-tat-tat*.

Jessica froze.

The knock again, more insistent this time.

She fumbled in the jacket pocket for the knife, but it wasn't there. Too late, she realised it was still embedded in the man at the station.

Another knock. The door rattled on its flimsy hinges.

'Tickets please,' came the man's voice. When Jessica didn't respond, he said, 'I know you're in there.'

'Uh, one second,' gasped Jessica. She flung the jacket around her shoulders and checked her face in the mirror. A couple of red specks here and there, but mostly clean. She opened the door a crack and saw a middle-aged man peering at her over round glasses. He smiled a well-practiced smile.

'Sorry, madam. Just need to see your ticket.'

'I...I don't have one,' she said, painfully aware of her stuttering voice.

He regarded her with something akin to pity. 'That's alright, love. You can buy one from me.'

'I don't have any money.'

The smile dropped from his face. 'Of course not. Typical. Well, I'd say that you have to get off at the next stop, but considering the next stop is the *last* stop, that threat doesn't carry much weight now, does it?'

'I'm sorry,' she said, positioning herself in front of the bloodstained basin.

'Forget it. Bloody junkies. If I find any evidence of...' he struggled for the right words, 'hashish, or...*PCP* in there, I'll be alerting the police, young lady. Now get out.'

She brushed past him and took her seat, the soft red carpet hiding the blood stains she left with each step. He gave her a final disgusted look and headed back up the train.

'Wait,' she called. 'You didn't check the last carriage.'

'No one ever gets on at this stop. You're the first person in months.'

'But what if...'

'What?' he demanded. 'My patience is wearing thin with this nonsense.'

What indeed?

What if someone's following me? Is that what she wanted to say? She glanced down the carriage and there it was, fleeting, a shadow at the window.

'Someone's there!' she shouted.

'Don't raise your voice at me, you wee brat. I know my job.'

'Can't you stay here with me? I'd feel...*safer* if you did.'

He shook his head, the moonlight casting shadows

across his face in the dim light of the carriage. 'I've got better things to do with my time than babysit drug addicts. Like finishing the crossword.'

She saw it again, movement in the next carriage, a face watching, pressed up against the glass then quickly withdrawn. Without her knife, she needed protection.

The inspector resumed walking.

'Wait! Please!' she cried.

Harrumphing, he turned to face her one last time, to give her a piece of his mind. Jessica stood before him, letting the tweed jacket that smelt of hay and earth and bird shit fall to the floor. The ticket inspector appraised her thin, naked body.

'Stay with me, please,' she said, a single tear rolling down her cheek. 'Don't leave me alone.'

The inspector checked his watch. Ten minutes until they arrived at the station.

He smiled and unzipped his fly.

4

'Keep me up to date,' said Cat.

Willow nodded and headed for the door in her yellow raincoat, slinging a handbag over her shoulder.

'I'll text you if I need any help,' she grinned. 'But I can handle myself.'

'You've always been good at that.'

'It's a tough world out there,' said Willow. 'If you can't take care of yourself, no one else is gonna do it for you. How do I look?'

'Hot AF. He's a lucky guy.'

'I'll be sure to tell him.' Willow opened the front door and stepped into the stairwell. 'See you later, bitch.'

'Back late?'

'Yeah. Got a shift tonight. Don't wait up.'

The door swung shut, the thunderous bang resounding throughout the empty stair, fading to a silence broken only by the click of Willow's heels on the faux-marble veneer. On the street, the wind whistled past her ears, a fine drizzle raining down. She checked her phone.

Here. Were u at?

'Jesus,' she muttered. Granted, she *was* late. Why did she bother doing her hair and make-up before stepping out into a storm? She'd need to do it all over again before work. CB would never let her get on stage looking like she'd been dragged through a hedge backwards. She supposed it didn't matter. CB preferred her to wear a wig anyway, said that men wanted long hair on a woman, not the pixie crop haircut Willow sported.

'I don't have standards, girls, but some of the customers do,' he was fond of saying. She knew the former was true, but wasn't sure about the latter. Onstage she often played a game for her own amusement. She would look the men in their eyes, see how many would meet her gaze. Few did, and even less would hold it. They had standards all right, but those standards were confined to tits and arse. She could get up there in full clown makeup and a shaved head, and they wouldn't care as long as she got naked. Still, CB was the boss, and she liked him. He was fair, and he always paid on time, which was more than could be said for other managers she'd worked under.

She texted Mitch to let him know she was on her way.

Mitch.

Who the fuck is called Mitch these days, she thought. *Imagine crying that out during sex.*

The rain drenched her jacket, the weather finally acquiescing to the demands of autumn. She looked up at the block opposite her flat. That creep was still at his window, watching her room. Well, he'd have to wait a little longer to get his free peep show.

A taxi roared past and she considered hailing it, then remembered she only had a tenner for the night. Mitch better have some money with him, or it was going to be a short date. He had insisted that he would pay for everything. On his profile he called himself an "old-fashioned romantic", which set alarm bells ringing. Often, the so-called nice guys were just as bad, if not worse than the meat-heads. They used fancy talk and compliments as a disguise, one as effective as a kid on his friend's shoulders wearing a trench coat.

As she walked, she peered through the windows of the bars and restaurants, the couples inside going about the familiar rituals. She wondered what they were talking about, what was being said, what lies told, what secrets kept. A bus drove by, the wheels grazing a puddle and sending a miniature wave of water over her stockinged legs.

'Fuck,' she snorted, as a passing group of teenagers laughed at her misfortune. The water pooled around her toes and she sheltered in a doorway, taking her shoes off and pouring the liquid out. The street was darkening, heavy storm clouds seething in the sky, and she thought about heading home and calling it off. No, that wouldn't be fair. And anyway, she was already soaked. Might as well get a couple of free drinks out of it before she had to dance naked in front of a hundred leering men.

What could possibly go wrong?

5

Jessica's bare feet slapped off Edinburgh's cobbled streets, the ragged jacket clasped across her chest by the single remaining button, hair plastered to her forehead by sheets of rain that lashed down. It was the closest she had come to a shower in weeks.

The streets were practically deserted; what day was it? Wednesday? Thursday? She didn't know. How long had she been down there, in that hellish place? Without daylight, there had been no sense of time. She could have been there for years.

No, not years. That was ridiculous. Absurd.

A group of students ambled towards her, pissed up and lairy, hooting and laughing. One of them wolf-whistled and tried to call her over. She crossed the road to avoid them, slipping down one of the myriad alleyways that criss-crossed the Old Town, leaving the amber lights of the street-lamps behind. She shivered beside a skip until they passed, closing her eyes.

Not far now. She was almost at her destination.

Something moved.

Jessica's eyes snapped open. It was probably a cat, or a fox. Her senses sharpened. The wind howled through the alley, carrying with it the Charon stench of rotten fruit and days-old rubbish. It was foul, but not as bad as decaying human flesh, a rancid smell that wrapped its grisly arms around your throat and kissed you as you wept in the night.

Someone was coming for her, the ghoulish form back-lit by the woozy glow of the lamps.

She slipped further into the alley, once more silently cursing herself for forgetting the knife. There, she became one with the shadows, a phantom. Should she run? Could she? Her foot ached, each step sending currents of agony shooting through her veins. Why hadn't she stayed on the streets, where there were people?

Where there were witnesses?

But she knew why. She was afraid. Afraid of people, of what they might do, of their capacity for evil, for utter, inhuman cruelty. Turns out that bad people don't stand around twiddling their moustaches and bellowing wickedly. They go to work. They have families. They're attractive.

'Jessica,' came the voice, honeyed and sweet. She blinked hard, unsure if it was in her head or not. 'Come back. We're not finished with you yet. We're only getting started.'

Leave me alone.

'There's so much to see, so much still to do.' Footsteps echoed off the walls, coming from all around.

Leave.

'There's no need to be afraid.' The steps slowed, the feet shuffling towards her. She clanged into a metal rubbish ban.

Me.

'We love you Jessica.' She could feel the breath on her

neck, her skin crawling like thousands of insects running rampant on her body.

Alone.

She heard the sound of a zipper as her hands raked through the trash and found a beer bottle, her fingers tightening over the neck. Hot liquid drizzled down her leg and she swung the bottle, catching the urinating student across the side of the head. The base of the bottle shattered, and the boy hit the ground, clasping his hands to his face, blood flowing freely onto the concrete as he howled in anguish. She left him weeping in a pool of blood and piss, ignoring his cries for help and hurrying down the alley.

He wasn't one of them. She had hit the wrong guy.

Bullshit. It could be anyone. They hide in plain sight.

The street narrowed, the buildings closing in. She rounded a corner and hit something with a bump.

Not something...*someone.*

The man didn't move, not at first. He looked at her with the cold eyes of a serpent.

'Found you, you cunt,' he said, unsheathing the six-inch hunting knife. Jessica stepped back and fell on her ass. She didn't even scream as the man took a casual step towards her. Killing was just business, after all. Jessica knew she was little more than an inconvenience, a fly buzzing around cattle. She crawled backwards, hearing the chink of the broken glass bottle.

It was still in her hand.

The man knelt before her, cloaked in shadow, and raised the knife, his free hand grabbing her by the lapels, hauling her up. The frayed button snapped, her jacket opening as she sat trembling. The man hesitated and Jessica thrust the bottle upwards, stabbing her assailant in the leg, the glass piercing his flesh. He dropped back, the bottle held in place, protruding from his thigh, filling with blood until it began to pour out of the bottle-top. In a second, Jessica was on her feet, pushing past. Ahead, she could see cars racing by. A girl walked alone, engrossed in her phone.

She thought she was going to make it until the blade punctured her skin, rammed between her shoulder blades. Her body stiffened, her back arched. She tried to yell, but no sound came out. Jessica worked her tired, aching legs harder, pulling away from the man, then felt the knife being removed.

A gurgling noise behind her, close by. It was her own lifeblood spurting out, gushing down her spine. The girl ahead of her stopped, squinting at her phone. Jessica wanted to shout out to her. She was mere feet away now. Another car shot past, a blur, a neon dream. She stretched her hands out, fingers twisted beyond recognition, her body shutting down, as the blade entered her again, lower this time, below the ribs. Something inside her burst. Something important.

I'm going to make it, she thought, as the hunting knife was yanked out of her, the serrated blade tearing a deep gash in her lower back.

I'm going to—

Then came the darkness.

6

Willow ran her hands through her hair. Fuck's sake, she was going to arrive looking like a drowned rat. Of course, if she had left on time, she would have avoided the worst of the weather.

C'est la vie.

Two taxis drove past, headlights illuminating the wet streets. She heard a phone ringing and realised it was hers.

It was Mitch. God, who phones anymore? Rain spattered the screen of her iPhone as it rang and rang. Should she answer it? She was nearly there.

Be patient, asshole, she thought. She was only, what, an *hour* late.

Whoops.

She waited for the shrill screech of the phone to subside, then stepped into the shelter of an alley to text him, praying he wouldn't leave a voicemail. If he did, then her only recourse would be to call the whole thing off. Her fingernails clacked off the screen as she typed.

On my way, dickhead.

No, that wouldn't do. Sometimes, she had to type out what she *really* wanted to say, before amending it to a more PG-friendly version. Sadly, this tactic did not work in real-life conversations.

On my way.

Behind her, Jessica staggered forwards, bumping off the walls, hot blood jetting from her ruptured flesh.

On my way, dickhead. ;-)

There, that oughta do it. God bless emojis.

'Help,' rasped a voice, but the downpour drowned it out. Willow hit Send and started to walk when the hand fell on her shoulder. She gasped and spun, her fist clenching into a ball. A woman walking alone at night can never be too careful. At least once a week Willow experienced one of those *Am I Going To Be Murdered?* moments that most men were unfamiliar with. In the last seven days she had been followed by a group of teenagers in a Citroen, catcalling and spitting at her until she managed to hail a taxi. She had no money, but the driver had taken her home for free after she told him the circumstances. A few days later, some smack addict had cornered her on the street demanding change for a packet of fags. Now *this*, some fucker laying a hand on her. Three times in one week — that was a record even for *her*.

And so as she turned, she was ready to look into the eyes of her killer, or her mugger, or her rapist. Well, she wouldn't make it easy for them. No fucking way.

She did not expect to see the scrawny girl, her lips drawn back in something resembling a snarl.

'Help,' she wheezed, taking Willow by surprise, blood

trickling from the corner of her mouth, her jaw slack, bulging eyes like two golf balls. She collapsed into Willow's arms, her body limp and heavy.

Dead weight, isn't that what they call it?

Willow cradled the dying girl, kneeling, bringing her down to sit on the pavement, unaware of Jessica slipping something into her open handbag. 'What happened?' she asked, the girl's eyelids fluttering, her body wracked by a coughing fit. She spluttered blood onto Willow's face, some of it getting in her mouth. Willow supported the girl's back, then almost retched as her fingers slipped into the gaping wound at the base of her spine.

Her nails scraped bone.

The girl hardly noticed. She was wearing nothing but an old tweed jacket, the kind some posh-as-fuck landowner would wear, except this one only had a single button and appeared to have been dragged from the trenches. Willow looked down the alley and thought she saw movement. Further down the road a couple strolled arm-in-arm, like the weather didn't matter as long as you were young and in love.

'Help,' screamed Willow. She grabbed her phone to call the emergency services, and the screen lit up with Mitch's number again. 'Fuck off,' she spat, struggling to reject the call, her shaking fingers ineffective on the rain-dotted touch-screen. The couple sped towards her, the man leaving the woman trailing behind.

'What's wrong?' he shouted.

'I think she's been stabbed,' Willow called back. The man reached her. He took the dying girl's wrist and checked for a pulse, then shouted to his girlfriend, who was still puffing her way towards them.

'Jackie, call an ambulance. Now!' He turned to Willow.

'Don't worry, I know first aid.' He gazed uncertainly at her. 'Are *you* okay?'

'Huh?' She realised the girl's blood was still dripping down her face and she wiped it away with a sleeve. 'Yeah,' she said. 'It's not my blood.' The man looked at her a moment longer, then turned his attention to the girl. Her body spasmed, and the stench of shit filled the air. His girlfriend had dialled 999 and was talking too fast, practically hyperventilating. She didn't know what street they were on. She started to cry, and Willow felt a pang of disgust.

'St Mary's Street,' she shouted, but it didn't matter. The girl was dead. Expired.

Snuffed out.

Her placid face was impossibly vulnerable. She wore the bloodstains like fragile jewellery, her full lips slightly parted. The man put his ear to her chest, listening for a heartbeat. He clasped his hands and held them over the girl's heart, pumping them repeatedly. He stopped when he heard the wet, squishy noise as blood flooded out the holes in her back.

'Too late,' murmured Willow, getting to her feet and shaking her head. 'It's too late.' She felt dizzy. The man ignored her, his girlfriend babbling incoherently. Willow stepped away from them, away from the corpse and the smell, and leaned against the wall. She stared down the alleyway, into the uninviting black void. The trail of blood led further in, and Willow followed, a strange primordial instinct drawing her in. The voice of the airhead on the phone receded, and she could no longer hear the thump of the man's hands on the dead girl's chest as he continued his futile attempt to restart her heart. Willow prowled further into the alley, the darkness greedily consuming her. Litter butterflies fluttered around her, shredded paper strewn along the gutter like tiny shattered ribcages. Water dripped from cracked drainpipes, splashing into a deep pool of blood.

This was it. This was where she had been stabbed.

Where she had been killed.

Anger roared over Willow, anger and frustration and shame. What gives people the right to kill, to take people's lives into their own hands?

'You bastard,' she said to the killer, unaware that he could hear her. She looked towards the street. A crowd had formed around the macabre scene, nosy neighbours and passers-by eager for a piece of the action, some to help, others to glimpse death. One guy filmed it on his phone, an older lady haranguing him to stop. People were shouting, screaming, crying. Where were the police, where was the ambulance?

Willow walked tentatively onwards, sensing something. A presence. Was the killer still here? She stopped. He could be right in front of her. She peered into the night, picking out rubbish bins and discarded cigarettes, but no murderer.

What if he's behind you? she thought. *What if you've passed him already?*

She swallowed, walking backwards down the alley, unwittingly getting closer and closer to the sharpened, blood-soaked blade.

Why had she come up this far? Why hadn't she stayed with the girl?

Because she was angry. Because she wanted to catch the bastard who had done this and beat the living shit out of him. Behind her a figure moved, swooping like a vampire, the knife raised, hovering over Willow.

Lightning forked overhead, the storm reaching its apotheosis, and for a fraction of a second the alleyway was flooded with light. Willow saw the shadow of the man, his arm raised, the sharpened tip of the blade inches from her skull, and then the light vanished and she was plunged into unfathomable darkness again.

She ran, the knife cutting through thin air where moments before she had stood. She didn't look back, instead just running, her shoes clicking off the ground, the ability to move quickly in heels one of the perks of being an exotic dancer.

Red and blue lights danced across her face as she emerged from the darkened passage. Someone screamed when they saw her, but Willow didn't care. She stared at the poor, dead girl on the pavement, at the paramedics racing towards her, at the boy comforting his weeping girlfriend.

They all knew it was too late.

7

THE RAIN TURNED TO SLEET, BATTERING THE WINDSCREEN OF the police car.

Willow rubbed her eyes and looked up at the burly detective sitting opposite her in the back seat, his pock-marked face resembling a crumpled paper bag, the street lights casting him in an orange glow. He scribbled something in his notepad.

'So you were the first one to find her?' Detective Stone asked, phlegm rolling around his throat. He lowered the window and spat onto the street, the wind whistling banshee-like through the interior of the car.

'I already told you that.'

He regarded her impassively. 'I like to get my facts straight.'

'Sure. Sorry, I just feel...' she trailed off, unsure *how* she felt. 'She came out of nowhere. Gave me a fright.'

Stone nodded. 'And she didn't say anything?'

'No.'

'I need you to think real hard about this.'

'She might have said *help*. I can't remember. It happened

so fast. I laid her down, and then—'

She remembered the wet sensation of her fingers slipping into the wound.

'And then what?'

'Then I saw that couple coming down the road. I called for them.'

'But they didn't see her emerge from the alley?'

'I don't think so.'

'So you're the only witness?'

Willow stared at him. 'Apart from the killer. You might want to try finding him instead of talking to me.'

'All in good time,' said Stone. 'Speaking of which, I can't help but notice you're covered in her blood.'

He let the statement hang like dirty laundry.

'I told you, she coughed it onto me. She was bleeding everywhere.' She fixed him with a glare. 'I thought you were taking notes?'

Stone smiled at her. 'I found it interesting, that's all.'

'You think I did it?' snapped Willow, regretting the words as soon as they left her mouth.

'I never said that, Miss...Zulawski? That's no' a very Scottish name now, is it?'

'Wow, you're good,' said Willow, sarcasm dripping like venom. 'I can see why you're a detective.'

'The finest in Scotland,' sneered Stone. 'Where are *you* from?'

'England. I was born in Brighton.'

'And your parents?'

'I don't see how this is relevant.' Stone said nothing. 'My father was Polish. A journalist. He moved here in the nineties. That answer your question?'

He smiled thinly. 'I suppose it does. No need to get your

knickers in a bunch, Miss Zulawski. Just checking your credibility as a witness.'

'And what has my name or my father got to do with anything?'

'Oh, nothing, I'm sure. Now, what do you do, Miss Zulawski? When you're no' finding dead girls in the street, that is?'

'Jesus,' said Willow, shaking her head. 'You're a piece of work, you know that?'

'Answer the fucking question.'

Willow's heart-rate increased. The blood was flowing again, and she clenched her teeth to stop herself saying something she shouldn't. She took a breath, then calmly said, 'You can't talk to me like that.' He waited. 'Fine. I'm a dancer.'

His eyes flickered. 'Oh, a dancer, eh? What kind? Ballet or tap?'

Willow could see where this was going.

'Exotic,' she mumbled.

'Speak up, lassie. Or would you prefer to answer in Polish?'

'I'm an exotic dancer. Over at Cannonball Joe's.'

'An exotic dancer,' he repeated, rolling the words around his tongue, enjoying the sweet taste. 'So you flash your wee fanny about the stage?'

'Fuck you,' said Willow. She grabbed the door-handle. It wouldn't give.

'Naw, fuck you.'

'Let me out. I need a smoke.'

'There's no smoking in a police vehicle,' said Stone, placing a cigarette in his crooked mouth. He pulled out a lighter embossed with the outline of a Wild West revolver, the silver dulled with age, and lit up. Stone took a draw and consulted his notes. 'So, a half-Polish stripper. Oh, the jury'll love you.'

'My nationality and job have nothing to do with this. Now unless I'm under arrest, you can't hold me here. I've answered your questions, I've told you everything I know. There was a man in the alley. He killed that poor girl, then he tried to kill me.'

'So you said. A shadow-man, am I right?'

They looked at each other for a long time. 'I only saw his shadow, that's correct. Then I ran. He was holding a knife.'

Stone closed his notebook and leaned back, blowing a mouthful of smoke out the window. Willow looked past him, at the paramedics trying to load the body into the ambulance. One of them slipped on the wet tarmac and fell to their knees, the gurney beginning to roll down the street. Someone cheered and Willow watched several people filming the gurney as it picked up speed on the shallow incline.

She looked away and noticed the detective staring at her legs.

'I didn't do it,' she said. 'You must know that, no matter how incompetent you are.'

'You're a wee charmer, aren't you?'

'I've been told that before, yeah.'

He smiled again, but there was no humour in it. 'CB Joe's, aye?'

'That's right. Six nights a week.'

'Alright. If I have any more questions, I know where to find you. Might even enjoy the show first. I ken what you Poles are like,' he said. He pressed a button and the doors unlocked. Willow stepped out into the torrential rain.

Before she closed the door, she peered in at the detective.

'You don't honestly think it was me, do you?'

He lit another cigarette. 'No. But a dirty wee Polish slapper? The tabloids would eat that shite up.'

She slammed the door and stormed down the street, not caring where she was going as long as it was away from that xenophobic arsehole. The problem was, she knew he was right. She could see herself emblazoned across the front page of the papers, a photo from one of CB's flyers of her in her underwear, with a headline like POLISH STRIPPER MURDERS LOVER IN JEALOUS RAGE or some other bollocks.

Her phone beeped at her. A text message from Mitch.

WELL DUCK YOU U BITCH
I HOPE U DIE U ABORSHON

She read it twice, walking aimlessly, her heart thumping in her chest. The third time, she started to laugh. By the fourth, she was in hysterics. She thought of Detective Stone, watching her from the police car, and that made her laugh even harder.

8

'OH MY GOD,' SAID EVE MURPHY, STARING WIDE-EYED AS Willow recounted her tale. 'And you actually saw her die?'

Willow nodded. 'Yeah. In my arms.' Eve placed a hand over Willow's. It was meant to comfort her, but Eve was always cold and Willow flinched from her icy touch.

'You okay?' asked Eve.

They sat in the dressing room at Cannonball Joe's, known colloquially to its patrons as CB's. Willow had decided to go straight to work. She wasn't due to start until eleven, but at least here the heating worked properly, unlike her and Cat's place. Willow had previously danced in a Glaswegian nightclub called Le Boudoir, which was as grotty as it sounded. Rat-infested changing rooms, a leaking toilet, ancient, decrepit wallpaper peeling from ugly plaster-board walls.

CB's though...it was something else.

The furnishings were all handmade by CB himself. A carpenter by trade, he had been forced out of business by a combination of the recession and IKEA, instead converting his workshop into a high-class strip club, the next logical step in his mind (and his mind alone). CB was unlike any boss Willow and the girls had ever worked for. He genuinely cared about their wellbeing. Why else would the dressing room have underfloor heating and a small library of well-thumbed paperbacks? As a bonus, he never expected any of the girls to perform extra-curricular activities with the clientele, nor did he demand any *favours* from them. He paid well, and he paid on time, the girls getting to keep all their tips. It was actually a pretty sweet gig if you didn't mind middle-aged perverts leering at you all night. Willow figured they were just as likely to leer at her in the street, so what did it matter?

'You okay?' Eve asked again, more insistently.

'Yeah, I'm fine. A bit rattled, that's all.' She smiled unconvincingly.

'Ask CB for the night off.'

Willow laughed. 'Come on. He's nice, but he's not a sucker.'

'Guess you're right,' said Eve. She left Willow and stood by the mirror, applying her makeup in broad strokes. 'You gotta paint for the back row,' she said.

'They could see that in the back row of the O2 Arena,' said Willow as she walked to the fire door, unbolting the heavy metal and stepping out onto the fire-escape. She lit up and smoked, trying not to think about the face of the dead girl, and failing.

'You really saw the killer?' said Eve from inside. 'That's so scary. What did he look like?'

'I didn't see him properly. I don't even know if it was a *him*.'

'It's always men,' said Eve matter-of-factly. 'Was he tall or short?'

'I told you, I just saw the shadow. He was holding a knife.'

Eve turned to look at Willow, one eye ringed with mascara. 'It could have been you, you know.'

'I guess so,' said Willow, too quietly for Eve to hear.

'Coulda been any of us. You carry protection, Will?'

Willow leaned on the metal balcony. 'You need a condom?'

'No, I mean like mace, or a knife or something.'

Willow tossed the butt and stepped inside, welcoming the warmth beneath her feet. 'A knife? Christ, Eve, we're not in the fucking Bronx.'

'It doesn't matter. Men are all at it these days. I've never felt so unsafe. I get the bus home every night now.'

'You live two streets away.'

'What's your point?'

Willow didn't have one.

A phone rang, the sound of The Ramones audible over the techno blaring from Eve's bluetooth speaker. 'That yours?' asked Willow.

Eve shook her head, turning up the volume on the speaker. 'Must be Maggie's.'

Willow nodded, forgetting all about it.

Eve applied the finishing touches to her face. 'Well, that's me due onstage. You sure you're alright?'

'I'm fine. Go on, get out there and knock 'em dead.'

Eve grimaced at her.

'No pun intended,' smiled Willow.

Eleven o'clock rolled around. Willow kept to herself, lurking on the fire-escape and smoking, peering through the windows of the building opposite. There wasn't much going on tonight. Lots of flickering lights from televisions, an old man eating alone at a table set for two, a man taking a bath behind frosted glass that left nothing to the imagination.

She showered and prepared for her first dance of the night, scrubbing the last spots of blood from her hair and face. When she stepped out, CB was waiting for her.

Willow wrapped a towel around herself and gave him an appraising glance. 'You the new girl? CB's standards are slipping.'

He laughed, prodding his beer gut. 'I'll have bigger tits than you soon.' He sat, his leather jacket screeching against the leather couch, making them both wince. 'Honestly Willow, enjoy your youth while you still have it. After forty it's all downhill.'

'I've got a few years yet, old man,' she chided. CB stuffed a cigarette in his mouth and offered her one. 'I thought this room was non-smoking,' said Willow. 'You said it damages the paint or something. That's why I skulk around on the porch like a voyeur whenever I need a pick-me-up.'

'Normally it is,' he said, 'but tonight's different.' He ran a hand through his thinning hair. 'I spoke to Eve.'

Willow took the cigarette and lit up. 'I'm fine, CB. Don't worry. I can handle myself.'

'You saw a girl die, Willow,' he whispered. 'If you're okay with that, then I'm even more concerned.'

'Eve's got a big mouth.'

'I know. It's gonna get her in a lot of trouble one day. But I'm not here to talk about Eve. Listen, if you need to go home, I can call in one of the other girls.' He held out an ashtray and she tipped the embers into it.

'Don't, I'm gonna stay. When I'm up there, you know, on the stage...that's the only time I get to forget about real life.

I'm like a character in a movie, and nothing else matters for those five or ten minutes. It's like I can become someone else. That make sense?'

'Nah, but I was always more of a craftsman than an artist. You,' he said, pointing the drooping tip of his cigarette at her, 'are an artist. The best dancer I've ever seen. You know how to work the crowd into a frenzy, tease them, give them a real show.'

'Cheers, pal.'

'And you've got the finest tits of all my girls.'

'Oh stop it, you're making me blush,' said Willow dryly.

CB laughed. 'You're an artist, but sometimes the boys out there just want some tits, arse and leg. It'd be nice if you could do a regular stripshow, to some Warrant or Mötley Crüe or something, once a week. For me?'

Willow smiled at him. 'You want me to compromise my art? Me, the great artist of CB Joe's?'

'No need to be sarcastic. You know I love that whole romantic aesthetic you've got going on, but maybe once a fortnight...' He looked at her. She turned away. 'Once a month...'

She crushed her cigarette. 'Once a month. Maybe.'

'I bet you could really move to *Girls, Girls, Girls*.'

'You're a monster, CB.'

'A monster who lets you keep your tips.'

'A monster who lets himself in while I'm in the shower.'

He coloured. 'Ah, that was a mistake.'

'Well out you go, I've got to get ready.'

He stood and moved towards the door. 'A shy stripper. Fuck me.'

'Never gonna happen, CB. I don't mix business with pleasure.'

He grinned at her. 'And which am I?'

She waved him away. 'Later, CB.'

Willow stood poised in the wings, the low hum of the cello rumbling throughout the club. She came out to quiet applause, the dim lights allowing her to see every face in the crowd, the usual mix of men and women. Every year there were more and more women.

The harpsichord picked out a delicate melody, one built on anticipation, a recurring motif in the music of Ennio Morricone.

Sorry, CB. No *Cherry Pie* tonight.

As she reached the pole and started to drift around it, the plaintive vocals of Edda Dell'Orso echoed out across the hall, the whole room watching in rapt attention. Some of the audience knew it was *Jill's Theme* from *Once Upon a Time in the West*, others didn't, and none of them cared.

The melody soared, Willow lost in the music, enraptured. She sank to her knees, running her hands down her body, stopping between her thighs. Willow forgot she was onstage, becoming one with the music, feeling the vibrations course through her.

She could die to this music, and die happy. The beauty of it was unearthly, magical. Her body moved in time, not to the music, but to the emotion. Then she was crawling, reaching out, desperate, haunted. A woman in the audience took her hand like she knew they would, feeling the softness of her sleeve, and then Willow pulled back, slipping out of the dress, letting it glide over her skin as the music built to a crescendo, Willow rolling onto her back, her fingers brushing her thighs, the lacy material of her underwear soft and cool to the touch. The audience held its collective breath, all except one, who stood in the back, unnoticed.

Glancing around to make sure no one was watching, they surreptitiously snapped a photo of Willow, then turned and left, striding through the red velvet curtains, down the stairs and out onto the street where they disappeared, just another lost soul wandering the rain-slicked streets.

9

Willow walked home, physically and mentally exhausted. Though it was close to three in the morning, she texted Cat to tell her about the evening's events. The rain had stopped, replaced by a biting wind that gnawed at her face with canine teeth, the puddles freezing before her eyes. She regretted not bringing trainers to change into.

When she got home, Cat was waiting, the kettle boiling in the kitchen. She filled two hot water bottles, and they hugged them as they sat on Willow's bed.

'Fucking police,' said Cat. 'Bureaucratic racists.'

'The worst kind of racists,' said Willow, her water bottle tucked beneath her dressing gown. 'They didn't give a shit. They think I killed her. Apparently being Polish makes me the number one suspect.'

'It's disgusting.'

'You'd think I'd be used to it by now,' said Willow. 'As soon as people hear my surname, they treat me differently. Less respect.'

'You could always change it,' said Cat.

'Never. It's my tribute to them. My parents.'

'You don't talk about them often,' said Cat, and it was true, she didn't.

'You know how I feel about heart-to-hearts,' said Willow. They sat quietly a while, then she said, 'There's not much to tell. They died when I was seven. A car crash. After that I was bounced around foster homes for years until one day I ran away. I expected someone to catch me, but no one ever did. I'm not even sure anyone looked for me.'

'That's awful,' said Cat, snuggling closer to Willow on the bed. Willow, who usually disliked physical contact, let her.

'I still miss them,' she said, 'even if sometimes I can barely remember what they looked like.'

'Don't you have photos?'

Willow shook her head. 'No photos, no videos. Just memories.'

That wasn't quite true. Tucked in her wallet was a photo snipped from a Polish newspaper, from her father's byline. He had broken the story of a child slavery ring operating out of Krakow. From her online research, she discovered he had gone undercover, and even been threatened with his life. It must have been the reason he left the country to set up home in a land that didn't care for him, that viewed him as an inconvenience.

'I should get some sleep,' said Willow after a while, though she didn't feel tired, her mind buzzing like a disturbed wasps' nest.

'Okay,' said Cat. She took Willow's hand. 'You want me to sleep on the floor? I don't mind, if you don't want to be alone. If you're scared...'

'That's the funny thing. I wasn't scared then, and I'm still not. I was stupid, and I was angry...but never scared.'

'Angry?'

'Yeah. Angry that someone would do this, and we'll never know who or why. This poor girl will be just another sad little mystery. A footnote. What's one more slaughtered female out there, eh?' Willow's eyes flicked to the window, catching her reflection. 'She deserves better.'

Cat stood, gave Willow a comforting smile, and headed for the door. Her hand paused over the handle, and she turned to Willow.

'I don't think you were stupid, going down that alley. I think you were very brave.'

'I should have stayed with her,' said Willow. 'Curiosity killed the cat, and all.'

Cat went pale.

'Sorry,' said Willow. 'Poor choice of words.'

Willow tried to sleep, but the grisly scene played over and over in her mind. The look on the girl's face, that look of abject horror, yet the eyes saying something different, projecting a weary, grudging acceptance. Was that what it was like to know you're going to die?

But where had she come from, and why was she naked, apart from that bizarre, incongruous jacket? As far as Willow was aware — and she had been watching keenly — the police inspectors hadn't recovered any clothes from the alley. Well, she hadn't fucking left the house like that.

She got out of bed and reclined on the chair by the window, an old but intricately carved one that CB had given her on her birthday last year. It creaked satisfyingly beneath her. She lit a cigarette, the orange glow illuminating her reflection.

Something on the street caught her eye.

A figure, clad entirely in black, standing by a lamppost.

Watching her.

Willow's heart caught in her throat. Her instinct was to jump out of sight, but she knew he'd seen her. Instead, she stared straight forwards, smoking, but keeping him in her periphery. She lifted the window and tipped the ash out. The man turned and left. He was too far away to make out any details. She watched him go and noticed his limp.

He *had* been staring at her, right? She couldn't be sure.

Well, what else was he doing there at quarter to four in the morning? Stargazing?

She closed the window and climbed into bed.

It was a long time until she slept.

10

WILLOW AWOKE FROM A RESTLESS SLEEP, CONFUSED AND hopelessly disorientated.

The Ramones were singing *I Wanna Be Sedated*.

Could she still be dreaming? Was Cat blasting out some punk-rock at — she glanced at the clock — five twenty-three?

'What the fuck,' she grumbled, sitting up, her head swimming. The music stopped, then looped to the start of the chorus. A ringtone. She vaguely recalled hearing the same tune at CB's while talking with Eve. She threw the covers aside and slithered out of bed. The song looped again, this time cutting out halfway through.

Silence.

Willow grabbed a cigarette from the nightstand and lit up, as the bedroom door opened and Cat poked her head through.

'Willow, it's late. Or early. I'm not sure. Please turn it down.'

'It's not me,' said Willow. 'I mean, it's coming from this room, but I don't know where.'

'What?'

'I don't know. Listen.'

The song started again, loud but muffled, like it was playing underwater.

'Did you change my ringtone as a joke?' said Willow.

Cat shuffled bleary-eyed into the room. 'Come on, I'm not funny, but I'm funnier than *that*.'

'So where's it coming from?'

Willow checked her jacket pockets, locating some chewing gum, an old LRT bus ticket and twenty pence.

'Check your bag,' said Cat, leaning sleepily against the wall.

Willow did, and found it straight away, nestled in between her purse and a paperback.

A phone.

She took it out.

'This isn't mine,' she said.

A white case protected the phone. Imprinted on it were four bloody fingerprints. Willow licked her finger and rubbed at one of them. The print came away.

'Oh my god,' said Cat. 'Is that...'

'Hers. The dead girl.' A cold shiver passed through Willow's body.

'But how?'

'She must have slipped it into my bag.'

'When?'

'I don't know,' said an exasperated Willow. 'It was crazy, confusing...could have been anytime. What I want to know is *why?*'

She turned the phone in her hand. She had to be careful now. This was evidence. Evidence that now had her fingerprints all over it...

'Shit.'

The phone went off again, The Ramones — freed from their handbag prison — blaring out at maximum volume. Startled, Willow let go, the phone — with absolute inevitability — striking the edge of the chest of drawers. She picked it up, tiny cracks forming an unsolvable maze across the glass. Luckily, the damage was confined to the corner, allowing Willow to read the Caller ID.

'Vinnie Sunset,' she said, then paused. 'That's the dumbest fucking name I've ever heard.'

'Answer it,' said Cat. When Willow didn't, she said, 'It might be a relative, or her boyfriend or something.'

Without thinking, Willow answered the call.

Silence on the other end. No, not silence. Breathing.

'Hello?' said Willow.

'Who is this?' A man's voice, deep and resonant, with the hint of an accent.

'Who is *this*?' She couldn't put her finger on why, but Willow was wary of giving out her name.

'You have my friend's phone.'

'Yes. I'm sorry.'

'Where are you? I'll pick it up.'

'I'm...look, I can send it to you. I don't mind. It's the least I could do.'

'No,' he replied too quickly. 'I'll come to you. Where are you?'

'Seriously...I don't mind.'

A pause. Willow checked the time. Almost five-thirty.

'What's your name,' said the man, breaking the silence and startling her.

'I don't want to say.'

More silence.

'You have my phone.'

'I thought you said it was your friend's?' She gripped it

so hard her knuckles whitened. There was a long period of oppressive silence.

'I'll be in touch,' said the man.

He hung up.

Willow flopped onto the bed and stared at the phone. 'Well fuck you,' she said, then felt guilty about it.

'Who was it?' asked Cat.

'I don't know. He wouldn't give his name. Unless Vinnie Sunset is his real name. Imagine the grief he must have gotten at school,' she said, trying and failing to lighten the strange mood that had descended.

'Why didn't you give yours? What if he doesn't know his friend's dead?' Cat sounded annoyed, and this irritated Willow.

'I didn't trust him.'

'Based on what, exactly?'

'Based on the fact that a girl snuck this phone into my fucking handbag before she was *murdered*, or don't you remember?'

Cat looked close to tears, and Willow sighed. Cat cried far too easily.

'Look, I'll phone him tomorrow,' said Willow. 'When the sun's up, like a normal person.'

Cat nodded. 'Vinnie Sunset,' she said. 'It *is* a weird name.'

'We can Facebook stalk him later. Knowing my luck, there'll be four-hundred Vinnie Sunsets in Scotland.'

The phone felt heavy in her hand. The lock screen displayed a photo of two black cats gazing disinterestedly at the camera, and the battery was down to seven percent. She unplugged her own phone and stuck the charger into this one.

'What are you doing now?'

'Just having a look.'

'You can't do that!' said Cat, her eyes wide. 'You need to take it to the police.'

'Aren't you in the least bit interested?'

'No, I most certainly am not.'

Willow bit her lip. 'Then go to bed,' she muttered.

Cat hesitated, then joined her on the bed, grumbling under her breath.

The phone wasn't locked, which struck Willow as odd. Who doesn't lock their phone these days, with a passcode or thumbprint or facial recognition? The screen was surprisingly barren, none of the usual social media apps present, almost as if it was straight out of the factory.

'There's nothing there,' said Cat, and Willow heard the relief in her voice.

'We'll see.' She tapped the screen.

'Photos...really?' said Cat in her most judgemental voice.

'Need to make sure it's hers.'

'You can justify anything if you want to,' said Cat, making no move to stop her.

The app opened, revealing a solitary thumbnail.

A video.

The image was black, and Willow moved to press it. Cat grabbed her wrist.

'Don't,' she said quietly. Willow looked at her and felt the sharp twist of fear in her gut.

'What's got you so spooked?' she asked, though she understood Cat's trepidation. It needled at her too, but for Willow it was an itch that needed scratching. She sometimes wondered whether she had inherited her natural curiosity from her journalist father.

'It's just a video,' she said, her finger hovering over the screen. In her head, she saw the face of the dying girl, the last flutter of her eyelids, the final tremble of her lip. She felt hot, too hot, and almost put the phone down. Something about Cat's demeanour was getting to her, or perhaps the realisation that she had seen a girl die was setting in, the dull throb of anger replaced by something more insidious.

Fear.

It was *fear* that tingled throughout her body, fear of what she would find at the simple touch of the screen. But why? After all she had witnessed tonight, how bad could it be? Hell, maybe it was nothing at all? She noticed the time of the video. Yesterday, at five-forty, only a few hours before the girl had been murdered.

She hit play, knowing that if she didn't now, she never would.

The image was dark, the gauzy film playing out like spectral imagery. Lines travelled up the picture, the way they do when a camera is pointed at a television set.

'What's happening?' asked Cat, and Willow saw she was looking away, staring at the blank wall above the dresser.

'Nothing,' said Willow. 'I can't see anything. *Wait*,' she snapped.

'What?'

Willow squinted at the three-inch screen. 'It's a girl.'

It was hard to tell at first. A gaunt white face shimmered into view, semi-obscured by a mask of digital grain as the camera struggled to contend with the lack of light. She seemed to be lying down, her blonde hair spread out around her head like a halo. She wore heavy makeup, dark circles around her eyes and lipstick smeared around her mouth and chin.

Willow tried to speak, but the words caught in her throat.

That wasn't makeup.

The girl looked into the lens, her mouth moving soundlessly.

'What's she doing?' asked Cat.

'She's saying something.' Willow nudged the volume to maximum, increasing the ambient noise, but no sounds escaped the girl's mouth. Metal clanged in the background over a steady hiss. The girl gargled and coughed, and what looked like blood — *it has to be blood* — spilled down her chin. The camera panned over her body. She was naked, and Willow thought she could see straps binding her to the table, though with all the distortion it was like looking through a snowstorm.

'Oh Jesus,' breathed Willow, her stomach tightening into a ball.

'What is it?' asked Cat, instinctively turning to look.

'*Don't*,' said Willow with unrestrained ferocity. Cat did as she was told.

The girl was missing a leg. Wasn't she? Willow couldn't be sure. She wanted to stop watching, to hurl the phone through the window, but she didn't. She felt compelled to watch, guided by a savage impulse she didn't understand. The left leg ended at the knee, the skin appearing ragged and loose. Something clanged again, metal on metal. Willow's throat was dry. She had never been more awake.

The camera travelled up the girl's body, her hands clawing feebly at thin air. It focused on her face, and then suddenly her face was gone. Willow jerked so violently that Cat screamed. There was a vicious, sickening crunch, and Willow wanted desperately to tear her eyes from the screen, to scrub them raw with bleach.

A blunt object protruded from the girl's smashed face. The image jumped and shook, moving down until the edges of a monitor appeared in shot and Willow knew for certain that the video was being filmed off a television screen. The ghastly sight of the girl vanished for one brief, merciful moment, and then the camera swung up again in time to see a thin white hand grasp the handle of the implement. It pulled at the object — was it a hammer? — struggling to remove it from the shattered skull, wrenching it free. The image shook, Willow horrified to discover it was her own hands quaking. Then the girl in the video gurgled, a deep, rasping croak that didn't sound human.

'Switch it off,' sobbed Cat, her hands covering her ears, tears rolling down her cheeks, but Willow couldn't, her own hands numb and useless. The camera moved away from the girl, towards the perpetrator of the heinous act. Though hard to discern through the darkening haze, it appeared to be another girl.

The hammer came down again, the camera operator too slow to catch the impact of the blow, but it caught the next one, and the next.

'Switch it off,' urged Cat. 'Please, Willow, switch it off!'

Things went silent for a while, except for the faint sounds of erratic breathing from the girl. How could she still be alive?

Then a female voice spoke with frightening clarity, a voice that must have been close to the recording device. It had to be whoever was filming the video off the monitor.

'Oh god, oh god,' she said, her voice cracked and guttural.

Willow felt sick, her head aching. The picture zoomed in to a close up of the girl's face, or what was left of it. Thank god the quality was so poor.

A harsh whirring sound blasted from the phone, and something long and thin entered the frame, a light source catching it and flaring. It looked like an electric drill. It drifted towards the girl's ruined face, towards her eye, and then came the sound of a door opening.

'Shit!' said a girl's voice, the image momentarily flashing away from the screen. It hovered, glimpsing a bare foot, then shot back. There was one final image before the video abruptly ended.

A chill ran down Willow's spine, her whole body tensed up like a frightened animal. She stared hard at the screen, at the last thing ever captured on it.

'Oh my god,' she said.

At first, she thought it was a blood-soaked rag, flat and shapeless and red, a disembodied eyeball in the middle, staring blankly into nothingness. Then the eye moved and looked directly at the camera, the rag tearing open, displaying teeth and a tongue.

The mutilated mess that had once been a face screamed.

Cat stumbled from the room, her footsteps stomping down the hall towards the bathroom. Seconds later Willow heard her retching.

The scream cut off and the phone slipped through Willow's fingers, landing face up on the bed. The single eye stared up at her with maddening intensity. Willow reached for a cigarette, but she fumbled the pack and it fell to the floor.

She put her head in her hands and started to cry.

11

'AND YOU'VE KNOWN ABOUT THIS FOR HOW LONG?' SLURRED Detective Stone from behind his desk. He sipped from a chipped coffee mug (TOO HOT FOR COPS, it said) and Willow wondered what he was actually drinking.

'I told you,' she said, almost to herself. 'I found it last night. The girl must have put it in my bag before she died.'

He regarded her over the purple bags beneath his eyes, that suspicious look never quite leaving them. Willow shifted uncomfortably, feeling like she had done something wrong. She supposed it was a special police superpower. Perhaps Stone was once a normal man who had been bitten by a radioactive detective? Normally, the idea would have made her laugh. But not today.

'And you just brought it in now?' said Stone.

'I was at work, then I went home to bed. It started ringing about five this morning.'

He smiled wryly. 'Ah yes, *work*. Good day at the office, was it? Anyone slip a tenner into your thong?'

Willow smiled angrily back at him. 'Customers use an app to leave tips.'

'What a wonderful world we live in. Is there an app for a blow job too?'

Willow looked Stone dead in the eye. 'I dance, and I'm good at it. That's all.'

'Aye, aye, sure. I'll send the boys round to have a look sometime. Might come myself...if you know what I mean.'

'Jesus...so you keep promising,' she snarled, refusing to break eye contact. 'Now, are you going to watch the video or not? Two girls are dead, you know. Maybe it's time to stop harassing innocent citizens and do your job.'

'Two girls?' said Stone, raising his eyebrows. 'Do you know something I don't?'

Fuck me, he's slow.

'The girl in the video,' she said, emphasising her point by gesturing at the blood-stained phone on the desk, 'and the girl last night.'

He took a drink and nodded. 'Ah yes. Miss Jessica Chalmers. Of course, I forgot. How silly of me.' He stared at her. 'Multiple stab wounds,' he said absently. 'The girl wasn't well. Looked like she'd been starved. If you ask me, it was a mercy killing.'

He was trying to get a rise out of her.

Willow forced her body to relax. Stone waited a moment longer, reading her like a porno mag, his eyes travelling down to her chest. She crossed her arms. This fucker was so seedy she could plant him in a field and grow a crop of arseholes. He smiled at her and turned to the iPhone.

'It's the only video on there,' she said, clasping her hands on her lap and waiting in dreadful anticipation.

The sounds of violence filled the cramped office like a noxious gas. Stone's brow furrowed as he paid attention for the first time since Willow had arrived at 9am that morning.

The strange metallic banging.

The breathing, the rasping.

The sudden thud of metal on bone.

Willow started to sweat. Why wasn't the window open?

Because it's October, and it's freezing outside.

She closed her eyes, knowing exactly when the high-pitched, gurgling scream would begin. After all, she had watched the video god-knows how many times last night. She pictured the face, that ghastly, screaming face, the eye betraying sheer terror amongst the broken porcelain death-mask.

She felt sick, like she might—

'I said, are you okay?'

Willow's eyes snapped open. Stone was staring at her, the phone face-down on the desk. Wind battered the window, which rattled in its frame from the onslaught. She uncrossed her legs and placed both feet on the ground, her hands gripping the sides of the chair.

'I'm fine. It's that video...' She shook her head as if to clear it from her mind. 'How do you do it? How do you live this shit every day?'

Stone smiled wearily. It was the first sincere emotion that had crossed his face. 'Gallons of whiskey,' he said. He took a bottle from his desk and offered it. 'Want some?'

Willow said she didn't. She felt awful enough. Stone took another swig and placed the bottle and the phone in his drawer.

'So? What do you think?' she asked. Her eye twitched from lack of sleep.

The detective rubbed a hand through his stubbly beard, the bristles making an irritating scratching sound.

'Load of bollocks,' he finally said.

'What?'

He laughed. 'It's fake! Anyone could tell you that.'

'No, no, it can't be. Did you see the look in her eyes? That girl wasn't acting.'

'I couldn't see anything, it was that bloody dark. Just some lesbians having a fumble. But don't worry, I'll be sure to take it home and investigate further,' he said, giving her a sly grin.

'Yeah, sure, after your wife has gone to bed, I imagine.'

'My wife's been dead for eight years,' said Stone abruptly.

Willow was caught off-guard. 'I'm sorry, I saw the ring and...' she mumbled.

'It's alright. I always wear it, to stop all the Polish strippers hitting on me cos I'm so bloody handsome,' he smirked.

'So that's it?' said Willow. 'You're not even going to investigate?'

'Listen, lassie. There's no body. If — and it's a big, fat fucking *if* — somebody died in that video, then it damn well wasn't Jessica Chalmers, because she died in the middle of fucking town last night, in *your* arms I might add. I've also got another body linked to her, some poor sod butchered in a train station. But no naked blonde girls tied to tables. Believe me, I'd be all over that case if it turned up. As it stands...no body, no crime.'

'But the video—'

'It's a blurry piece o' shite,' roared Stone, pounding the desk with his fist. He leaned forwards, getting right into her face, close enough for her to smell the whiskey coming off his breath in waves. 'Anyone can make a video. That's two lassies shagging, then someone with ketchup on their face. It's a porno for freaks.' He moved closer, his nose almost touching her own. 'What about you?' he whispered. 'You a wee blood freak? You get off on death, aye?'

Willow tried to recoil, but he placed his hands on the back of her chair, forcing her to stay. 'What are you doing?' she said. 'What the fuck are you talking about?'

He laughed and let go, sitting down as if nothing had happened. 'I told you. It's fake. You find them all over the internet. Once a year some poor concerned mother finds a stash of this shite on her son's computer and brings it in to me, some slut getting rammed then someone pretending to kill her. That's all this is. See it all the time, usually the Poles or the Russians.' He smiled. 'No offence.'

'It's more than that, and you know it.' She wanted to leave but found herself rooted to the chair. 'You need to find out who that girl is and—'

'Don't tell me how to do my job. I don't come into your work and tell you how to flash your fanny and suck off some boy for smack.'

'Fuck you,' said Willow, getting to her feet and heading for the door.

'Any fucking time, doll,' grinned Stone, as the door slammed shut behind her. He watched her through the glass panel as she stormed down the corridor, then took the phone out of the drawer and tucked it into his trouser pocket.

'Any fucking time.'

~

The screaming rattled around inside her brain. Willow hit pause halfway through the video and rested her head in her hands. When she looked up she was staring into the haunted eyes of the blonde girl, frozen in time like a piece of art.

Who was she? And who was her killer? She scrolled

through the timeline, stopping at the brief shot of the killer, but it was hard to make anything out. The person was also naked, she thought, but she couldn't determine a gender, their body thin and flat-chested, their hair short, their skin bleached.

Her mind wandered to who had filmed the original video. Willow was positive that the girl from last night had shot the footage on the phone. Perhaps she had stumbled upon it somewhere, and filmed it as evidence before making her escape.

Whilst totally nude.

Sure, why not? Maybe she would have been next? Was there some cult out there, kidnapping women and killing them? But why film it? For pleasure? Or money?

A headache gnawed at her and she washed down some Ibuprofen with a Coke. This wasn't her line of work. Murder should never be normalised, and yet every time she watched the video it *did* get easier, right until the end. Sometimes, she stopped before the flattened, smashed face opened its mouth and started screaming. She didn't need to see it again — it was there whenever she closed her eyes.

She took her headphones off and selected iMovie on her Mac, then opened the Untitled folder on her desktop, the folder where she had stored all the information from the dead girl's phone.

Jessica. That was her name. Use it. Jessica Chalmers.

She dragged the video into the Project Media section and double-clicked, the video appearing in a window.

Willow navigated to the midpoint of the timeline and paused the film. The image was dark, obscured by shadows and tracking lines and digital grain. She hit an onscreen button that looked like a magic wand and the picture adjusted, taking on a blue tint.

It was not helpful.

She dragged a slider bar and the image darkened considerably.

'Shit.'

She dragged it the other way, the screen brightening but revealing no new details, the background still unidentifiable. There seemed to be only one light source from somewhere in the corner of the room. She moved through the film frame-by-frame until she found something in the background, a white square. It looked like a sign. Willow zoomed in on the picture. An EXIT sign? She couldn't be sure, so she zoomed in further, until the screen broke up into a mass of useless pixels.

She played around for a while, and when Cat knocked on the door to tell her dinner was ready, she found Willow inches from the screen.

'You'll get square eyes sitting that close to the telly. That's what my mum used to say, anyway.'

Cat had been weird all day, skipping uni and pottering around the house like last night hadn't happened and everything was normal, fine, *tickety-boo.*

We all have our ways of dealing with things. At least she hadn't seen the video.

'Just checking something,' muttered Willow.

'What'd you say? Doesn't matter. Tea's ready if you want.' Cat waited a while, then left, off to water the plants again or rearrange the furniture, anything to keep her mind busy.

Willow didn't notice her leave. She stared at the screen, into the eyes of the girl. Her tortured face filled the monitor, blending with Willow's own reflection.

'Who are you?' she asked, and then a tear rolled down the girl's cheek and Willow realised it was her own.

12

THE WARM WATER CASCADED OVER WILLOW'S SHOULDERS. IT had been a long night, the crowd less receptive than normal, the applause muted. Perhaps it was her own fault. There was too much going on inside her head for her to commit to the performance with her usual gusto. She felt distracted, and also...what? Depressed? Was that it? Something about that video had really messed her up. Not just watching someone die — fuck, that was bad enough — but the idea that someone had murdered them. To see the victim's face, to hear her whimpers and moans and cries...how could someone stand there and attack her until she was no longer recognisable as human?

She stepped out of the shower and felt the warmth of the underfloor heating on her wet feet.

CB, you're a lifesaver, she thought. *A sleaze and a perv, but a lifesaver too.*

Wrapping a towel around her waist, she padded through to the dressing room and parked herself on the leather couch. She was still sitting there when Eve came offstage twenty minutes later.

'Hey Will, how's it going? That was shite,' she continued, not waiting for Willow's response. 'Just did two slots back-to-back cos Jane called in sick, but we all know she's on holiday with that cunt from the bank, and she's going to turn up next week with an allover Mallorca tan and CB's gonna hit the roof.'

Willow nodded as if she was listening.

'And he wanted me to dance to dubstep tonight! I mean, you ever tried dancing to dubstep? It's not sexy, no way. I was like, "CB, you're my boss and all, but leave the music up to me, okay?" and he was all, "You'll do what I say or else you'll be out on your arse," and you know what I said Willow?'

'Huh?'

'I said, "Well this arse is about to get out there and make you a lot of money, so..." Willow, are you even listening?'

Willow looked at her. 'Umm, yeah, you were saying something about your arse?'

Eve headed for the shower. 'Not quite, Will. Close, though. And why are you sitting with your tits out?'

'I'm posing for a Renaissance painting.'

Eve didn't understand, and stuck her tongue out in response. When she got out of the shower, she found Willow sitting naked in front of the mirror.

'Have you had a fucking stroke or something?' she asked, compassion not being one of Eve's stronger personality traits. 'You're acting weird.'

'Got a lot on my mind right now.'

Eve plopped herself in the chair next to Willow and spun to face her. 'Boy trouble?' she said in her most sympathetic voice. 'You can tell me.'

'Boys? Fuck no. This is real trouble.' She looked at Eve. 'Can I trust you?'

She knew she couldn't, but Eve said she could and

Willow, wanting someone to talk to, told her about the phone and the video.

'Oh my god,' said Eve, nodding appreciatively at this extraordinary gossip that had landed right in her lap. She placed a hand on Willow's knee, her skin almost dry now, and gave Willow what she thought was her most intense look.

'Can I see it?'

'The video?'

'You kept a copy, aye?'

'Yeah, but it's fucked up.'

Eve smiled at her. 'Come on, Will. You're not the only one with a dark side. I wanna see,' she pouted, the face of someone used to getting their own way.

'I mean…if you really want to…'

'I do.'

Willow took the phone from her bag, unlocked it, and handed it to Eve. She dressed as Eve watched the video, trying to ignore the sounds that had bothered her throughout her performance tonight. She put on her t-shirt, not noticing it was inside-out. The video finished with the cut-off scream and she saw Eve typing away at her phone.

'What are you doing?'

Eve didn't look up. 'Sending this to my phone.'

'Why?'

The girl shrugged. 'I think my boyfriend would like to see it. He's into some freaky shit. This one time, he asked me to lie totally still while he fucked me, like I was dead. I wasn't allowed to make a sound.'

'That sounds like a healthy relationship.'

'You gotta keep it interesting,' remarked Eve, hitting Send and passing the phone back. 'Your shirt's inside-out, by the way.'

Willow didn't care. Eve's attitude towards the video fascinated her.

'You don't think it's real?' she asked.

'Dunno. Probably not.'

'But a girl was killed, and that was the last thing on her phone.'

Eve started dressing. 'Doesn't mean anything. If I died tomorrow, you wouldn't *believe* some of the shit on my phone. With my Google history, I'll be on an FBI watchlist.'

'I guess so.'

'Everyone's hiding something, Will. Even you have your little secrets.'

Eve turned away with an unfamiliar expression on her face. It looked to Willow like thoughtfulness.

'See you tomorrow then,' said Eve, as Willow slung her bag over her shoulder and left. The door closed with an audible *click* and she waited until Willow's footsteps disappeared down the hall. She glanced around the dressing room in case someone was there, listening in, but she was alone. Heart racing, she took out her phone.

This was it. Her ticket out of this dump, out of this life of stripping and being ogled by men. She wanted more. She wanted to be rich, to be looked after, waited on hand-and-foot. She wanted servants and butlers and maids and chefs and personal trainers.

A voice answered and she cleared her throat.

'I know what you're doing,' she said, pleased with the authority and gravitas she had injected into her little act. All the best dancers were great actors, that's what CB had told her once. 'And I have proof. It could fucking bury you.'

'Who is this?' said the voice.

'It doesn't matter. Just know that I have evidence, and I'm going straight to the police unless you pay me ten thousand...no, *fifty* thousand dollars. Wait, no, I mean pounds. Fifty thousand pounds. Bring it in a suitcase to...' She thought hard. It had to someplace public, but also quiet. She should have considered it before phoning, but she was too excited. 'Bring it to the old bandstand in Princes Street Gardens at nine tomorrow morning. Be there...or else. What's that? Okay, fine, six. Ten thousand at...dammit, I mean fifty thousand pounds at six tomorrow morning. I'll see you there. I'll be wearing a red jacket.'

She hung up, pleased with how it had gone. The red jacket was a nice touch.

All the best dancers were great actors, CB had once said.

Eve, however, was neither.

13

WILLOW HUNCHED OVER THE LAPTOP LIKE A GARGOYLE. IT WAS 3am. She had downloaded a copy of Final Cut Editing Software from Pirate Bay and spent the last two hours watching YouTube tutorials on how to work the damn thing. Worst of all, the videos were invariably voiced by American boys who were, at most, fifteen.

It was a ridiculous, fiddly program, with hundreds of filters to choose from, most of which seemed to do the same thing, while the rest did nothing at all. Every change she made had the opposite effect, obscuring the image further. She stopped for a while and sat smoking by the window, the night chill invading the room. Looking out at the rain-soaked streets, she watched people hurrying by. They looked so innocent from a distance. As each passed, she wondered if they had the capacity to kill.

'Jesus, you're losing it,' she said to herself. It was good to acknowledge it. It made her feel like she was still sane.

Her thoughts turned to Detective Stone. He had mentioned another body with a possible link to Jessica. Willow didn't read the papers, and actively avoided the news, so she had heard nothing else about it. She closed Final Cut for the evening and fired up Google.

The BBC apparently didn't deem it worthy of coverage, but there was a short piece on the Scottish News website. The article said that a girl had been stabbed, but there was no mention of other victims.

She Googled 'Edinburgh Stabbing' and a photograph of Jessica Chalmers gazed at her from the top of the screen. She looked a lot younger, *years* younger in fact. Rounder in the face, with sparkling eyes and flowing brown hair. The next result was a video. Willow clicked it, and it redirected her to Twitter, playing automatically.

Jessica Chalmers lay bleeding on the pavement, surrounded by a group of onlookers. A young man rhythmically pumped his hands on her chest.

'Stop filming!' shouted an unidentified voice. Someone else laughed.

'Oh my god,' said the man holding the phone. 'It's about nine o'clock, and we found this girl on the street.' He turned the camera away from Jessica and pointed it at his own bearded face. 'It looks like she's dying.'

'Switch that off ya sick cunt,' shouted someone. The man ignored the heckler.

'What happened here?' he continued. A siren wailed in the distance. 'Is it a gang slaying? Or a serial killer? I was on my way to band practice — check us out on Soundcloud, real guitar rock with Kevin and The McAllisters — when I stumbled upon this horrifying scene.'

The camera turned back to Jessica. The man kneeling by her had given up. He looked like a ghost, his hands dangling limply by his sides, his head shaking.

'She's dead,' he said. He looked at the camera. 'For god's sake stop filming, can't you see she's fucking *dead*?' He got to his feet and started towards the camera. The image cut to black for a second, then resumed with a closeup of the bearded man. A trickle of blood ran from his nose.

'He fucking hit me, man,' he said. The camera tracked towards the crime scene again. The ambulance had arrived, and the paramedics were attending to Jessica's prone body. In the background, Willow could see herself getting into the police car, Detective Stone holding the door open.

The bearded man continued. 'I've deleted that part of the video for now, because rest assured I'll be talking to the police. I can film whatever I want, there're no laws out there. This is in the public interest, aye, so the police can't cover it up, and that wanker fucking leathered me. Well, it's all recorded, so *I'm* gonna have the last laugh.'

Wait.

Willow hit pause, then scrubbed through the timeline.

There.

She full-screened the video and hit play. A man walked away from the scene, dressed in black. Well, walking wasn't the right word. He was limping, like the man Willow had seen from her window the evening of the killing, the man who had stood and watched her from the street.

The video ended, and Willow instinctively stared out the window. There was no one there now. Even her personal voyeur across the road must have gone to bed.

They know who I am, she thought. *They know where I live.*

So why was she still alive?

Because you have nothing on them.

'Not yet,' she growled, suddenly feeling very alone.

She climbed into bed, drew the protective shroud of the covers around her and went to sleep. At one point she woke to find herself in an industrial building, water dripping from huge chains that clanked overhead, the walls of her bedroom covered in obscene graffiti. A girl was on top of her, naked, beautiful, and drenched in blood. She lay helpless as the girl kissed her, her hand finding Willow's crotch, the other holding a hammer. She brought it down hard and fast, the bell of the hammer striking her square in the forehead.

She woke up sweating, checked her skull was still intact, and didn't go back to sleep.

14

THE CITY OF EDINBURGH SLUMBERED, THE CURTAINS DRAWN, the sun nowhere to be seen. Eve passed a lone jogger huffing his way through the streets, and a harried looking woman walking two excitable pugs, the dogs determined to sniff every inch of the pavement. Few cars were on the road, and Eve realised she should never have agreed to meet so early.

It was too quiet.

Still, fifty-thousand pounds, eh? Not bad for a morning's work.

She reached the gate to Princes Street Gardens, the large public park that sat in the ancient shadow of Edinburgh Castle, and found it was locked.

'Fuck,' she said. Of course it was. According to the sign it didn't open til seven. She looked around the empty streets, through the fine mist that had settled. Not a soul was watching. Headlights cut through the fog and vanished, the number twenty-six bus carrying its passengers to work like the ferryman on the River Styx, and then all was silent.

What to do?

She couldn't wait until the park opened. If she missed the meeting, she might not have the guts to go through with it again.

That left one option.

Placing her foot on the fence, she hauled herself up. Working the pole at CB's had given her tremendous upper body strength, and she made it over with ease, landing stealthily on the wet grass. She moved away from the road, wary of being spotted by the groundskeeper. Did this place have groundskeepers? Did anywhere, or was that an invention of children's comics? Now would not be a good time to find out.

Keeping low, she dashed from tree to tree, then checked her phone. Almost six. She cursed herself for sleeping in. She wanted to arrive early, to be the one in control. Too late for that. She had already been tricked into meeting alone.

Stupid!

She walked into a low-hanging branch and shook last night's rain all over her. Why were there no lights? Determined not to lose her bearings, Eve headed towards the glow of Princes Street. That way, she would have to cross a path at some point, a path that she could follow to the bandstand. Sure enough, her feet found concrete and she turned left, pleased with herself. She hugged her red jacket tightly around her and shivered. The jacket would make her easy to spot, and that was dangerous. What if they were—

No, don't think like that.

Instead, she fantasised about how she would spend her newly acquired riches. The first thing she would do would be to go on holiday. Somewhere exotic and far-off, like Zante or Ibiza. She would leave her dumbass boyfriend behind unless he paid his own way. This was *her* money, not his. Hell, maybe she would retire there and live the life of a princess, waited-on hand-and-foot by her servants.

Something moved in the bushes and she stopped, her throat small, breaths coming with alarming difficulty.

Think of the money!

Yes, the money. It would all be hers, and soon!

Another sound, a different direction this time. Birds? Foxes? A squirrel?

'Hello?' she called out, unable to disguise the tremor in her voice. 'Who's there?'

She turned sharply, turned again, but all she could see were shimmering ethereal outlines.

'I've come for my money,' she said, and thought she heard someone laugh.

She whirled on the spot, searching for clues and finding none, then stepped back and slipped, landing heavily and winding herself. The dewy grass soaked through her yoga pants, and as she got to her feet tears formed in her eyes. She wanted to be anywhere but here, alone in the middle of nowhere.

No, not alone. That was the problem.

Shadows scuttled through the mist, the vague impressions of trees swaying languidly. She walked backwards, hands up in submission, too afraid to speak. Something touched her shoulder and she screamed.

A tree. A fucking tree.

Eve laughed in spite of herself. It wasn't funny, but the release felt good, and then hands gripped her hair, pulling her head back as cold metal pressed against her throat.

'Hello Eve,' said a voice in her ear.

'Please,' she whispered. 'I'm sorry. I won't tell anyone, I swear.'

'Oh Eve,' said the voice. *'You're gonna die.'*

She threw her elbow back, striking hard. The grip loosened, the knife dropping to the concrete path. Eve pulled free, a handful of hair tearing from her scalp.

She ran.

The ground was slippery and maintaining balance was difficult but not impossible. Hell, she had danced on stages that were positively *soaked* with booze. She could do this.

Fuck the money. All that mattered now was getting out of here alive.

And then what? She would have to flee the city, maybe even the country. They wouldn't stop, not until she was—

Lights! Up ahead, a passing car.

She heard the laughter again, that cruel, mocking sound.

You're gonna die.

No way. Not today.

The footsteps were gaining on her. Branches slashed her face as she worked her legs, the mist near-impenetrable. She turned and saw a dark figure behind her, a ghost in the fog, and then she hit the fence full-force, smacking her forehead.

She stumbled back, rubbing her brow and blinking away stars, putting two hands on the metal and one foot on a lower spike for momentum, trying to haul herself over. Panicking, her hands slipped and she dropped, the metal spike piercing through the flimsy sole of her Converse trainers and puncturing her foot. She yelled in agony and tried again, lifting herself from the ground, but her foot was stuck, impaled on the spike. Hands grabbed her jacket, yanking her down, her bones crunching as the wrought iron forced them aside and burst out the top of her shoe. The man took her by the head, lifting her up towards the fence, and for one crazy moment she thought he was going to help her over.

Then he positioned her chin over one of the spikes, the metal peculiar against the soft underside of her jaw, and before she could cry out for help he forced her head down. Her skin offered no resistance, tearing away as metal met flesh, ripping through her jaw and into her mouth, slicing easily through her tongue until it met her hard palate.

Then the man started pounding on the dome of her skull, harder and harder until something cracked and Eve's head slid down the remainder of the spike, her jaw coming to rest on the bar of the fence, blood fountaining from her mouth like a grotesque garden ornament.

Within the hour, the morning drizzle had dispersed the fog, and the woman who found Eve's carcass hanging there like a pig in a slaughterhouse would never fully recover from the shock.

15

The rain thrummed off the coffin lid as Jessica Chalmers was laid to rest. Willow clutched her handbag to her chest, out of place and uncomfortable. It wasn't just that she didn't know anyone — it was churches in general. She could count on two fingers the amount of times she had been inside one.

Her parents' funeral. Her friends' wedding (they had divorced a year later).

And now this, the funeral of a girl who had died in her arms just a few days prior. She glanced around the churchyard, at the mourners dabbing their eyes with expensive handkerchiefs and muttering about how she was so young, gone too soon, such a waste.

The service took place outside, the crowd gathering around the grave and struggling to hear the minister's words over the traffic on the other side of the old stone walls.

Life goes on, she thought. *Except in here, in graveyards, where time forever stands still.*

She had woken early to attend. Cat was already at uni, and Willow was thankful she didn't have to explain where she was going. Cat couldn't seem to grasp the seriousness of the situation. She had pushed the video from her mind, perhaps as a means of self-preservation. For Willow, it wasn't that simple. The only way to make amends was to bring to light the reason Jessica had died. To expose the truth, however ghastly it was.

So you're here to snoop, then? Looking for clues? Gonna question her family on this of all days?

No, she wouldn't do that. Well, not unless the opportunity presented itself...isn't that what her father would have done?

The minister droned on about Jessica taking her place by God's side, his voice little more than white noise. Jessica's mother dropped a rose onto her daughter's coffin as it was lowered into the ground, then retreated to the safety of her husband's arms. The pair were a handsome couple in their fifties. Jessica's father wore an eye-wateringly expensive suit, his greying hair cropped short. The stoic mask of his face betrayed no emotion. Jessica's mother, on the other hand, wept against her husband's shoulder. She wore all-black, each item from a designer label.

Willow caught the father's eye and realised she'd been staring. She looked away, embarrassed.

So far, no one had questioned her presence, but she supposed that was bad form at a funeral. A single photographer lurked outside the gates, snapping away with a telephoto lens beneath a golfing umbrella. Halfway through the service, he left. A young girl's death wasn't particularly newsworthy these days.

It's the new normal.

She watched the journalist get into his car and drive off, no doubt to chase another coffin. As the vehicle turned the corner and vanished from sight, Willow spotted a figure by an oak tree in the corner of the cemetery. A girl, her dark, curly hair tied back in a ponytail, loitering in the shadow of the ancient tree as if afraid to come any closer, the rain bouncing off her black jacket.

People began shuffling away from the grave in single file. The service was over.

The priest said something about the wake, and then closed his worn bible and trudged back to the chapel, his black robes dragging through the mud. Willow opened the pamphlet she had been given on arrival, adorned with photographs of Jessica throughout her short life. There she was as a baby, then as a toddler, excitably opening her presents on Christmas morning. The most recent was a school photo, and Jessica couldn't be more than ten or eleven in it. She was nineteen when she died, so where were the shots from the last decade?

According to the pamphlet, the wake was to be held at Jessica's parents' house, a five-minute walk from the church. She didn't know why, but she followed the crowd. Did Jessica have no friends? She could see no one under the age of at least forty, apart from the girl by the tree. Willow scanned the grounds for her, but she was gone.

'Like a fucking ghost,' she whispered. The sky rumbled overhead and she fumbled in her pocket for a smoke, following the procession of mourners out of the cemetery.

~

The house was located in Morningside, one of Edinburgh's most affluent areas. A two-storey brick mansion, with a driveway leading to a double garage, and exquisitely trimmed topiary lining the garden, tall enough to keep out prying eyes and unwanted visitors.

But what are you *doing here?*

She had no answer. In the vestibule, a man in a waistcoat and bowtie waited, balancing a tray of champagne glasses. He offered one to Willow and she took it. The man regarded her with sad eyes and nodded gravely, saying nothing.

She wandered into a lavish room, a table set out with sandwiches and finger-food, the mourners milling around making half-hearted small talk and sipping their drinks. In the corner was a bar, well-stocked with wines and champagne, where most of the men had gathered. Jessica's father staggered through the crowd towards them, people parting to let him pass. One of them patted his shoulder and solemnly nodded, but he ignored the group, reaching over the counter and pouring himself a whiskey. He looked haggard, as if the strain of remaining so unemotional was taking its toll.

Just leave, thought Willow. *You don't belong here. You're nothing but an interloper. A grief tourist.*

She looked over to a bay window lined with heavy velvet curtains, in front of which sat Jessica's mother, weeping softly into her hands, while a lady with white hair and a black veil comforted her. She thought she saw movement in the garden, and stood on tip-toes to get a better look.

'I don't think I know you,' said a voice. Willow spun, coming face-to-face with Jessica's father. He looked at her through rheumy eyes. 'Were you one of Jessica's friends?'

'Ummm,' said Willow.

Speak, you idiot!

'We knew each other a little,' she managed.

No sense in bringing up the gory details.

'Jessica was an enigma,' he said. 'I suppose no one ever truly knew her. Perhaps not even herself.'

‘I’m sorry,’ said Willow, but he wasn’t listening.

‘No father should outlive his daughter,’ he said, a tear running down the ragged lines of his cheeks, disappearing into his well-trimmed, greying beard. He took a sip of whiskey and stared into space. ‘No father should outlive his daughter.’ He left her, heading back towards the bar, slamming the now-empty glass down and reaching for the bottle.

‘So sad,’ said an older woman, and Willow realised the lady was talking to her. ‘She was such a sweet girl. I taught her the harp, you know.’ The lady smiled. ‘She was a natural. I thought she’d end up playing the Royal Albert Hall. And now...’

‘Now she’s dead,’ finished Willow.

The woman leaned in closer. ‘Apparently she was on *drugs*,’ she said conspiratorially. ‘Not that I’m one to gossip, of course.’

‘Of *course*.’

‘A drug-induced freakout, that’s what I’ve heard. She killed a man, you know.’

‘So I’m told.’

The lady looked closely at her. ‘How did you say you knew Jessica?’

‘I didn’t,’ said Willow, walking away.

Time to go.

As usual, her subconscious was right. She placed her glass on the mantel next to a photo of a Chalmers family picnic and slipped into the hallway as the woman muttered something behind her. The man in the waistcoat was no longer there, the drinks tray resting on a chair that looked more expensive than Willow’s entire flat, full of empty, lipstick-smeared champagne flutes. Willow opened the door and stood a moment, watching the rain fall. A little girl in a yellow mac splashed through the puddles, a lonely voice calling for her to come home.

Without fully realising why, Willow slowly turned until she faced a winding, carpeted staircase. The hallway was empty, the soft murmur of idle chit-chat leaking through the closed door.

She took a tentative step towards the staircase, waiting, hoping for someone to appear and stop her, but no one did.

She gripped the bannister and started up the stairs, leaving the hum of voices behind. Glancing over her shoulder, she expected to see someone telling her that this area was off-limits, but she was alone.

At the top was another long hallway lined with doors, the only light coming from the rain-speckled windowpane at the end of the hall. She glanced through a gap in the first door, at the plushest bathroom she had ever seen, and kept walking. She would find no answers in there.

Answers? To what, exactly?

She would know when she found them.

She moved to the next door, passing a series of framed black and white photographs of decaying urban buildings and parks. There was a scrap of paper stuck to the door, one edge torn as if ripped from the pages of a notepad. Written in felt-tip, and surrounded by glitter-glue stars, it said,

"JeSSicaS RooM"

Willow smiled. The handwriting belonged to a child. Jessica probably hadn't lived here for years. Feeling ridiculous, she turned to sneak back down the stairs when she heard a shallow bump from inside. A thin sliver of light escaped beneath the entrance. Was someone in there? She paused, pressing her ear to the door, hearing nothing but the elegant strains of classical music playing from below. She looked down the hall, at the staircase beckoning her back to normality. All she had to do was descend those stairs, leave the house, and get on with her life. Problem solved. She had no business here. Life was complicated enough without trying to solve a murder like some amateur gumshoe. After all, the police were on the case.

The police. Like they give a shit.

'Fuck those guys,' said Willow.

She heard the whisper of footsteps on the stairs, then turned the handle, nudged open the door and stepped inside.

It was a child's bedroom, the walls decorated in garish pinks and purples, adorned with framed posters of horses and Minnie Mouse. The room smelled sweetly of summer grass, of childhoods spent outdoors, and forgotten secrets. The window was open, rain splashing over a wooden chest and pooling on the carpet.

The bed was undisturbed, but each dresser drawer jutted out like obscene tongues. She noticed the bedside cabinets had also been rifled through. Someone had been in here recently. Had the person found what they were looking for? Or had she scared them off?

What if they're still in here...?

Her blood seemed to freeze in her veins, her eyes — the only part of her able to move — darting around the room, settling on the wardrobe, the door half-open. Willing her body to function, she stalked to the wardrobe, her fingers finding the handle. She threw the door open and stepped back, smiling when all she found were rows of expensive designer dresses. Beneath them sat a painted wooden jewellery box atop several shoe boxes. Willow knelt and lifted the music box's lid. A tiny ballerina rotated before an oval mirror, and a piece of music she recognised as Swan Lake tinkled delicately.

She smiled, feeling nostalgic for a childhood she'd never experienced, one in which she'd been loved unconditionally by parents who hadn't died when she was seven, where she had wanted for nothing and grown up surrounded by laughter and games and other children, rather than being shunted from home to home, never settling in or settling down. She supposed a lot of that was her fault. After a while, she'd just stopped trying.

She fought back the strange melancholy waking within her, and slid open the drawer of the music box. Inside was a heart-shaped silver locket. She lifted the jewellery and it dangled from her fingers, catching the light as it rotated. Willow snapped the locket open. On either side of the heart were photographs of two girls. She recognised the first immediately; it was Jessica, smiling, pretty, happy. She looked so different. Willow squinted at the other photo. It was a girl of a similar age, dark curls springing over her shoulders.

It was the girl from the funeral, the one sheltering far from the rest of the mourners.

Who was she? A friend? A sister? A lover?

Footsteps stomped along the hall. Without thinking, Willow pocketed the locket and stood, heading for the exit. Before she reached it, the door burst open.

'What are you doing in here?' cried Jessica's mother, flanked by two older men with grim expressions, their faces carved in granite.

'I'm sorry,' stammered Willow. 'I was looking for the bathroom.'

The woman looked past her, to the bedroom in disarray, the clothes and belongings piled on the floor and spilling over the lip of the drawers. Her bloodshot eyes widened and she pointed a shaking finger at Willow.

'You...you've been going through her things! How could you, on the day of her...her...'

'It wasn't me,' said Willow, knowing how feeble that sounded.

The woman struck her across the face with surprising force. 'Get out!' she shouted. 'Get out of my house! Get out of Jessica's—'

But at the mention of her daughter's name, the woman dissolved into tears and slumped against the door frame, one of the men catching her.

The other man, bland and featureless like a slug in a suit, took Willow by the arm.

'This way, please,' he said in a stiff voice, 'or we'll have no choice but to call the police.'

Willow allowed him to lead her to the top of the stairs, then shook free.

'Okay,' she said, 'you can let go. I'm leaving.'

His deep-set eyes brimmed with casual fury. 'Just make sure you do.'

Willow started down the stairs. She paused halfway and turned back. 'Tell her I'm sorry for her loss,' she said. The man didn't reply.

As she stepped out into the rain, she heard Mrs Chalmers weeping through the open window. She looked up at it, and then down to the garden below, at the trough of churned grass and mud where someone had landed and made their escape. Tracks led away from the house, turning to muddy footprints on the paved path. In a matter of minutes, the rain would wash them away.

Willow shoved her hands in her pockets, her fingers brushing the cool metal of the locket. She knew she should return it, maybe slip it through the letterbox, but something in her subconscious stopped her.

She turned her back on the house, put her hood up, and disappeared into the afternoon rain.

That evening Willow sat with her laptop on her knees, headphones on, watching a screaming Japanese lady being methodically sliced apart, limb from limb. It was a film called *Flower of Flesh and Blood*, part of a series of movies known as *Guinea Pig* that she had read about on Wikipedia whilst researching so-called 'snuff' movies.

Flower of Flesh and Blood was a well-known faux-snuff movie that had caused Charlie Sheen to contact the FBI back in the 90s, believing it to be real. In the film, a young woman is kidnapped by a gap toothed man in a samurai helmet, then tied up and slaughtered. It should have been shocking. It should have been nightmarish.

Willow stifled a yawn.

'Bullshit,' she said to herself. She had found the movie online, on YouTube of all places. The special effects were convincing, there was no doubt about that. But to mistake it for a snuff movie? Sheen must have been on some good crack that day. The lighting and tracking shots were too slick, the sound effects ridiculously over the top, and the acting — whilst not *bad* — paled into insignificance against the real thing.

It was always the eyes that gave it away.

Still, it was a step up from the previous film she had watched, a little gem called *Snuff*. That one had been a 1970s exploitation flick about a sexy all-girl biker gang embroiled in a Charles Manson-style siege, with the last five minutes being a pretend snuff film in which the actress's heart is pulled out of her *stomach*. Even Willow, who had failed high school biology, knew better than that.

She clicked further along the timeline. The samurai was fondling the woman's intestines, letting them ooze through his fingers. It was gross. It was icky.

What it wasn't, was *real*.

'Oh Jesus, Willow, what are you *watching*?'

Willow turned towards the voice. It was Cat, her face ashen. Willow defensively slammed the laptop shut.

'Don't worry, it's fake,' she said, but her protestations fell on deaf ears.

'It's sick, that's what it is. Haven't you seen enough?'

Willow wasn't sure how to answer. She thought for a moment, before settling on, 'It's research.'

It was the best she could come up with.

'But the police told you that video was fake. Why are you still thinking about it?'

'They didn't look properly. They didn't care.' Willow looked away and placed a hand on her laptop. 'Hell, they're probably in on it.' She glanced out the window, into the depthless black of the night sky. The moon was huge, and she felt like she could reach up and pluck it out of the void.

'Look,' said Cat, 'I just came in to tell you I'm putting some pasta on, though now I'm not so hungry.'

'I'm alright, thanks.'

Cat didn't leave. 'You should eat something. You don't look well.'

'I'm fine.'

She turned back to her laptop and lifted the screen, watching Cat's reflection in the monitor. After a while, her flatmate left her alone. She opened a new tab and searched for *Faces of Death*, washing two caffeine pills down with some whisky, feeling like Humphrey Bogart in some old film noir. The only difference was, people believed him. One of the benefits of being an old, straight, white male, she supposed.

She found *Faces of Death* readily available on multiple streaming platforms, but gave up after about twenty minutes. Like *Guinea Pig*, most of the footage had been faked, and none-too convincingly. She switched it off, lit a smoke and fired up Jessica's video again, scrutinising the image for information. There had to be a clue, some vital piece of the puzzle she had missed. If only she could find it!

Halfway through her third viewing, she realised she had to be at work in an hour. Willow had never felt less inclined to get on the stage and dance for the pleasure of others. The thought made her sick. Well, that and the vodka she had been drinking. She looked at the bottle and saw it was almost empty. Had it been full when she started? She couldn't recall.

The room swayed when she stood. God, she was drunk. She *never* drank before going onstage, but tonight was different. It was going to be very different indeed. She walked as soberly as possible into the kitchen and grabbed a knife and a pair of scissors, then slipped back into her room without alerting Cat.

There was work to be done.

16

CB Joe sipped his whiskey and nodded at Ethel to refill the glass. Behind the bar, Ethel sighed — she did everything with a sigh these days — and did as instructed.

CB nodded once more at her. The pair of them communicated solely in nods, sighs, and the occasional grunt. The music was too loud for anything approaching conversation, which was fine for both of them. Ethel had been CB's secretary back when the club was still a workshop, a cantankerous old battle-axe who knew how to deal with obnoxious customers. When CB had told her he was closing down the woodwork shop and turning it into a strip club, he had expected her to hand in her notice. Instead, she had asked how long until the new place opened, gone to Spain for two months, and returned in time for opening day. She was a hard-worker, never late, and hated small-talk.

She was CB's dream employee.

He turned his attention towards the stage. One of the new girls was giving it laldy on the pole, spinning round and round, legs out, then upside down, back to front. He didn't know how they did it. Once, after closing time, Willow had convinced him to give the pole a go, and in doing so he had nearly broken his back. Bloody Willow! She was up next. He slugged down more whiskey and waited. Willow always put on a show. This girl right now, she was good, and had a cracking pair of chebs, but she was no artist. There was no drama, no romance. As much as he chided Willow for her theatricality and self-indulgence, he knew it was what the punters wanted to see. Not all of them, mind. Some were just here for the tits and fanny, but fewer and fewer. Those lads usually visited one of the bars on Edinburgh's Pubic Triangle. CB had a NO STAG DO policy, strictly enforced by himself and, should the need arise, Ethel. Ethel Nitrate, that was what Willow was fond of calling her. He smiled.

It always came back to Willow.

The girl left the stage in high heels and a thong, stumbling as she did so, and the bar filled up with patrons. CB hopped behind to give Ethel a hand. Some studenty-looking cunt asked for a cocktail and CB slammed down a beer instead and took ten pounds payment, no change. The boy sheepishly scurried back to his seat.

Music began to drift over from the speakers, and CB stopped to watch. He didn't like what he was hearing. The music was dark, violent, the atmosphere of the club changing. He recognised it from somewhere, an old film. It always was with Willow. She came onstage, moving lethargically, almost drunkenly, the temperature seeming to drop several degrees. CB took a deep breath, expecting to see it cloud before him.

'What the fuck are you doing?' he muttered.

Her face was pure white. At first he thought she wore a mask, but as she slithered into the light he could see it was paint. Her eyes were ringed with thick black lines, crudely applied, and she wore a dress constructed from hundreds of strips of a shiny black fabric which hung down to her knees. He squinted. In the glare of the lights, it looked like it was made from videotape.

The dangling strands parted as she stalked to the pole, never once making eye contact with the audience. It was unlike her. Something was different. Something was wrong.

'Can I have a drink?' shouted a rake-thin asshole propping up the bar, a panama hat balancing on his head.

'Fuck off,' snapped CB, leaving the bar and walking closer to the stage as Willow wrapped herself around the pole like the snake in the Garden of Eden. Up close he could see her black dress had been sliced into shreds from the neck down, which created the videotape illusion. The way it swooshed around her body gave tantalising glimpses of skin, and it was clear she wore nothing underneath but knickers and a lace garter around one thigh.

CB's heart stopped when he noticed the knife tucked into the garter.

The music got louder, all strummed harp, deep, frightening brass and pounding drums. It was music to get drunk and kill to, not to arouse the passions of a paying customer.

No one moved except Willow, the crowd enraptured as she swayed seductively, her body a poisonous chalice from which they all drank. Intoxicated, CB felt a stirring in his groin. He reached for his whiskey and knocked the glass from the table, as Willow took the knife from her garter and spun languorously by her thighs, the dark hair of her wig trailing. She slid down the pole until her back touched the stage, and pushed herself towards the crowd, holding the metal blade above her breast. It glinted in the light.

That better not be real, thought CB.

She hooked the knife into the collar of the dress and sliced through it with a flick of her wrist, the fabric spilling to the floor like dark blood, then held the tip to her throat, tracing it down her chest and between her breasts, towards her stomach. CB wanted to rush the stage and stop this madness, but his feet were blocks of ice. It was so quiet you could hear a stripper's knickers drop, the music ebbing to nothing, then coming back more visceral than ever as Willow's knife passed her belly and reached her underwear, tugging on the waistband and carrying on until it hovered over her crotch.

She leaned her head back, looking out over the audience, black make-up running in tracks from her eyes. She raised the knife higher and CB started towards the stage, barging between tables, knocking one over, not pausing as the music reached its apex and Willow brought the knife down between her legs.

The crowd gasped. Someone screamed.

'Get the lights on,' hollered CB as he clambered onto the stage, thumping his knee as he did so and ignoring the sharp pain, his eyes focused on Willow as she lay still, the handle of the blade jutting out between her thighs.

'Should I call a doctor?' said someone in the crowd.

'Is she okay?' said another.

Willow stood as CB puffed his way towards her, the knife lodged in the stage. She quickly bowed, and ran into the wings.

'Hey she's fine,' called a disgruntled punter. 'I want my money back.'

Normally CB would have throttled the customer, but not today. He raced after Willow, heading for the dressing room.

'Bravo,' shouted a voice that CB recognised, one he hadn't heard for a long time. He stopped, gazing out into the lights, shielding his eyes with his hands, but he couldn't see, couldn't find the source.

Alice Cooper's *Poison* surged from the speakers, and CB glanced left, one of the new girls standing nervously in the wings, waiting for him to get offstage. He staggered past her as she wandered out to cheers from the crowd, his mind frantic and confused.

He had to find Willow.

~

She burst into the dressing room and threw on a robe.

'You okay, hun?' asked Linda, but Willow ignored her, heading through the fire escape and onto the metal stairs outside. She lit a cigarette with fumbling, clumsy fingers and waited for CB, shivering in the cold.

She finished her smoke unhurriedly, and went back inside. CB was sitting on the couch.

'Well, if it isn't my star attraction.' He held out his hand, the blade resting on it. 'I believe you left your big fuck-off *knife* stuck in my stage,' he roared. She tried to grab it, and he snatched his hand away. 'I don't think so. See, I have a no deadly weapons policy in my club. I never mentioned it before, because I figured you weren't a total fucking idiot, but maybe I had you all wrong.'

'Give me my knife,' purred Willow.

'I should fire you, y'know.'

'Yeah? And who's gonna take over? That girl before me looked like she was having a fucking seizure.'

CB shook his head. 'At least she wasn't in any danger.' He sniffed the air. 'Are you drunk? You fucking reek of booze.'

Willow held her hand out, staring at him. 'My knife.'

They locked eyes, and CB reluctantly placed it in her palm. Something about the way she acted frightened him. She held the knife, catching her reflection in the mirror. She didn't recognise the strange, blank-faced girl staring at her. Holding the weapon like an explosive device, she tucked it in a drawer.

'Listen Will, I need to talk to you,' said CB.

'Jesus, I was trying something new,' said Willow, rubbing the bridge of her nose. She had a headache that wouldn't quit. 'I don't wanna talk about it right now, okay?'

'It's not about the show,' said CB, his voice softening.

'Then what is it?'

'It's Eve, Will. She's dead.'

17

They sat in the claustrophobic space that CB called his office, Willow staring at her hands. There was barely enough room to fit two people ('It's easier if one of them is on their knees under the desk,' CB liked to joke), but Willow sat opposite her boss regardless, the tips of their shoes touching.

'Eve's dead?'

CB put his hand on hers. 'I'm afraid so, aye. Her sister rang in. I planned on catching you before you went onstage, but the bar got busy, and...I'm sorry, pal. I know you two were close.'

They weren't that close — Willow had always found Eve sweet but vacuous — but she didn't bother CB with that information. He let go of her hand and Willow leaned back until her head touched the wall.

'What happened?'

CB stuffed a cigarette in his mouth and offered the pack to Willow. She took one without thinking. 'She might have been murdered,' he said.

Willow's arms broke out in gooseflesh as CB spoke, the

early evening light shining through the slats in the blinds. 'They found her...' he searched for the right words, '...*impaled* on a fence in Princes Street Gardens at about seven in the morning.'

'What the fuck was she doing there?'

CB took a long draw.

'Fuck knows. Didn't she go to some fitness thing?'

'That was on a Wednesday,' said Willow, as if it mattered. Her eyes travelled to the walls of the sparsely decorated room. Posters from the legendary Cannonball Joe's Halloween Nights hung in tatters from decaying Blu-tak, one featuring Willow dressed as Elvira, hitching her dress up to her navel and smiling coyly. The desk was free of clutter, except for a white desk fan and several Polaroids of topless young women, the latest batch of potential recruits. CB must have dug the photos out as soon as he heard Eve was dead. He was nothing if not efficient.

She thought back to the last time she had seen Eve. Yesterday, in the dressing room, when she had shown her the video.

It couldn't be related, could it? Actually, scratch that from the record.

It *had* to be related.

'CB, can I ask you a question?'

He nodded, wearing his most sensitive face like an ill-fitting suit. 'Aye, love. I'm, uh, here for you.' Normally she would have dragged this out, making him feel as uncomfortable as possible, but today was different. She came right out with her question.

'You're a sleazy bastard, right?'

Relieved, CB burst out laughing. 'Aye, I suppose I am.'

'And I bet you've seen plenty of sick shit.'

'I've seen things. I'm not always proud of it, but aye, I've seen what you might call some "sick shit".'

'You ever see a film where the actress is killed?'

CB stopped smiling. He looked at her intently, mulling the question over. 'You mean like a snuff film?'

'That seems to be the term, yeah.'

'No, I've not. I'm not sure they exist.' He stubbed his cigarette and lit another. 'Growing up, we used to watch things like *Cannibal Holocaust* and shite like that. Saw one called *The Killing of America*, compilations of people dying on camera, some real, some fake. Nowadays there're thousands of websites with that stuff, if you go looking. There was one called Rotten, pictures of dead folk, car accidents, crime scenes, in amongst a bunch of porn. I suppose sex and death have always gone hand-in-hand. Me, I always preferred the sex. Never had any interest in watching folk die.'

'But what about videos where the whole point is that the person is murdered on camera?'

'A myth, I reckon. Terrorist beheadings, drug cartel slayings, you can find all that shite. But something like that made for commercial gain? No chance. Where would you sell it?'

'On the dark web.'

'I don't know what that means,' chuckled CB.

'It's like the internet, but totally anonymous. You can buy drugs, order assassinations, whatever you want. If you wanted to, you could sell a snuff movie there.'

'Aye,' said an exasperated CB, 'but who would *buy* it?'

'Some sick fuck rich prick.'

'It doesn't happen. Not in Scotland anyway.'

'We're too civilised, right?' said Willow, running an accusatory eye over the topless snapshots on CB's desk.

'That's just business, Willow. You know that. *You're* my star attraction.'

Willow nodded, playing with a ring on her finger. CB waited a moment before speaking.

'Why do you ask? About the snuff movies, I mean.'

'Because I found one.'

CB snorted. '*Balls* you did.'

'I'm serious. That girl who died — she hid her phone in my bag.' She leaned in closer, lowering her voice. 'There was a snuff film on it, and I think that's why she was killed. The other night, I showed it to Eve.'

CB flicked on the desk fan. Even in the throes of autumn, the office felt like a sauna, particularly when occupied by more than one person. The fan whirred, gaining speed and blowing the Polaroids from the desk. They let them fall.

'There's no such thing as snuff,' he said, though he didn't sound as convinced as he had moments before. He picked up a pen, clicking and unclicking the nib. Every time he did, the lady on the pen's clothes disappeared, then reappeared.

'I can show you,' said Willow.

'You have it with you?'

She nodded hesitantly.

CB exhaled. 'Then I suppose I'd better watch it.'

She cradled the phone in her hand. 'The last person I showed this to is dead. The person who *gave* it to me is dead.'

'That's a risk I'm willing to take.' He wiped sweat from his brow and Willow handed him the phone, sitting in silence as he watched. The final scream cut off as usual, leaving CB staring at the grotesque face that haunted Willow's every waking moment.

He gave the phone back to her, his palms clammy.

'Fuck, it's hot in here,' he said, cranking the dial on the fan.

'What'd you think?'

He pondered. 'Kinda difficult to see. It's too dark, filmed off a telly, shaky camera. Can't you make it brighter?'

'I've tried. It just seems to bleach everything out.'

'What about enhancing it? In the movies, they can enhance the...y'know, *pixels* or something?'

'I don't work for MI6, CB. That's a little out of my remit.'

'Well, I dunno then. I can't tell what's going on.'

'That's what the police said.'

CB sat up. 'You showed *that* to the police?'

'Yeah. Why?'

Was it her imagination, or was his face colouring?

'Ach, only wondering. And what, they didn't believe you either?'

Willow tucked her phone away defensively. 'That's right. But now Eve's dead...'

'Leave it, Willow. That thing on your phone? It's a lot of fuckery. A trick of the eye. You notice how the camera moves away before the first hit? It's so they can replace the actress with a dummy or something. Then that bit where you see the feet of the person filming it? There'll be a wee hidden edit there too. It's not real.'

Willow stood, the chair clattering against the wall. 'Yeah, so people keep telling me, before they turn up dead.'

She turned to leave and CB grabbed her wrist. She glared at him and he let go, leaving light red marks on her skin.

'I'm sorry,' he said. 'Listen, you're upset about Eve. So am I. Take the day off tomorrow, I'll get one of the new lassies to cover your shift.' He shuffled backwards, the chair scuffing the floor, and opened a drawer, rummaging through the contents and emerging with a handful of notes. 'Here's thirty pounds,' he said, holding it out towards her. 'It's not much, but go shopping or whatever it is you lot do for fun.'

'I don't want your money.'

'Take it,' he insisted.

She clasped her hands to prevent her from taking the cash. Thirty pounds wasn't much to some people, but it was a big deal for her. She could surprise Cat by bringing home some groceries, or buy them both a takeaway one night.

'No,' she said firmly. 'This is something I have to do.'

CB shook his head and tucked the money back in the drawer. As he did so, she noticed his eyes flicker to something in the drawer. He hesitated a moment, then slammed it shut. Willow half-opened the door and CB said, 'For fuck's sake, leave this snuff shite alone. It's not worth it. That sort of thing fucks with your head.'

'That's easy for you to say,' said Willow, as she left the room. 'It's not men being killed, is it?'

The door closed behind her, leaving CB alone, the desk fan cooling the perspiration that trickled down his face. He bent and picked up the scattered Polaroids.

'It never is, Willow,' he said.

18

SHE TRUDGED THROUGH THE DISMAL STREETS IN A DAZE, THE smell from the breweries stinging her nostrils, her breath fogging in the cold.

She debated grabbing a coffee, but ghoulish fantasies played over and over in her head. She cast her mind back to last week, when her biggest concern had been whether she could afford groceries, or if it was toast and microwave noodles until payday.

Now, she was mixed up in murder and a possible snuff movie ring.

Entirely of your own volition, by the way.

Maybe CB and Cat were right. She should drop the whole thing, take a few days off, and go on holiday.

And let more innocent women get slaughtered for someone's amusement?

She stopped walking, the realisation of where she was dawning on her like morning to an insomniac.

She looked to her left, to the alley where Jessica Chalmers had died less than a week ago, and felt a lump in her throat.

'Jesus.'

In all that had happened since, Willow had almost forgotten about it, if it was truly possible to forget someone dying in your arms, holding them as they shuddered their final breath.

'I'm sorry I couldn't help you,' she said, sitting herself down on a wooden bench opposite the alley, not caring that the rain drenched her jeans. 'I'll find who did this to you, I promise.' She ignored the looks from passersby, regarding her with either thinly veiled contempt or suspicion.

Let them stare. She was used to it. She had long since come to terms with the fact people liked to look at her. Hell, she'd made a living out of it. Whether they stared at her because she was dancing naked in a club, or because they thought she was a crazy homeless person sitting on a bench in a storm, it didn't matter. It was all the same. People love to watch, even if they're too afraid to admit it in public, let alone to themselves. Others were willing to pay good money for the privilege. She thought of the video, of that screaming face, wet with blood, and wondered how much someone would pay to watch *that*.

How many times had *she* watched that video over the last few days?

That's different, though. I'm watching it to uncover the truth.

But truth comes in many forms, her subconscious argued, *and you might not like what you find.*

The rain let up, and she searched for her last cigarette, looking up in time to see a girl mooching by the alleyway, carrying a wreath of white flowers. Willow kept her head down, stealing furtive glances. The girl looked around the street, as if afraid she was being watched. Her curly brown hair was pulled back into a ponytail, the kind Cat referred to as a council estate facelift, and when she removed her glasses to wipe the raindrops from the lenses, the whites of her eyes were red with tears.

Willow's heart quickened.

The girl from the funeral.

She placed the wreath against the piss-stained wall and said something only she could hear. Then, as the mystery girl took off up the alley, Willow left the bench and followed, almost knocking over a tourist staring dumbly at a map in her haste.

This time she was ready. This time she would get answers. She ran, the girl not looking back at her, her hands firmly in her pockets.

'Wait,' shouted Willow, her voice booming off the narrow walls of the alley. The girl kept walking. There was no way she didn't hear. 'I need to talk to you! I saw you at the funeral.'

She was closing the gap. Another couple of steps...

She placed her hand on the girl's shoulder. 'Hey, I'm—'

The girl spun around, a blur of motion, her left hand rising to Willow's neck. In it, a flash of dirty silver, flakes of rust or paint or blood dotted down it, the knife scraping across her throat. Willow threw herself back, thumping into the wall mere inches behind her, the girl sticking to her like seaweed on a drowned corpse, the tip of the knife pressing hard into Willow's jugular. She raised her chin, trying to pull away, but there was nowhere to go.

The girl's eyes narrowed through her prescription glasses.

'Don't move or I swear to god I'll cut your fucking throat.'

19

WILLOW TOOK SLOW BREATHS, EVERY EXHALATION PRESSING the tip of the blade closer. She looked into the eyes of the girl and saw nothing, two black dots in a cold and unforgiving ocean.

'There's been a mistake,' said Willow.

'I do the talking,' said the girl through clenched jaws. Willow felt the warm trickle of blood running down her neck. 'Who the fuck are you?'

'Willow. Willow Zulawski.'

'And why are you following me, Willow Zulawski? Did Vinnie send you?'

'I don't know who that is,' she answered, so fast the words blended together into one long syllable. 'I just wanted to talk. I saw you putting flowers down where that girl got killed. Where *Jessica* was killed.'

A glimmer of softness came over the girl's face. 'What do you know about her?'

Willow considered lying, but settled on the truth. It was too stressful a situation to come up with and maintain a convincing lie.

'I saw her die. Right here, the other night. I was out walking, going on a date, this guy I met on—'

'Stop fucking babbling.'

'I'm sorry. She, uh, she came out of nowhere, covered in blood. I tried to help her but it was too late.'

The girl stared at her. 'So why did you follow me?'

Willow swallowed. 'I need to talk to someone who knew her. I think I know why she was murdered.'

'And why was that?'

'She gave me her phone. There was a video—'

'You have her phone?' snapped the girl. There was something different in her eyes now. Desperation.

'Not anymore. The police have it.'

'Convenient.'

'I swear, I'm telling the truth. Look,' said Willow, stuffing a hand into her pocket. The girl pressed the knife harder into Willow's throat.

'Slowly,' she said.

Willow carefully removed the heart-shaped locket and held it out on her open palm. The girl looked down in disbelief, her eyes rimmed with tears.

'Where did you get that?'

'I found it in her room. In an old music box.'

The girl smiled wanly. 'The one place I didn't look.' She visibly relaxed, stepping away, placing the knife in her jacket pocket. She took the locket from Willow and held it.

'Thank you,' said the girl, and Willow didn't know if she was talking to her or to Jessica.

'Who was she?' said Willow softly. 'Who was Jessica?'

The girl flinched at the mention of her name.

'She's my girlfriend. *Was* my girlfriend.' She shook her head, tears mixing with the rain. 'She was crazy. I'd never met anyone like her.' She smiled sadly. 'Posh as fuck, like. Her family are old money, Morningside types.'

'Yeah, I was there after the funeral. I saw you outside.'

The girl wasn't listening. 'She hated them, would do anything to piss them off. I guess that's why she started seeing me. A girl from the wrong side of the tracks, or some shite like that.'

'What about the video?'

'Oh, she got into pornos. I don't know if it was for the money, or to upset her family, or if she just enjoyed it. I didn't mind, she only did hetero stuff, real vanilla shit. Those guys with the big dicks don't know what they're doing. They could never satisfy her. No one could, I suppose. Not even me.'

'This was more than sex,' said Willow. 'They were—'

'I don't want to know.' The girl's shoulders slumped. 'I warned her not to get involved, but she said she needed the money. She'd gotten into smack. I think her parents drove her to it.' She looked away, talking to someone that wasn't there. '*They put you under so much pressure*.'

'But don't you care what she died for?'

'No,' she answered sharply. 'No, I really don't. The less I know, the better. She got mixed up with some shady bastards. Dangerous people. Don't go sticking your nose in places it doesn't belong. Trust me.'

'She died for this!'

The girl broke eye contact, looking down the narrow close. 'She died long before this. The girl they killed was just an empty, broken shell.'

'But they're *murdering* people!'

The girl grimaced. 'You think they won't kill you too? And me? Keep up, and you'll soon find out.'

'Are you threatening me?'

'No. You seem like a nice girl. I think you have a good heart. So consider it a warning.'

She turned to go and Willow stopped her. 'You mentioned Vinnie earlier. Who is he?'

For a moment, it looked like she wasn't going to get an answer. Then the girl spoke. 'She used to talk about him. I only know the name, preferred to stay out of it. That was a world I didn't want to visit. I'm not sure people come back from there.'

'Wait, please. I need your help.'

'Drop it. For the sake of you and anyone who loves you, forget the whole thing.' She started walking.

'At least tell me your name.'

The girl turned back. 'My name's Lina, and we will never see each other again. I'm heading out of town, and I suggest you do the same.'

'I need to know what happened,' said Willow.

Lina stopped, wiped her glasses again. 'Why do you care?'

'Because someone has to,' said Willow. 'Because if I'd made some different decisions, that could have been *me* in the video.'

Lina watched her a moment, the rain drizzling down her face. 'Or me,' she said after a while.

'You ever hear about *the less dead?*' said Willow. 'It's people who live on the fringes of society. Minorities, sex workers...you think a junkie or a prostitute's murder is as newsworthy as a politician's, or a millionaire's?'

'It should be,' said Lina, 'but it's not.'

'Exactly. The police have swept Jessica under the carpet, and whoever did it will go on. It could be us next,' said Willow.

'It's not the same,' said Lina. 'She made some bad decisions, she—'

'So did I. I take drugs. A few years ago I made some pornos for cash. So fucking what? Does that mean I deserve to die for some sick fuck's entertainment? Am I inferior, am I disposable, because of who I am? Of where I come from?'

She stopped, wiped away a tear that mingled with the endless downpour. Lina stood silently, watching her. She pulled a key from her pocket and slipped it into Willow's hand.

'Thirty Slane Street. Flat five. She lived there a while. They might have been there already, but if not, maybe you'll find what you're looking for.' She leaned in and kissed Willow on the cheek, her lips cold. 'Good luck,' she said, 'and thank you for the locket. You don't know how much it means to me.' She turned and walked away.

'I'm sorry I couldn't save her,' said Willow.

Lina didn't stop.

'You can't save someone who doesn't want to be saved,' she called back. Then, to herself, she said, 'You can't save someone who's already dead.'

20

SHE CONSIDERED GOING STRAIGHT TO JESSICA'S FLAT.

If it hadn't been almost midnight, she would have, but now the buses weren't running, and she couldn't afford a taxi, so Willow slogged home through the rain, setting her alarm for six in the morning. The key felt like it was burning a hole in her pocket, and she gripped it in her fist in case it magically vanished.

By the time she arrived at her front door, her feet ached and her stomach grumbled, so she changed the alarm to seven. God, she was tired. She needed answers, but could hardly keep her eyes from closing. All she wanted was to go home, munch some noodles, and try to get some badly needed sleep. It didn't seem too much to ask, so when she opened the door and found Cat talking to Detective Stone, she almost turned round and went back outside to wait in the cold.

'Ah, Miss Zulawski,' said Stone. 'Welcome. We've been waiting for you.'

Willow looked at Cat, who offered an apologetic shrug.

'You'll have to wait a little longer,' she yawned. 'I'm going to bed.'

'I'm sorry, but this is not a social visit, charming as you two young ladies undoubtedly are. Why don't we all sit down and have a chat?'

'Apparently I don't have a choice.'

Stone slouched in an armchair, while Willow and Cat took the sofa.

'What's this about?' said Willow. 'I've had a long day.'

Stone smirked. 'Aye, you've been a busy wee bee, haven't you? Out all day, your friend tells me.'

'Most of it. So what? Why don't you cut to the chase and we can get this over with?'

'Fair enough.' Stone folded his hands on his lap. His shirt was too small and strained over his gut, patches of skin visible between each button. 'How well did you know Eve Murphy?'

'We worked together.'

'And?'

'And what? We worked together. End of story.'

'You know she's dead?'

'Oh Willow!' gasped Cat. She ignored her.

'I heard, yeah. Murdered.'

'Well,' said Stone, sipping from a hip flask, 'Nobody said anything about *murder*. That's pure conjecture at this time.'

'So why are you here?'

'Why not? You think I'd only come to see you if I thought she had been killed? That's quite a connection you're making.'

Cat blanched. 'You don't think Willow—'

'He doesn't,' she interrupted. 'He's just run out of ideas already. Are you interviewing everyone at the club, or just me?'

Stone made an approximation of a smile. 'Everyone, naturally.'

'But you're not paying them a house call, are you?'

'Well, not everyone is such accommodating hostesses as yourself and Miss...'

'*Howards*,' said Cat. 'Listen, I don't like the way you're talking to us.'

'And I don't like the way everyone around Miss Zulawski seems to end up dead. It's something that should concern *you*, Miss Howards.' He turned to Willow. 'Where were you around six this morning?'

'I was asleep.'

'Any witnesses? Bring home any of your johns from the club for some extracurricular work? Or perhaps you two are...well, *y'know*.' He chuckled.

'You're a pig,' said Cat. 'Willow *was* here. I can confirm that.'

'And what do you do, Miss Howards? A drug pusher? A pimp? Maybe a grave robber?'

'I'm a nursing student, thank you very much.'

'I see.' Stone turned his attention back to Willow. 'We didn't find a phone on her, which her poor mother says is highly unusual. I wondered if you knew anything about that?'

'Why would I?' asked Willow.

'Well, other people's phones have a funny way of finding you, don't they? And it's odd that hers should go missing, stolen from her body as it hung there like a slab of fucking meat, yet her cash or credit cards were untouched. Doesn't that strike you as unusual?'

'Phones are worth a lot of money.'

'They are indeed, Miss Zulawski. They are indeed. May I see your phone?'

Willow flashed him an empty smile. 'No, you may not.'

'That's fine. Thought I'd ask. No reason.' He placed his hands on the side of the armchair and heaved himself up. 'Well, it's late, and I wouldn't want to keep you two up.'

He handed Willow his card. She refused to take it, so he left it on the table. 'If you do remember anything, please call. It's such a pleasure to talk with you. You too, Miss Howards. I always had a thing for nurses. Something about the uniform...' He pretended to shiver and laughed.

'The door is that way. You can see yourself out,' said Cat.

Willow smiled, not used to seeing her flatmate this assertive. Without another word, Stone left. Cat stalked to the front door, checked through the peephole, then slid the chain into place.

'And that,' said Willow from the living room, 'is why I don't bother going to the police.'

21

Lina closed the front door and stood, soaked to the skin, in the hallway of her flat. There was nowhere to hang her coat, so she dropped it onto the floor next to some scuffed trainers and pizza restaurant flyers.

Water dripped from the tips of her fingers, drumming on the hardwood with monotonous regularity. She took her glasses off, wiping the lenses with her thumb, and placed them on a shelf that hung crookedly on the wall.

Her waterlogged shoes squelched as she walked to the bathroom. There, she kicked them off, then stripped, chucking her clothes into the empty washing basket beneath the sink, before covering herself with a dressing gown and running a bath.

The encounter with that girl had shaken her. What was her name again? She couldn't remember. It had all been too confusing. Someone had been following her for days now, of that she was sure. And that poor girl tonight...she had almost *killed* her.

Willow!

Yes, that was it. Willow. She had almost killed Willow, an innocent girl.

Wasn't she?

What if this Willow was the one who'd been following her? And now she had gone and blabbed everything she knew...well, not quite everything, but enough.

She panicked. Jesus, what if she *was* one of them? What if they had sent Willow to kill her? She pulled aside the flimsy curtain and looked out the second-storey window.

The room was filling with steam from the hot water, and the glass was clouded. She rubbed it with her palm. Was someone out there? Dammit, where were her glasses? She darted from the room and found them, racing back to the window.

He was gone. Or had anyone ever been there at all? Was she paranoid?

It's not paranoia if they really are trying to kill you, she reminded herself.

She untied her wet hair, the curls tickling her neck. At least the hot water still worked. She dipped her hands in, chasing away the numbness. When she took them out, they were bright red up to her wrists.

Fuck it. She would leave tonight. No sense hanging around any longer than necessary. Leaving the taps running, she wandered into her bedroom, pulled an old rucksack from under the bed, and stuffed her clothes in. Some socks and underwear, jeans, leggings, a few tops. She reached into her robe and clasped the silver locket.

That was all she needed. Everything else — the TV, the kettle, the towels, the radio — could be left behind. She opened the locket and looked at Jessica's lopsided grin. It made her smile, something she hadn't done for a while, and it felt good.

'Time to start over,' she murmured. 'But I'll never forget you, my love. Never.'

A knock at the door.

Lina jumped. She left her half-packed bag on the bed and stepped barefoot into the hall.

'Who is it?' she asked, the words catching in her throat.

'Delivery.' A man's voice. She looked at the old clock and saw it was after eleven. Who delivers parcels this late?

'I haven't ordered anything,' she said shakily.

'It's a special delivery. Flowers,' said the disembodied voice, flat and bored. 'I was supposed to deliver between six and eight, but they must have got lost in the back of the van.'

'Leave them on the doormat,' she shouted.

The water continued to pour into the bath, the bubbles rising.

'I need a signature,' said the voice behind the door. He paused. 'I can't go without one.'

'I'm taking a bath,' called Lina. 'Just leave them at the door, please.' Did she sound as afraid as she felt?

'I need them signed for. It won't take a minute, then I can go.'

She crept up to the peephole and peered through, but all she could see was darkness. Perhaps the stair-light outside was broken again? Or was the man still there, staring back through the peep-hole at her...

The phone rang and she screamed. It was the landline. Who the hell knew that number?

'You okay in there, madam?' asked the man on the other side of the door. 'Do you require assistance?'

'No, I'm fine,' she said.

The phone continued to ring.

'Is something the matter? Do you need me to break the door down?'

'No!' she shouted. 'Just leave the flowers and go, please.'

'I need a signature,' he repeated.

Lina staggered through to the living room and picked up the phone.

'Hello?'

A voice on the other end, thin and raspy. *'I know you're in there,'* it said.

'Leave me alone!' she shouted, slamming the phone onto the cradle.

Steam filled the hallway, spilling out through the crack in the bathroom door. Lina hugged her gown tight across her chest and wandered back into the hall.

'Are you still there?' she asked.

There was no response.

The phone rang again. She ran through and picked it up, screaming, 'Fuck off!' down the receiver.

It was time to leave. To hell with the bath, she had to get out right now.

But what if that man was still outside?

What if *he* had been sent to kill her?

Alternatively, he could be a deliveryman doing his job, and running late.

An angry rap at the door.

'Excuse me, but I'd like to go home now. Do you want the flowers or not?'

Lina fell to her knees, hyperventilating.

'Please,' she said, 'Just go. Fuck off and leave me alone.'

'Fine,' the man shouted. 'But if you put in a complaint about me...' she heard him grumble as he trudged down the stairs.

She waited until she was sure he was gone, then unlocked the door and peered out into the stair.

A large bundle of roses lay on the doormat.

Lina snatched them up and closed the door, her heartbeat settling. She checked on the bathwater — almost ready — and then brought the flowers into the kitchen. There was a card attached, and she tore open the envelope.

'I'm sorry I haven't been there for you recently,' it read. *'I hope one day things can go back to how they were. Happy birthday. Love, Jessica.'*

Lina blinked away tears, unprepared for the emotion that threatened to overwhelm her. 'Happy birthday,' she whispered, as if she couldn't believe it herself. It *was* her birthday. Her twenty-fourth. With all that had happened, she had forgotten about her own birthday.

Her iPhone rang from the bathroom, but she ignored it. She broke down, flowers in hand. Jessica must have arranged the delivery weeks ago. And now here they were, a birthday gift from beyond the grave. 'Why did you leave me?' she asked quietly. She smashed the flowers across the linoleum floor, sending petals floating gracefully around the room.

'Why did you leave me!' she screamed.

Her phone continued to ring, and she hurled the roses against the wall, forcing herself up and staggering to the bathroom. The water was spilling over the sides of the tub, and she thought of the time she and Jessica had flooded their downstairs neighbour's flat by keeping the water running while they fooled around in the bath.

She smiled at the memory, then turned off the taps, grabbing a towel and laying it on the ground, the water saturating it. Steam billowed through the room, making it hard to see. She looked for her phone and saw the screen light up like a beacon in the night, a tiny lighthouse through the fog.

Lina picked up her phone. She knew who was calling,

though she wasn't sure how they had her number. Those bastards.

Ah well, she didn't need a phone anyway. There was no one left for her to call. She aimed it at the wall and got ready to throw, until her eyes caught the Caller ID.

Home Phone, it said.

Her home. *This* home.

The call was coming from the landline in the living room.

She didn't know why, but she answered it.

'Hello?' croaked Lina.

It was the last thing she'd ever say.

22

THE NEXT MORNING, WILLOW SAT ON THE TOP DECK OF THE number sixteen bus, watching the people on the street scurry about their lives.

Leith was the polar opposite of Morningside, where Jessica had once lived with her parents in that sprawling mansion. Despite the slow gentrification and influx of students to the area, its rough edges were still visible.

Some of the pubs were already open, or perhaps hadn't closed. The greying patrons gathered outside, smoking, huddled together to stave off the cold. A bicycle clung to the railings, stripped of its tyres, handlebars, and seat. Down one street stood several police officers, the area cordoned off for an investigation.

Willow reached her stop and got off, checking Google Maps for directions. She walked down a side street, surrounded by crumbling tenements that swayed in the breeze like drunks staggering home after a night out, their chimneys stabbing at steely clouds pregnant with rain.

What if she was too late? Had someone already visited the flat and robbed it of whatever secrets it held? She supposed she would never know if they had, some vital shred of evidence having disappeared long ago. And anyway, what did she hope to find? A signed photo of the killer? A written confession?

She clutched the key fiercely and carried on, dodging the dog shit that spotted the pavement. Soon, she found herself on Slane Street. Untended gardens and overflowing rubbish bins flanked the road, while on one side of the street an overgrown children's play area festered. Two youths perched on the swings, too old to be doing so. One swigged from a bottle of Buckfast and passed it to the other, back and forth, back and forth.

As she walked, she wondered how one solitary key would grant her access to both the main door *and* the flat, but upon arrival, the answer was obvious.

The stair door was gone, the number thirty scrawled in magic marker on the chipped tiles. The tiny garden in front of the property had been paved over, a cornucopia of weeds muscling their way through the cracks, and the window that overlooked it had been boarded up with flattened cardboard boxes and masking tape.

'Inviting,' muttered Willow under her breath.

She looked around, saw no one apart from the kids, and snuck inside. The lower level was dark, the morning sun too low to shine through the skylight three floors above. Music drifted throughout the stair, coming from much higher up.

A man lay passed out across the first floor landing, his face coated with a film of sweat. Willow watched him a moment, checking he was breathing. His shirt was unbuttoned, the scrawny chest beneath undulating gently. She tiptoed over him and continued her ascent until she reached flat five. The blue door had several swastikas daubed on it, along with *junkie slut*. She inserted the key, and then a realisation struck her.

Someone else could live here. But wouldn't Lina have mentioned a flatmate? She knocked, three sharp taps with her knuckles, and waited, the key nestled in the lock.

To her right, a door opened, startling her. A middle-aged man dressed in pyjama bottoms and a scraggly white vest regarded her lazily.

'What you up tae?' he wheezed, a cigarette between his lips.

Willow thought fast. 'I'm from the letting agency. Just checking up.'

The lie seemed to work. The man nodded thoughtfully.

'Good. That fucking music's been playing for days. I was gonnae smash the door down.' He gestured behind him. 'My bairn's trying to sleep in here.'

'I'll make sure they keep it down in future.'

'They? There's only one of them.'

'Jessica?' said Willow, seizing her chance. 'Did you know her?'

'Nah. Folks here keep tae themselves. Seen her come and go, like. Nice enough. She's not fae Leith, though.'

'What makes you say that?'

'Her accent. Posh, like they cunts fae—' He stopped, embarrassed, and corrected himself. 'I mean, like they yins fae Stockbridge.'

'Aye,' said Willow, finding herself subtly broadening her own accent in some weird, chameleonic defence mechanism.

'Better get back,' said the man. 'Mind and tell her to shut that music off. My bairn cannae sleep.'

'I will.'

She waited, but the man just stood, watching. She

smiled at him, then turned the key and let herself in, waiting to hear his door close, a sound which never came.

Weirdo.

She wanted badly to peek out and see if he was still there, but what would she do if he was? She let the door slam shut and stood in the hallway of Jessica Chalmers' flat.

The smell hit her first, rancid food and the acrid stench of weed permeating the air. She gagged, turning her head to the side as if *that* would make a difference. Her fingers fumbled for a light switch and found one. Absurdly, the bulb was red, bathing the room in a garish crimson glow. A single pair of ratty looking trainers sat lonely by the wall, and a fridge hummed in the corner.

She looked at the fridge, sniffed the air, and decided against opening it.

The music grew louder, and she followed it, passing through the hall with muted footsteps and entering the living room. It reeked of death, an irony not lost on Willow. She made for the window, throwing open the ratty curtains and letting some light in, half-expecting the furniture to turn to dust as the sunlight hit it. The window was stiff, but she heaved it up — a few inches, that was as far as it went — and thrust her head out into the cool morning air, gulping down great lungfuls.

Over the drone of the music, she heard a dull thudding sound. Ducking back inside, she looked for the source. It came again, the soft pounding.

It was coming from the wall.

Willow crept over towards the old hi-fi system, a relic of the 90s if ever there was one, and hit STOP on the cd player, putting the infernal song out of its misery for good.

'*Thank fuck,*' shouted a muffled voice. '*My bairn can sleep now.*'

Willow didn't respond. Without the music, the room was eerily silent, save for the low rumble of the fridge and the beating wings of a few dozen flies that were already trying to make their escape through the open window.

There was a sofa with a crude throw draped over it, multiple cigarette burns and unidentifiable stains marring the fabric. For one moment, she felt like she was back in the dressing room at her first club, Le Boudoir.

It was not a happy memory.

A filthy sleeping bag lay on the floor like a used condom. Next to it balanced a coffee table, one leg buckling where it was taped together. On top of the table rested a mound of drug paraphernalia, spoons and foil and lighters. Willow knew it well. Too many of the girls she had worked with over the years had been hooked on that stuff. She was willing to give most shit a go, but had always steered clear of heroin. She had seen what it could do to a person, and it wasn't pretty.

In the corner of the room was a narrow worktop, a microwave balancing precariously atop a washing machine, garments spilling out like it had been disembowelled. Next to the microwave was a knife block. Curiously, there were no knives in it. It was the kind of detail Willow wished she hadn't noticed.

The only other point of interest was a calendar hanging askew from a rusted nail.

September, it read, beneath a generic photo of a babbling brook on a hillside. Only one month out of date, surprisingly. She flipped back to August and noticed several dates circled in black ink, and within the circle was the letter V.

V for Vinnie?

Maybe...maybe not. She had hoped for so much more than this, the student flat from hell, pungent and revolting.

She took one look into the bathroom and decided to move on to the final room, rather than unleash the plague of flies that had taken up residence.

Did the police know about this place? Did anyone, apart from Lina?

A heavy padlock barred the last door. She tried the key, but it was too big. Rattling the padlock with her hands didn't help either, so she walked into the kitchen and grabbed the empty wooden knife block. She tested the weight and hoped it would do the trick.

Back in the hall, she raised the block above her head and brought it down on the padlock. It appeared to have no effect. She tried again, this time etching a small dent. A door opened somewhere in the stair and she held her breath. Footsteps echoed throughout, trailing away to nothing. She wiped her brow and went back to work. It was noisy, and sure enough the man next door started knocking on the wall again, shouting something about his bairn.

'Shut up,' she growled.

She brought the wooden block down one more time and the padlock clanged to the floor, followed closely by the bludgeoning implement. Her arms ached, and she stretched out her limbs, her joints popping, releasing as much tension as she could spare.

She rested her hand on the door, ready to open it, then paused. Something in the back of her mind told her not to enter. It was Detective Stone, it was Cat, it was CB, it was Lina, all telling her to give up and go home, that she was treading on thin ice, that she wouldn't like what she found, and all the other boring clichés people say when they have something to hide, or are too afraid to act.

Well, not her. She was doing this for Jessica Chalmers, and all the other anonymous dead girls throughout history. It was what her father would have done, she was sure of it.

Taking a deep breath, she pushed open the door and stepped inside.

23

THE ATMOSPHERE WAS AS STALE AS A NEGLECTED ATTIC, DUST floating ethereally through shafts of light, as if the air itself was a tangible, creeping terror. Covering her mouth, Willow hit the lights.

The room — like the others — was sparsely furnished. A bed frame lay dead against the wall, the mattress covered by several thin blankets of indeterminate colour. There was a panel heater in the corner with a few socks and knickers draped over it, and a bundle of clothes piled in front. At the far end of the room was a large and rather antique-looking wardrobe.

Willow walked towards it, stepping over a pizza box and some paper plates. She looked down, thought she saw something moving on them, and focused her attention on the wardrobe.

If there were maggots, she didn't want to know. She could deal with a lot of things, but not maggots. They repulsed her. She considered maggots the vultures of the insect world, and was undecided as to whether that was an insult to maggots or vultures.

Willow stood before the wardrobe, her hand resting on the knob, struck with a sense of deja vu. Hadn't she been here just yesterday, poised in front of a piece of furniture in a house belonging to Jessica Chalmers? Was she doomed to repeat this act for eternity as penance for some unknown sin?

A sticky substance covered the handle. Blood. It dribbled down the wood to where it had once pooled on the floor, now a dark stain beneath her feet. Her hand was shaking, and she threw open the door before she had a chance to change her mind.

A selection of knives lay on a shelf, the blades coated rust-red. She moved to pick one up and stopped herself.

Fingerprints.

She pulled a pair of leather gloves from her pocket and slipped them on, making a mental note to wipe down any surface she had touched.

The light switch...the knife block...the door handle...

What else? She had to think. God, why was everything she did always so half-assed?

Because you're not a professional. You're a dancer, and a damn-good one. Stick to what you know.

Fuck *that*. No one else seemed to care, not even Lina, the one person who might have helped her. What did Lina know that she wasn't telling? Everything? Willow doubted it.

If she knew everything, she'd be dead.

The thought sent another chill skating down Willow's spine. At what point did *she* become a problem, a problem that needed to be dealt with? They knew who she was, and where she lived. She glanced over her shoulder and listened, hearing nothing but her own heartbeat. From far down the street a car alarm wailed monotonously.

She inspected one of the knives, not sure what she was looking for.

The murder weapons?

There were no clothes in the wardrobe, an old-fashioned television and a chunky VCR taking up the bulk of the space. Piled on a shelf were four or five videotapes, all blank, the white labels scratched from the cassettes, leaving a sticky residue. With a gloved hand, Willow pressed the button on the twelve inch telly and it churned into life, presenting her with a screen of snowy static. She picked up one of the tapes and a piece of paper slipped out from underneath. She stooped to pick it up.

It was a photograph, a Polaroid of a girl Willow didn't recognise. She was naked, a knife held to her throat by an unseen assailant, tears running down her face. She flipped the photo and there, written on the back, was a sequence of numbers that meant nothing to her.

Outside, a car door slammed.

She stuffed the photo in her pocket and inserted one of the tapes into the VCR. The screen was blank for a long time, apart from the PLAY symbol in the top right corner. She didn't remember the last time she had used a VCR. One of her old foster homes had one, along with a collection of Disney films, but that had been long ago, and she hadn't lived there for more than a few weeks.

An image filled the screen.

It was Jessica Chalmers. She stood in what appeared to be some kind of studio, her hands clasped nervously in front of her. She wore black leggings and a blue t-shirt several sizes too small.

'What's your name?' said someone offscreen.

'Jessica Chalmers,' she smiled, her voice echoing and distorted.

'Nice to meet you, Jessica. My name's Robert, and this is Laura. What part are you auditioning for?'

'Topless wench number one,' Jessica answered, somehow keeping a straight face as she did so.

'Okay, great. So let's do a scene. In this one, the reanimated corpse of Robert Burns is coming up the stairs to get you.' Jessica nodded along. She looked younger, maybe a year or two, fresher faced, slightly heavier. The offscreen voice continued. 'I think to make it more real, you should do the audition topless. That okay with you?'

'Sure,' said Jessica, and she moved to lift her t-shirt. Willow hit STOP and ejected the tape. This dumb shit wasn't what she was searching for, though she wondered if the film about a zombie Robert Burns had ever actually been made, and if so, how bad was it?

She selected another tape and slammed it in, the old video machine making its crazy mechanical noises. Her stomach lurched as the picture filled the screen. It was a boy, nude and emaciated, his wrists bound with thick black straps. He sat alone, blindfolded, in some sort of industrial building.

'Help me,' he said, his voice a choked squawk. The camera pulled back, revealing more of his surroundings; the bare walls, the cracked and peeling wallpaper, a smashed EXIT sign above a closed steel door, the floor littered with debris. There was a large boiler nearby, but the place looked like it had been abandoned for years. It *had* to be the same location as the video on Jessica's phone. This time though, the image quality was much better.

This was it, the proof she so badly required.

The boy whimpered as a figure walked into frame. It was a young woman wearing a white apron. She turned to the unseen camera operator and gestured for them to follow. She smiled, and Willow recognised her as Jessica Chalmers.

In her hand she held a straight razor.

'Oh god,' said Willow, her legs suddenly less than steady.

She knelt by the boy, who screamed as she touched his face, scrambling away from her.

'Please,' he said. 'Please...'

Jessica grabbed his head and slammed it off the wall with an audible crunch. He yelped, curling his body into a foetal position.

'Get up,' she shouted, the boy reluctantly complying. She forced him onto his hands and knees, then sat on his back. The boy snivelled and wept behind his blindfold, the camera moving in closer. Jessica's face filled the screen, and she bit her lip in an attempt at seduction, but Willow knew that look, had seen it in the dead-eyed stare of a thousand junkies. Her eyes were vacant. Willow doubted she knew what she was doing. The camera panned down her body, her collarbones jutting out through the taut flesh behind the butchers apron, then continued down to the boy's exposed back.

Jessica traced her fingernail down his spine and the boy shuddered. She lifted the apron and rubbed her crotch against him, grinding her hips, and then placed the razor blade at the base of his neck.

Willow heard footsteps, and it took her a moment to realise they were coming up the stairs. She stepped back from the TV, glancing into the hall.

The screaming started and she whipped round to the screen as Jessica dragged the blade down the boy's spine. At first it looked like it wasn't hard enough to break the skin, but then the flesh opened and fresh blood spurted out, running in rivers down his back, flowing towards Jessica's open legs. She grabbed his bucking body by the hair as she raised the blade again and brought it down on the opposite side of his spinal column in one endless, unbroken cut.

Jessica slid off the man and stood behind him, her legs glistening with his blood. She knelt, facing his bare ass, and placed one hand on a buttock, the other bringing the razor up towards—

Her stomach lurched. Head swimming, Willow ran from the room and into the bathroom, the bile rising in her throat. The stench was unbearable, and the toilet was a clogged-up horror show.

You can't be sick in here. You'll leave DNA.

As if she had a choice. She threw up in the bath, vomiting until her stomach was empty and her head pounded like a marching-band drum. She had to get out, had to get some air. Struggling to breathe, Willow stumbled from the bathroom towards the front door, her outstretched hands reaching for the lock.

A fist pounded on the other side, and she froze, terrified.

A body slammed into the door and the flimsy lock rattled. Someone was trying to force their way in. Willow didn't know what to do, her mind a juggernaut racing out of control. She backed away as the door buckled. Any moment now...

She ran into the bedroom, searching for somewhere to hide.

The bed.

She moved towards it, then remembered the TV was still on. As she raced to switch it off, she caught a glimpse of what was onscreen, an image so revolting, so horrifying, she knew she would never forget it.

The door smashed open and she threw herself under the bed, shuffling as far into the corner as possible. Adrenaline coursed through her veins, her fingers moving of their own accord, opening and closing, as the intruder entered the flat, heading straight into the bedroom, black workboots stomping across the floor.

Willow watched from her low vantage point, cursing her inability to act. But she was scared, scared for her *life*. The man — she was sure it was a man by the way he walked — proceeded to the wardrobe, the door creaking open.

The evidence.

He dropped a heavy black bag on the floor and scoured the wardrobe, soundtracked by the sharp sounds of plastic videotapes being shoved around, picked up, put down. One of the knives fell, landing on the handle and ricocheting across the floor, coming to rest under the bed. It stopped inches from Willow's face. She saw the man's feet turn, and then he was heading towards the bed as she lay helpless. He got down on his knees and a black-gloved hand appeared, groping along the floorboards. She pulled her head back until it touched the wall. The man couldn't seem to find the knife, and he stooped down, readying himself to investigate further.

Do something, she urged herself, but she was trapped.

The one thing she decided to not do was close her eyes. If she was going to meet her killer, then she was damn-well gonna look that fucker in the eyes.

Footsteps in the hall. The man paused, standing with a grunt. Willow watched from under the bed as another person entered. All she could see were his maroon slippers.

'Fuck you doing?' said the man. 'Ma bairn's tryin' tae sleep next door!'

The man in the work-boots stepped forward with surprising speed. There was a sound, a mini explosion of violence, and then the man in the slippers went limp, the fight over as quickly as it had begun. He dropped to his knees, then collapsed onto his side, blood gushing from a wound in his neck. He clawed at it, facing Willow, three feet from her. She wanted to turn away, but couldn't. The man stared at her, eyes widening. He tried to say something.

No, mouthed Willow. He couldn't give away her location!

He reached out towards her, fingers seizing at thin air.

'Help,' he wheezed.

She looked past him. The killer was facing the other way, going through the wardrobe again. Willow pushed the man's hand away, his fingers stained with dark blood.

'Please,' said the dying man, blood spurting from his mortal wound, his eyeballs rolling back into his head. The video tapes smashed off the floor behind him, and the killer brought his heavy boots down on them, stomping until they were destroyed beyond repair. Then he lifted his bag and placed it on the bed, the mattress groaning, pressing down on Willow's back.

A new smell filled the air as liquid splashed around the room, on the floors, on the bed, over the dying man. Willow recognised it immediately.

Gasoline.

Oh god, oh shit, oh fuck.

Every fibre of Willow's being urged her to get out, to *escape*, psychotic killer be damned. She was going to die here, burnt alive. She was going to die, going to die, *going to die.*

Her whole body vibrated with panic. The bed felt like it was crushing her, getting more cramped, and she would be stuck here, unable to move until the fire roared over her and *she couldn't move, god she couldn't move, the fire, the fire, the fire...*

The sharp *whick* of a match from the hallway, and then the room lit up.

It wasn't the explosion Willow expected, as a constant diet of Hollywood action movies had led her to believe. It was more gradual, the flame meandering through from the hallway like a curious snake. Then it touched the wardrobe and the whole thing ignited with a muted roar. The man by the bed caught fire, his eyes shooting open. He tried to scream but his punctured throat prevented it. He shook, his skin blackening before her, the eyes the first to go, popping in the skull, his lips blistering and oozing. She crawled out, the flames licking the wardrobe, but the killer was still in the hall. When she looked back towards her feet, she saw the fire had reached the bed frame, scorching the wood. There was no time. She made her move, scrambling free, and then the footsteps were coming back, the killer returning.

She retreated, watching from beneath the bed as the work boots reappeared. Her back felt hot, the bed sheets on fire. Soon the whole room would be ablaze. Flames danced before her eyes, and then the killer turned and left. Kicking her feet against the wall, she pushed herself free, the heat prickling her skin. The front door closed, and she took one last look at the neighbour. He was no longer recognisable as human, a charred shapeless mass consumed by fire.

She stumbled from the room, keeping low to avoid the smoke, and made her way out the door and into the stair, gasping for breath, ready to hit the stairs running. Then she remembered the words of the dead man.

Ma bairn's trying to sleep.

Willow hesitated. She could hear the quick steps of the killer making his escape. If she hurried, she could catch up to him, follow him, confront him. It might be her only chance. She put a hand on the bannister and paused, looking back at the open door of the neighbour's house, almost obscured by the thick, choking smoke spewing from Jessica's flat.

'Fuck it,' she said, darting past the smoke and into the hallway of the neighbouring flat. How long until the fire spread, or the smoke made its deadly journey into the other homes?

She hurried into the first room and found nothing but stacks of newspapers piled high like a makeshift fort. A hoarder's paradise, but no child. She kicked open the next door, a bathroom, and carried on. The layout seemed to be the same as Jessica's flat, which meant the last room would be the living room and kitchen.

'Fire!' she heard someone in the stair scream as the unyielding black fog of smoke invaded the flat. Willow covered her mouth and nose, her eyes stinging, and then she saw it.

A wooden crib by the window.

She raced over, grabbing the swaddled bundle and holding it to her chest, hurtling through the house. She made it into the stair, coughing, and passed Jessica's flat, the heat from the blaze momentarily staggering her, forcing her eyes shut.

People were evacuating their homes, screaming as they did so, pushing past each other. One man knocked into her and she fell, gripping on to the curiously silent infant in her arms, shielding it from the impact as best she could. She got to her feet and continued down the staircase, and then she was outside, blending into the gathered crowd, most of them in pyjamas and dressing gowns, one poor woman wrapped in a towel, shivering, watching as her house and all her worldly possessions went up in smoke.

In the distance, she heard sirens.

She looked at the occupants, and the occupants looked at her, ashen-faced and cradling the tiny bundle in her arms. What now? What the fuck should she do now?

The baby laughed.

'Ha ha ha ha,' it gurgled.

Faces turned to look at Willow in bewilderment, their eyes watching her, judging her.

'Ha ha ha ha,' said the baby again. It sounded—

Willow pulled back the blanket, gazing at the blank stare of a plastic doll. It fell from her hands, hitting the pavement and bouncing into the gutter. Someone somewhere screamed.

'Ohmygod she killed that baby!' said a voice.

Willow backed away, looking at her hands, shaking her head. The baby laughed again, but it was a lower sound, deeper, as if the batteries were dying.

'It's not real,' she whimpered.

'Somebody stop her!' cried another voice.

High above, a window shattered from the heat.

'Get away from the building,' said someone, as broken glass showered over them, slicing their clothes and cutting their skin. It was the distraction Willow needed.

She looked at her empty, trembling hands, then up at the fast-approaching lights of the fire engine. She turned and ran.

'Ha ha ha ha,' gurgled the plastic baby, face down in the gutter. Then the fire engine pulled in, crushing the doll beneath its massive wheel.

By that point, Willow was long gone.

24

SHE RAN UNTIL SHE COULD RUN NO MORE, HER ACHING LEGS forcing her to a premature stop. Heart pounding mercilessly, Willow stumbled and fell, grazing her palms on the concrete. Two young men from outside a nearby pub rushed to her aid, helping her to her feet.

'You alright?' asked one.

'I'm fine,' said Willow, backing up, wishing to get as far from other people as possible. She started away from them, mumbling, 'Thank you,' before hurrying on, unable to think straight.

Images tortured her mind like a rusted blade to the temple. The ghastly video, Jessica holding the razor, dead eyes above a heroin smile, while the laughter of the doll played on an endless loop. She lurched down a side-street and stood panting. She closed her eyes, but still she saw the doll falling to the pavement, its round head bouncing, and the shocked look on the faces of the building's occupants.

So much for subtlety, she thought, and laughed. It was a strange, childlike laugh, one she didn't recognise. Had she grabbed the doll instead of the baby? Surely not. There was nothing else in the crib. Was there? The neighbour was a crank, a nutter, tending to a piece of plastic as if it were his own flesh and blood.

You'd better hope so.

The man was dead now, another corpse for the fire, another body for no one to care about. The poor didn't matter around here. They were little more than an inconvenience harnessed by aspiring politicians, led around by the nose with the pretence of improving their lot in life, when all they had to look forward to was a smoke and a drink and a million-to-one chance of winning the lottery. She thought back to Jessica's house, to her affluent parents. Why had the girl given it all up to live like this?

Jessica.

The murdered was also a murderer.

She had cut that boy up, tortured him, abused him. What she had done was—

She tried not to think of it.

Please, he had begged as she sliced through his skin as if peeling an orange. *Please...*

So why had *Jessica* been murdered? If anything, this revelation made matters even more perplexing. The deeper she dived, the muddier the waters became.

Willow looked around and realised she didn't know where she was. It was becoming a habit. Checking her watch, she saw it was eight in the morning. She wanted to go home, but Cat would be there, and she would have to tell the whole story, what she did, what she saw...

No, she couldn't do that. She shoved her hands in her pockets and kept walking, following the sound of traffic. Her fingers brushed something and she remembered the photograph. Pulling it from her pocket, she stared at the image for a long time, at the weeping naked girl, the knife at her throat. On closer inspection — too close, some might say — Willow spotted a latticework of scars down the girl's chest and shoulders and arms, some white and faded, others raw, angry and bleeding. What had gone on after this photo had been taken? Who was the girl, and where was she now? Buried in a mass grave? Maybe the other videos would have held the answer...and maybe not. Now she would never know.

Maybe there are *no answers.*

'I don't believe that.'

She cursed herself for not having gone to the flat last night. She could have watched the rest of the videos, called the police, gotten proof...so why hadn't she?

Because it was dark, and you were afraid. It's okay, nothing to be ashamed of. You have every right to be scared. You might be next.

'Shut up,' she whispered, unaware she was doing so.

It didn't pay to think like that. Fuck doubt, and fuck fear. You can't live your life ruled by fear.

She flipped the photo and looked at the bizarre configuration of numbers printed on the back.

56.051894, -2.629404

It wasn't a phone number. The only thing Willow could think of was coordinates, which she vaguely remembered from her brief time in school, on the days she wasn't skiving class. Figuring it was worth a try, she opened the Maps app on her phone and hammered the digits in. Before she hit Enter, Willow paused, flashing back to the video in Jessica's flat, thinking of the background of the location. It was her first time seeing it with clarity, not obfuscated by shoddy camerawork and tracking lines. There was something about it she couldn't place, something...familiar, like she had been there before.

Or somewhere similar. Or it's your imagination.

No, there was a clue, just within reach, but the more she tried to find it, the further it slipped from her frantic grasp.

Relax. Don't force it.

She pictured the razor blade glinting, and behind it the peeling wallpaper revealing crumbling, damp brick like exposed musculature, raw and bloody.

Shaking her head in frustration, she turned her attention back to the phone and the potential coordinates. She tapped enter and the map zoomed in.

Bingo.

The numbers were coordinates, alright. Coordinates for the arse-end of nowhere on the Scottish coast. She zoomed in further, but it was a random beach to the east. Had she input the numbers correctly? Christ, it was 2019. Who the fuck uses coordinates these days?

The beach was three hours by public transport; a bus, a train, and a long walk. She checked her watch again, as if more than two minutes could have gone by, then shoved the photo in her pocket and went looking for a bus stop.

There was someplace she needed to be.

25

THE TRAIN TRUNDLED THROUGH THE COUNTRYSIDE FOR almost two hours, determined to stop at every village station it passed, before reaching its final destination in the quaint coastal town of North Berwick. Stomach rumbling, Willow bought some crisps and a sandwich with her last three pounds, then waited for the bus in the shadow of Berwick Law, a small hill with a whale's jawbone displayed at the summit.

The bus made the journey twice a day, and when it finally arrived an hour later, Willow was the only person waiting at the stop. Determined to conserve her phone battery, she stared out the window at the rolling dunes of golden sand that ran alongside the track. The sun was already dipping low, cascading orange sparkles across the sea. Aside from the seagulls that crowded round faraway fishing trawlers, there were no signs of life.

Where the hell was she going?

'Last stop,' said the driver, and Willow got off. The bus pulled away, churning up dust and gravel, leaving Willow alone. A bizarre near-silence descended, only the faint sound of the waves lapping against the shore remaining.

She headed down to the beach, figuring she couldn't get lost if she stuck to the coastline.

The quietness was brutal, and Willow wanted anything but to be alone with her thoughts. Images jostled in her head, fact and fiction jumbled together. The first video, *Faces of Death*, the photograph, the Japanese *Guinea Pig* movies, the video in Jessica's flat, the baby doll, Detective Stone's face, Jessica dying in her arms...

It was getting harder to remember which nightmare scenes were plucked from reality, and which were the deranged fantasies of her subconscious playing their cruel and savage tricks.

The violent red of the sun gave way to cool blue moonlight, reflecting off the sea with haphazard beauty. She checked her phone (still over fifty percent battery, thank god) and saw three missed calls from Cat.

She worries too much, thought Willow.

While she still had a signal, she called CB to tell him she wouldn't be in tonight, but he didn't answer, so she tried calling the club instead. When no one answered *there*, she sent a text.

A car roared past in the distance. It wasn't the first she had heard, and it gave her hope that she could hitch a ride home after she found...whatever it was she was looking for.

And what was that?

She didn't know. The coordinates pointed to an empty area slap bang in the middle of the sand. Maybe the numbers weren't coordinates, and this was a wild goose chase?

Would that be so bad?

She only wished someone believed her. She needed

support. Did she honestly think she could do this on her own?

You've been on your own your whole life.

True. She had known Cat for two years, CB for three. How well did she really know either of them, and how well did they think they knew her? She remembered something Jessica's father had said at the funeral.

Jessica was an enigma. I suppose no one ever truly knew her. Perhaps not even herself.

Was the same true of Willow? Sometimes her doggedness and determination surprised her, while other times she felt ashamed of her inability to act. She recalled that very morning, lying on the floor, hiding underneath a bed as the killer she sought murdered a man, so scared she thought she might piss her pants. What would she do if confronted by him again? Did she have the strength? The courage?

She noticed a light out at sea. A boat? No...a speck of land offshore. As she advanced, she saw it was a rocky outcrop with one building on it, tall and white.

A lighthouse.

The main beam wasn't on, just a single light near the top. She recalled a bad date, during which her potential suitor told her that most old-fashioned lighthouses had been decommissioned. This guy, whose name she had forgotten, had been nice but terribly dull. If you end up talking about decommissioned lighthouses on a first date, things are not going well.

'X marks the spot,' she said.

She had arrived. The cloudless sky illuminated the grass and the sand and little else. A boat bobbed in the shallows, while an ancient wooden sign warned of the dangers of swimming, and gave the times for high and low tide.

'Well,' she snorted. 'That was worth the trip.'

'Looking fae something?' Startled, Willow spun in the direction of the voice. 'Or are you lost? This is nae place for a wee lassie to be wandering.'

A man stepped out of the shadows. He flicked on a torch and the beam hit Willow in the face, obscuring her vision. She held up a hand to block the light.

'And such a pretty wee thing too.'

'Get that out of my eyes,' said Willow, unable to disguise the tremor in her voice. Thankfully, the man complied.

'Only cos ya asked nicely,' he said, his voice slick with sarcasm. They stood in silence, looking each other over. The man looked around fifty, and wore blue jeans, a white vest, and a leather jacket, like he'd come straight from a high school production of Grease. The shotgun tucked under his arm suggested otherwise.

Danny Zuko this guy was not.

'Now, I asked you a question. Lookin' fae something?' Willow didn't answer. The man glanced down at his shotgun, then back to her. 'Ah, dinnae mind this,' he sneered. '*Protection.*' His sagging face grinned.

'I was told to come here,' she said, projecting confidence.

The man ran the torch up her body and nodded. 'Aye. And who told you?'

She had no time to think. 'Vinnie,' she said, hoping that was the right answer.

'Makes sense. Will you be participating in tonight's activities, or just watching?'

'Watching,' said Willow, not understanding what he meant. It seemed the safer option.

'You're early then. Come on.' He turned his back and motioned for her to follow. Against her better judgment, she did.

The man waded into the sea towards the boat, the

moonlight catching the dull grey of the outboard motor. He shot her a disdainful look.

'I've no' got all night,' he spat.

Willow took a deep breath. No one knew she was here. She wasn't even sure where *here* was.

What fresh horrors awaited her on the island?

She slipped off her shoes, picked them up, and walked into the freezing water.

She was about to find out.

26

THE BOAT RIDE TO THE ISLAND TOOK A MATTER OF MINUTES, but it felt like hours.

The man said nothing as he navigated the craft through the water, deftly avoiding the treacherous rocks that lay below the surface, wind howling across the choppy waves. He killed the engine as they neared a haggard-looking dock jutting out from the shore, letting them glide up alongside it. Safely docked, he tied the boat with a thick rope and held it steady.

'Out,' he said.

Willow hoisted herself up. The man put his hand on her ass as she got out and she shot him a look.

'Just tryin' tae help,' he smiled.

'Sure. I bet you're a *real* helpful guy.'

'A man does his best.' He placed his shotgun on the dock and climbed out after her. 'This way.'

Wooden decking had been laid out along the path, leading to a white building, and beyond that, the lighthouse. Willow fought back the instinct to ask the man where they were, and what was happening. He hadn't been surprised to see her, but she supposed she wasn't the first young woman to make this journey. She wondered if any of the others were alive to tell the tale.

The decking gave way to a well-trodden path that stopped at the old cottage. The man walked past it. Willow tried to peer through the windows, but there was only black nothingness behind the filthy glass.

The lighthouse towered over them, a blank white monument that obscured the moon and bathed them in pitch black shadows, the torchlight suffocatingly insignificant. Willow paused and craned her neck to see the top.

The man stopped. 'Here we are. Ah'm Boone, by the way.'

'Willow,' she said, caught off guard.

Oh yeah, use your real name. Fucking brilliant.

'Willow, eh? You're a wee smasher, aren't ya? Gie us a twirl, aye?'

'Excuse me?'

He took the shotgun from under his arm and rested on it like a walking stick.

'Ah said gie us a twirl. I wanna see ya.'

What the fuck am I doing here, she thought, spinning half-heartedly around.

'Slowly,' he drawled. 'I want a good look.'

Willow took a deep breath and turned again, slower this time, the torch a spotlight. She saw her shadow, hideously extended, and thought of the old internet myth, The Slender Man.

'There, you happy now?' she said, as she turned to face him.

He grinned at her. 'Ah'm always happy, me. Aye, ah'm wan o' they happy-go-lucky cunts. You ever wanna wee cuddle, you ken who tae ask fae. Aye, ol' Boone, happy to help, that's me, you wee fuckin' slut.'

He walked up to her and smiled in her face. With nowhere else to go, Willow stood her ground.

'Are we gonna stand out here all night?' she said.

Boone flicked the flashlight beam towards the doorway. 'Come on. You're lucky, it's ladies' night tonight. Free entry,' he sniggered. He looked at her. 'You comin' or no'?'

She didn't have a choice. They walked through an old oak door that creaked like it was auditioning for a haunted mansion, Boone leading the way, Willow close behind. He smelled of cigarettes and Lynx deodorant, and his jeans had a rip below the left arse cheek that flashed pale, hairy leg at her like a grotesque winking eye.

'You cold?' he said. 'Want me tae warm ya up?'

Willow didn't answer. He led her up a dimly lit spiral staircase. It was a lot bigger inside than she had anticipated, though the spartan furniture looked like it had lain undisturbed for centuries. They climbed up and up, as Willow quietly panicked.

Where was this shotgun-toting freak taking her?

Idiot!

She had forgotten the first rule of investigating a snuff-porn ring — don't go into abandoned lighthouses with greasy slobs carrying guns. It was good life advice all round. And yet...

The heady thrill of excitement throbbed deep within her. She was getting closer. Closer to what, she wasn't sure. To solving the mystery? What even *was* the mystery anymore? It didn't matter. This was progress of some sort. And if it came down to it, she would defend herself.

'Here we are,' he said, stopping abruptly enough that Willow bumped into him. The way he pressed up against her breasts, she doubted it had been an accident. He pushed open a weathered wooden door and stepped inside, then struck a match and used it to light a single candle. He popped the lit match in his mouth to extinguish it, turning and grinning at her as he did so.

'Yer early,' he said, leaving the room and standing in the doorway. 'Gonnae have to wait a while.' He adopted a grotesque mockery of her voice, and said, 'Posh cunt probably brought a *book* with her.'

'How long?' she said, secretly dreading the answer.

'You got somewhere to be?'

'I guess not.'

Willow squeezed past him, the door slamming shut behind her. The room was empty except for the table and a wooden chair facing an old mirror. The floor was sticky, her shoes making a slurping sound with every step.

She sat down and waited for something to happen.

~

The next two hours crawled by. If there had been a clock, she would have expected to see the hands moving backwards.

At six-thirty, she checked her phone, got up, and tried the door, unsurprised to find it locked. The candle had burnt itself a quarter of the way down, wax pooling at the base of the metal holder. She took out a cigarette and used the flame to light it, hoping to conserve her smokes. She only had a couple left, and didn't know how much longer she would be here.

What if no one comes back? What if you're locked in here, miles from anyone, left to die?

It was one of her greatest fears. Ever since she had read

about someone being buried alive when she was a child, Willow had been afraid of the same thing happening to her. Left somewhere, unable to escape, clawing at the coffin lid or the door or the window until her fingernails snapped off and she curled into a ball, awaiting death.

Stop it.

Would that be worse than being killed in one of those videos? At least they were over quickly. After the initial assaults, the body hopefully went into shock, and if you were very lucky, your mind would shut down too.

Buried alive though, meant you were left with the one thing that can do more damage than a hammer or a knife or a chainsaw — your own mind, the cruelest weapon of all. Willow had never been able to control her thoughts. She dwelled on things, obsessed over them.

Particularly death.

It was a topic that both repulsed and fascinated her. She thought often of her parents' death, and of how people would react to her own passing. She thought about her friends dying, though she didn't have many. She thought about suicide — never considering it, just thinking about what it would be like — and she thought about cancer, and what it must be like to have a terminal disease. Willow had come to terms with thinking about death, but was never sure if it was a healthy or unhealthy topic to dwell on.

At six-forty-five, a noise outside brought her back to the present. Footsteps, and a door closing. She waited for the pins and needles in her legs to subside, then went to the door and pressed her ear to it, listening. She heard nothing else.

The same thing happened fifteen minutes later. More people arriving. But who, and for what?

Could this be it? Could this be where the videos were

shot? Was she about to have a front-row seat for the latest attraction? No, that wasn't likely. The lighthouse was bigger than it looked, but not as big and wide as the room from the video. This was something different.

Suddenly the mirror lit up.

Willow jumped, flattening herself against the door.

It was a room...another room beyond the mirror. She crept forwards, heart racing, staring through the two-way glass. The only furniture in the adjoining room was a bed and cabinet, an exposed bulb dangling from the ceiling like a fat spider.

There were two more mirrors reflecting the bed back at her. Who was behind them? She knew no one could see in, but still she snuffed the candle and sat waiting.

The bed sheets moved. There was someone under there. Willow put her hand to the glass then hurriedly pulled it away.

Don't be daft, no one can see you.

Minutes passed before the door opened and a man walked in, a huge man, naked apart from a featureless white mask. He stopped before the bed and gazed into the three mirrors one at a time. Willow felt sure he was looking right at her. She moved to the side, out of what she suspected was his eye-line, but the mask made it hard to tell, the eyes thick black pools of tar. It reminded her of the face paint she had applied the other night in CB's.

With one huge hand he stripped the sheets from the bed, and Willow's heart stopped. It was a girl. She lay there in her underwear, trembling up at the intruder beneath light blonde hair that framed her soft, delicate features.

Her lips moved, but Willow could hear nothing, the soundproof glass isolating her own heavy breathing.

Oh god it's happening, it's fucking happening.

Where was the camera? Was it hidden? Or was this a special private screening?

Get out, get out, get out.

It was too late for that. She was here now.

The man climbed onto the bed, straddling the girl and pinning her arms. She looked up at him. Was she smiling? He leaned over her, opened the drawer of the cabinet, and took something out. A condom. He stretched it out and snapped it over his dick.

He's not going to kill her. Why would he wear a condom if he was going to kill her?

It didn't make sense, but nothing did. Willow knew she had to escape, alert the authorities...and she *would* do that. Soon. First, she had to wait a minute. See how this played out. She might need to give a description or something. It was the right thing to do, she was sure of it. Her vision fogged and Willow realised it was her own breath, her face an inch from the glass.

The man let the girl's arms go, then grabbed the waistband of her underpants and tore them from her body in one savage motion. The blonde gasped but didn't scream. Instead she reached a shaking hand towards the mask and tenderly stroked her fingers down the hard material as he spread her legs and guided himself inside her. She didn't fight back, didn't strike him. She let him in and arched her back, then put her arms around his neck. Pulling herself up, she kissed his mask, running her tongue over it, then raked her nails down his chest, leaving angry red welts.

He shoved her away and smacked her across the face with the back of one burly hand. Willow felt the blow and recoiled. The girl looked up at the man, licking a thin trickle of blood from the corner of her mouth. She smiled and said something.

He backhanded her again.

'Stop it,' said Willow, though no one heard.

The girl was laughing at him now, as his hips thrust and he pounded away. He raised a fist again.

'Hey,' shouted Willow, no longer concerned about her own safety. She hammered on the glass. 'Stop!'

The man hit her with a closed fist and the girl barely reacted. She just took it, smiling the whole time. Willow battered the mirror. She ran to the door and rattled the handle, slammed her shoulder into it, but it wouldn't budge. She raced to the mirror in time to see the blonde spit a mouthful of blood onto the plain white mask. It ran down the smooth surface, dripping onto her chest.

The masked man had a knife in his hand.

'Oh god, no,' said Willow, backing up and tripping over the chair. She landed clumsily, then got to her feet and grabbed the chair with both hands. Without a second thought she swung it at the glass. It bounced harmlessly off.

The man raised the knife high. He stopped a moment and turned and looked at the mirror, *through* it, at Willow.

Somehow, behind that mask, she knew he was smiling.

27

THE KNIFE PLUNGED INTO THE BLONDE'S ABDOMEN.

Willow tried the chair again, putting all her strength into it. The glass cracked a little, but not enough.

The masked man pulled the knife free, dark red blood flowing thickly onto the mattress. Woozy and staggering, Willow brought the chair up again. The cracks hustled across the glass like ice on a frozen pond.

One more hit should do it.

The girl jerked violently as the man stabbed her again. The mirror shattered, the chair flying through, crashing into the bed, and then the man was up and on his feet, his hard-on undiminished. He ran, bursting through the door as Willow kicked loose shards of glass from the frame and clambered over, the masked man's head knocking the bare lightbulb, sending it swaying from side to side like a pendulum. Glass crunched beneath her feet as she made her way to the bed, to the grisly mess of the dead girl, her eyes open wide, staring.

The eyes never lie.

She put her fingers to the girl's neck, searching for a

pulse, and then the girl grabbed her by the wrist and pulled her down, wrestling Willow onto her back. She leaned in close and kissed her.

'I'm okay,' she whispered in Willow's ear, the urgency in her voice unmistakable.

'But—'

'Shut up and kiss me. We have to make this look good. They're watching.' She kissed Willow's neck, running her tongue towards her ear, flicking the lobe and leaving a trail of red saliva. 'They're always watching.' She guided Willow's trembling hand to her belly, to the wound, the stab wound that should have killed her. It was slippery with blood, but cold. Too cold. Willow slid her hand around the soft skin, feeling for cuts or lacerations and finding none. She looked into the blonde's eyes and saw fear.

'Make it convincing,' the girl whispered. 'Can you do that?'

Willow didn't respond.

The girl pulled her close, her lips touching Willow's ear.

'They'll kill us if you don't,' she said.

Willow nodded, adrenaline flowing through her like a raging torrent. She placed a hand on the girl's face and left a bloody print.

'I can do it,' she said.

The blonde slapped her across the face and forced her down on the bed. She slipped a hand under the pillow and pulled something out.

'Take this,' she said, her fingers finding Willow's lips, forcing their way inside, placing something on her tongue, something small.

A pill.

'Swallow,' she said, taking Willow's shirt and ripping it open, the buttons popping, one of them landing on the concrete floor. She buried her face in Willow's breasts, running her tongue between them.

'Who are they?' asked Willow quietly.

'Hit me,' said the girl. She put her hands on Willow's throat and squeezed. *'Hit me,'* she snarled. Willow slapped the girl across her cheek. In response, the blonde balled a fist and struck Willow in the side of the head. Stars exploded in her vision. She couldn't think straight. The girl's breasts pressed against her own and Willow shuffled down and kissed them. The blood tasted sugary-sweet.

It was not unpleasant. Excitement tingled through her body as her hands explored the girl's bare skin. The lightbulb swung above them, getting further and further away until it was little more than a twilight glint, and then thousands more lit up around it, sparkling in the night sky, millions of miles away.

The pill was kicking in, and kicking in *hard*.

'What is this place?' she moaned.

'Go to Edinburgh,' whispered the girl, her voice so close it was like she was in her head. *'Cannonball Joe's. Ask for CB.'*

'No,' said Willow in disbelief, but her mind had loosened, floated away from her. She tried to speak but couldn't form a sentence, let alone demand answers. CB was involved? No! Not CB...she looked up at the girl and wondered who she was...where was she...man, she was on the good shit now...she hadn't taken a pill for years...it felt good...blissful...good...blissful...

The blonde rubbed her hands over the bloody mess of her stomach and placed them on Willow's breasts, smearing the liquid across them, staining her white bra. Her hands went to Willow's jeans, working the fastener free, tugging them down over her hips. Willow lay still, guiding the girl's head to the warmth between her legs, but the excitement had faded now, though she couldn't remember why. Her eyes were drawn to the mirrors, to her own gore-streaked reflection staring back at her through half-lidded, drugged eyes.

She thought she saw movement behind the glass, a ghostly impression.

Someone was watching them.

But who?

28

WILLOW WOKE UP ALONE.

That, in itself, was not unusual, but this was different. It took her several moments to parse through the insanity of the previous night, sorting reality from the dreams that crawled up from the dark well of her subconscious and haunted her sleep. Her head throbbed and her limbs ached. What was in that pill? It had knocked her *right* out. She lay a while, staring at the lightbulb above her hanging unmoving from its frayed cord. The girl was gone, a large bloodstain on the sheets where she had lain.

Not *real* blood, of course. The whole thing was fake.

Not everything, thought Willow, remembering the stinging slaps from the girl, and the way she had choked her. Still, the murder — the so-called snuff killing — was a sham. What was it Stone called it? Porno for blood-freaks? So that was it, then. Everyone had been right. There was no such thing as snuff movies.

That, however, failed to account for the ever-increasing trail of corpses. Jessica, Eve, the neighbour...that's a whole lotta murder over some special effects. Plus, there was no way that video was shot in this cramped, unfurnished room. Was this some sort of sideline business, a way to audition potential recruits? That idea made more sense than anything else she could come up with, so she decided to run with it for now.

Groggily, she sat up, looking at herself in one of the two remaining mirrors. A curious red-faced devil stared at her, the blood dry and cracked on her face. She badly wanted a shower, or at least to wash away some of the scum that clung to her, burrowing into her pores.

Was she still being watched? Was someone on the other side of the mirror right now, peering in, looking at her? Her clothes were strewn across the room and she gathered them and put them on over her blood-caked body, fastening the few buttons that remained on her shirt, just enough to maintain the illusion of decency. There had to be a sink somewhere. She couldn't go home like this. Cat would have a fit.

Leaving the room and its grotty memories behind, she headed down the stairs on unsteady legs. At the bottom she found another door and entered without knocking. What was the worst she could find?

There was a dirty wash-hand basin in the corner, and she ran the cold water over her hands, scrubbing her face raw. She wanted to leave right away, but one thought nagged at her.

You're never going to come back here, are you?

'No,' said whispered.

So do some fucking investigating. This might be your last chance.

She turned off the tap and stood a moment, staring at her own washed-out reflection in the dirty mirror above the sink. There was a sticker of a rainbow in the bottom corner, a unicorn frolicking underneath it, as if once upon a time a family had lived here. She traced her finger over the sticker, then headed up the stairs.

The porthole windows on the staircase let her know it was morning, the misty haar seeping inland from the sea beneath a cloud-throttled sun.

At the top of the stairs, she faced the room she had spent the night in, and to the right was the room Boone had initially shown her to. But there had to be at least two more, so she headed left, following the circular walkway until she came to them. The first door was half-open, and she stepped inside. It was the same as her own chamber, empty but for a single chair and a snuffed candle on the table. Six crushed cans of Tennent's lay on the floor. She left and walked further round, coming to the final door. Inside was exactly the same. The room stank of stale cum and cigarettes. An ashtray, overflowing with butts, perched beside the candle.

'Classy,' said Willow, wishing for a cigarette of her own. She checked her pocket. One left. She lit up, and was about to leave when she noticed something metallic glinting by the chair. She knelt to investigate, exacerbating the throbbing aches in her body, and found a silver lighter.

'Jesus,' she said, recognising it the moment she picked it up by the engraving on the side. A Wild West six-shooter. She had seen it before, once, in the police car after Jessica's death.

Stone. Detective fuckin' Stone. Oh Jesus...

Was he there last night? Was he in on it? It made sense now. Well, some of it.

She shoved the lighter into the pocket of her jeans and rushed down the stairs, feeling nauseous. The fresh air hit her hard and she staggered around the lighthouse and vomited. Waves lapped against the shore of the desolate island, and she sat for a while, feeling sorry for herself.

A tear rolled down her cheek and she wiped it away.

The island looked different in the morning light. Peaceful. Respectable. The clouds parted, the lighthouse gleaming in the brilliant sun. The tide was out, the beach of the mainland closer, almost within swimming distance.

She hoped it wouldn't come to that.

Seagulls squawked nearby. She lumbered over to the edge of the land and peered over a cliff. Thirty foot below her the gulls flocked and crowded over one another, jostling for position, their white feathers stained crimson. They were eating something, stringy pieces of flesh drooping from their beaks.

'Enjoy yersel'?'

The voice startled her and she turned to face Boone. His leather jacket was unbuttoned, and despite the chill he wore nothing beneath it, his belly making a bid for freedom over his jeans. The wind blew his previously slicked-back hair across his forehead like insect legs.

'That was no' quite what we had planned for the evening's entertainment,' he said.

She tried to speak but words deserted her.

'Get in the boat,' he said after a while.

The shotgun dangled from his hand and Willow didn't argue.

He ferried her across the sea and stopped a few feet from the beach. She left without a word, wading through the shallow water and taking off in the direction of the train station.

She didn't once look back.

Willow dozed for much of the return journey, apart from when she saw the conductor making his rounds from carriage to carriage. Then, she had hidden in the toilet stall, holding the door closed but not locking it, so that the ENGAGED sign did not show. It was an old trick from the days when she couldn't afford to eat, let alone use public transport.

She waited until he left, and then the temptation of the toilet became too much and she vomited again. Unable or unwilling to stand, she spent the rest of the journey curled on the carpeted floor of the stall, not caring about the cleanliness, or lack thereof.

Her dreams came in fitful starts, ugly with half-glimpsed horrors, seeming to play out on an old VHS tape in her mind's eye, the images flickering between colour and black-and-white. She dreamed of Lina, who knew everything and yet said so little, the one person who could help her.

You should have listened to her and stayed away.

Too late for that now.

The train ground to a halt and the automated announcement proclaimed they had arrived in Edinburgh Waverley. Grabbing the toilet bowl for balance, Willow got to her feet and disembarked. It was lunchtime, and the station was heaving with tourists arriving for the October holiday. Or were they going home? What date *was* it, anyway? What day of the week?

She meandered down comfortingly familiar roads, the wet streets sparkling in the sun like a midnight sky. It was oddly appropriate — in the last few days, Willow's entire world had turned upside down.

But how did everything fit together?

Detective Stone was part of it, of that she was sure. He had been there last night, watching her, as he had once promised to do. The idea appalled her. To think she had gone to him, trusted him, bringing him Jessica's phone, giving away the only piece of evidence like the good little lapdog she was.

Stone. Boone. The mysterious Vinnie Sunset. Those were the three names at the top of her list.

No.

There was another name. It suddenly came to her with dreadful clarity, the blonde girl whispering it in her ear.

Go to Edinburgh. Cannonball Joe's. Ask for CB.

'No,' groaned Willow, her legs buckling beneath her as the memory flooded back. Not CB.

It couldn't be true.

It *couldn't* be.

29

WHEN CB ARRIVED TO OPEN THE CLUB AT FOUR-THIRTY, Willow was waiting for him, a pile of cigarette butts around her feet.

'You're keen,' he said, eyeing her warily. 'You look like a bag of shite. If you're sick, keep your bloody distance, I've a busy week ahead. Cannae be getting a cold.'

'I need to talk to you,' was all she said.

'Fine. I've got new curtains arriving in an hour, you can help me put them up.' He shoved the key into the lock and opened the door, motioning for Willow to enter. 'You giving me the silent treatment?' She stalked past him into the building without a word.

The club was as quiet as a morgue. CB bent and picked up the mail, sorting it into piles as he made his way to the boiler. He hit the switch. When nothing happened, he slammed his fist off the metal. The boiler choked into life, the pipes rattling and spluttering.

He shook his head and turned to Willow. 'Damn boiler.' He saw the knife in her hand and stopped. 'What's that for?'

he asked, glancing at the weathered blade. 'Gonna chop some potatoes?'

'I woke up in a lighthouse this morning,' she said, and thought she saw CB flinch.

'That's a funny place to wake up,' he said absently, staring at a hand-written letter on the top of the pile. He folded it and stuffed it into his pocket, placing the rest of the letters on the cloakroom counter.

'I met a man called Boone. Do you know him?'

He refused to meet her gaze. 'Can't say I know any Boones. Knew a Ben once.' He paused, thoughtful. 'He was a right wanker.'

'Met a blonde girl too. She told me to come and see you.'

'I do know a few blondes, to be fair.'

'Would you stop *fucking* with me!' shouted Willow. CB said nothing. She took a breath, forcing herself to calm down, and said, 'I know you're involved. You can't talk your way out of this.'

He stared at the door as if considering making a run for it, then mumbled something inaudible.

'What did you say?' said Willow sharply.

He finally looked at her and sighed, his hands flat on the counter. 'I said...*I told you to leave it alone.*'

The admission hit her like a freight train. She stumbled and CB moved to catch her.

'Get away from me!' she cried, brandishing the knife, thrusting it at him, slicing his hand.

He backed off. 'Willow...put the knife down,' he said calmly, specks of blood dripping onto the floor. 'It's not what you think. Come into my office.' He looked imploringly at her. 'Please.'

With that, he turned, hesitant, perhaps fearing she

would attack him. Willow let the knife fall from her hand and it clattered on the floor. 'How could you?' she said.

He looked at her from the office doorway. 'I told you...it's not what you think. I didn't do anything.'

She walked unsteadily towards the tiny room where CB waited behind his desk, the fan on its highest speed setting. She took a seat.

Bad move. What if he's got a gun in his desk and shoots you?

Don't be ridiculous. It's CB. Your employer. Your friend.

He began to speak and Willow interrupted.

'Did you know Jessica Chalmers?'

CB exhaled exaggeratedly. 'Christ, which one is she? All these bloody names.'

'She's the girl who was murdered, the one who's video I showed you.' She shivered. 'The one who died in my arms.'

He nodded gravely. 'Aye, her. Too many dead girls around, these days. Hard to keep track.'

'Is that meant to be a joke?'

'No joke. Just the truth.'

'You knew her, didn't you? All this time, and you knew her. You bastard.'

'I knew her, yes,' he said, 'but not *well*. Christ, I only met her once. One of the girls brought her to see me. She was looking for work.'

'And?'

'And you know my policy. I don't hire junkies. Too unreliable. Anyway, punters don't go for that look. Too skinny. A sack of bones rattling around onstage, that's what she would have been. I told her I couldn't hire her, but...'

'But what?' demanded Willow.

'But that I knew people who might. People in the industry.' He shook his head. 'No, no, it's not what you're thinking.

I gave her the numbers of *legit* places, all above board, mostly.'

'*Mostly*,' spat Willow with disdain.

'Will, she was in a state. Track lines up her arms, scabs round her mouth, no tits. No fucker would hire her unless they catered to a...a different market, so to speak.'

'You're disgusting.'

'I was trying to help her.'

'You murdered her.'

CB slammed his uninjured fist off the desk, rattling the pens that jutted from his empty coffee mug.

'I did nothing of the sort,' he bellowed. 'I gave her contacts and sent her on her way. She made her own choices.'

Willow clenched her fists. If she still had the knife, she would have stabbed him there and then.

'Where did you send her?' she managed to say.

'Bunch of places, all small time. Niche markets, mostly fetish stuff,' he said, sliding open a drawer and pulling out a card. 'But she probably went to see Vinnie.' Willow snatched the card from him and held it between her fingers like it might bite her.

THE SUNSET PALACE
ADULT MOVIES FOR ADULT MINDS

'Vinnie Sunset,' she said.

'Aye, Vinnie Sunset,' repeated CB. 'You know him?' Willow shook her head. 'He's a strange man, Will. Very strange indeed. Deals in violent porno, nasty, hard-edged shit. He used to sell them out of his own shop. But he doesn't kill people, if that's what you're thinking.'

'And you sent Jessica to see him?'

CB leaned in his chair and looked at his bloody hand. 'I don't presume to tell anyone what to do. We make—'

'Our own choices. Sure.' She flipped the business card over. Written on the back, in a tasteful font, was the address of The Sunset Palace. 'Did Eve ever work for them?'

'Not that I know of.' Then, quietly, he said, 'I'm sorry.'

'Me too.' She got up and made for the door.

'He's dangerous,' said CB.

Willow turned to face him. 'Why didn't you tell me this before?'

'I couldn't,' he said.

Willow nodded. 'That's what I thought. I quit, by the way.'

He offered her a pained smile. 'I know. Goodbye, Willow. I hope you find what you're looking for.'

She shot him a disgusted look and stormed out of the office.

~

'Cannonball' Joe Stephens sat alone at his desk, waiting to hear the main entrance slam shut. He had just lost his best dancer.

More than that, he had lost a friend.

With shaking hands, he pulled out his phone and called someone. They answered — as they always did — on the first ring.

'Sunset Palace, this is Vincenzo.'

'It's Joe,' he stammered. 'She took the bait. She's on her way.'

Vinnie started to say something, but CB hung up and slammed the phone face-down on the desk.

He sucked in his gut to allow him access to the drawer,

and rummaged through the contents. He came across dozens of Polaroids of naked girls, several OVERDUE notices marked in bright red, and a half-eaten Digestive biscuit before he found what he was looking for.

A black compact revolver. It was illegal, unregistered, but he had owned it for years. One of the girls had left it behind after taking off into the night, and he had kept it hidden in his drawer like a mysterious artefact ever since.

CB placed the weapon on his desk with a metallic thud, then sat and stared at it for a long time. He pulled the handwritten envelope from his pocket, noticing it had no stamp or postal mark, and tore it open.

Tears stung his eyes as he read the letter. There was a photo paper-clipped to the back. He looked at it, then tucked it into the drawer with the rest of the photographs. He picked up the revolver and checked the chamber.

The coldness of the barrel against his temple made him nauseous, and he broke out in gooseflesh.

'I'm sorry, Willow,' he whispered, his finger on the trigger, squeezing, *squeezing*. 'I really am sorry.'

A knock at the door.

'Hey CB,' came the voice from the other side. 'It's Allison. I know I'm early, but can I get an advance on this month's pay?'

'Come back later,' said CB through gritted teeth, not recognising the voice as his own.

'It's my mum's fiftieth on Saturday and I need to get her a present.'

'Go away,' he snarled. Christ, he'd have to wait til she left.

'You okay, CB? You sound stressed.'

'I'm fine!' he roared. He rubbed his eyes, the gun feeling

alien in his hand. His finger relaxed and he lowered the gun, tucking it in amongst the photographs.

'Just leave me alone,' he said, his voice cracking. *'Please.'*

He heard the girl mutter something, then her heels clicking as she walked away. He took one last look at the weapon, then closed the drawer, put his head in his hands, and wept.

30

I HOPE YOU FIND WHAT YOU'RE LOOKING FOR.

The words bounced around Willow's head as she staggered from Cannonball Joe's and weaved her way drunkenly through the streets.

'Fuck you,' she mumbled. The sun was setting. What time was it? She leaned against a car and the alarm went off. Ignoring it, she carried on down the street. She needed to go home, to lie down, but she couldn't, not now. Not when she was so close.

Cars splashed through puddles, spraying tidal waves of neon light across the pavement. Faces blurred by. She felt they were all looking at her. Maybe *everyone* was in on it.

Killing girls is the new trend, Willow. Didn't you get the memo? The next season of Keeping Up With The Kardashians is wall-to-wall slaughter. It's gonna be a smash hit!

Her phone vibrated in her pocket. It was CB. She let it ring, waited until he had given up, and called Cat, hoping she would lend her the money for a taxi home. No one answered, so she dialled the house phone instead. To her surprise, Cat picked up.

'Hello?'

'It's Willow,' she said, grateful to speak to someone normal, someone she trusted. 'I need help.'

'I think you have the wrong number,' said Cat, and hung up.

Willow felt drunk, the world spinning like an out-of-control carousel. She dialled again.

'Hello—'

'It's *Willow*. Don't hang up. I—'

'I'm sorry, there's no one of that name here. Please stop calling,' came the curt response, followed by the sound of the receiver slamming into the cradle.

'Well, fuck *you*,' said Willow, staring at her phone. She didn't understand. Why wouldn't Cat talk to her?

A hen party rumbled past, the group's bright pink t-shirts visible through their transparent ponchos, yapping in broad Scouse accents. Willow moved to the side, eyeing them suspiciously. A middle-aged couple strolled beneath the shelter of an umbrella, paying her no attention. At the last moment, the man glanced at her.

Willow's heart stopped.

'What are you looking at?' she barked.

The couple hurried on. She spotted a man smoking out of his third-floor window. He was watching her.

Probably wondering who the weird, aggressive drunk is.

No. He was one of them. She slipped into the shadows, her foot nudging a discarded beer bottle. It rolled across the concrete, and she picked it up, hurling it towards the man. She missed, but the glass shattered against the wall.

'Hey, what are you doing? I'll call the police!' he shouted, but she was gone.

Soon, she found herself in a heavy-metal bar, raucous music blaring over the speakers, drowning out the chat of the patrons and the voices in her head. She ordered a double vodka and downed it, then ordered another. A man stood beside her. She took a drink and fiddled with the business card.

THE SUNSET PALACE
ADULT MOVIES FOR ADULT MINDS

She had to go, had to pay Vinnie Sunset a visit.

Another drink first. Some Dutch courage.

She flipped the card and read the address for the twentieth time. It wasn't far. She could reach it by foot.

I'm sorry, Willow, she heard CB say, and at that moment she truly hated him. She noticed the music was quieter, distant sounding. When she turned to look, everyone in the bar was staring at her, frozen like statues before Medusa.

It's not real. It's your imagination.

She closed her eyes, but didn't dare look round again. The man beside her moved closer, leaning on the bar, his arm covered in tattoos. He was flirting with her, complimenting her hair and her eyes and her smile. She pictured him naked and hog-tied, a pair of pliers in her hands, removing his teeth one-by-one, until his mouth was nothing but blood-smeared gums.

'Excuse me,' she said, pushing past him and making for the exit, horrified at her own twisted thoughts.

It's getting to you, said a talkative voice as she roamed the streets, heading in the general direction of The Sunset Palace, but taking an increasingly circuitous route. *But you still have a choice. Tear up that business card and forget about the whole thing.*

Before she had a chance to think about that, a phone rang and she screamed.

'You okay?' asked a lady as she walked past, and Willow nodded, trying to force a smile. The ringtone was *I Wanna Be Sedated* by The Ramones. She groped in her pocket and pulled out her phone.

Funny, she thought madly, *I don't remember changing the ringtone.*

She answered, comforted by the fact she *knew* it would not be good news.

'Willow?' said the voice. It took her a while to recognise it.

'Cat?' she slurred.

'It's me, Will. You okay? You sound bad.'

She ignored the question. 'Why'd you hang up on me?'

Cat snorted. 'Jesus, the police were here.'

Willow took several deep breaths and slumped against the wall, sliding down into a crouch. 'What did they want?'

'They were asking all these questions, they wanted to know where you were.' Cat paused. 'They said you killed someone.'

The phone almost slipped from her hand. It took every fibre of self-control to hold on to it. The sickness rose again, the street spinning.

'Will...you still there?'

'Who?' she said.

'Who what?'

She took a deep breath. 'Who do they think I killed?'

'I dunno, some girl. They showed me a photo, but I'd never seen her before. They wouldn't tell me much. I told them I don't know where you are.'

'What did she look like?'

'Who?'

"The girl in the photo?'

'Oh.' Cat thought for a moment. 'Young, blonde, pretty.'

'The lighthouse...'

'What lighthouse? Willow, you're not making any sense. What the hell are you mixed up in?' Cat was near hysterics.

'I can get proof,' said Willow. 'I know where to get it now. The Sunset Palace. I can show them.'

'Show them what?'

Willow smiled crookedly. 'I know who did it, who's behind it all. CB told me everything. I thought the coordinates would take me there, but that's only part of it. It's bigger than that.'

'Coordinates? What are you talking about? *Please*, just stop. Either hand yourself in, or run. Get out of the city.'

'I didn't kill her,' said Willow. She could hear Cat crying down the phone. 'At least, I don't think I did.' She remembered the seagulls feeding outside the lighthouse, their beaks and feathers red, and laughed. 'Don't worry,' she said, aiming for reassurance and falling somewhere between patronising and insane. 'I'm going to get proof.'

She hung up and switched off her phone.

After a while, she managed to stand.

'I didn't kill anyone,' she said to herself. 'I *couldn't* kill anyone.'

But even she had trouble believing it.

31

CAT PACED THROUGH THE FLAT BITING HER NAILS, resurrecting an old habit she had kicked in her teenage years.

She wandered room to room, trying to clear her head. The police visit had rattled her, but at least she knew Willow was innocent. After speaking to her on the phone, however, she suddenly wasn't so sure. How deeply was she involved? How far would she go, how low would she sink?

She stopped outside Willow's room and put her hand on the door, as if waiting for permission to enter. The police had spent hours in there, every drawer opened, the contents abandoned on the floor. Her computer was gone, and a nail polish had been knocked over, the crimson pouring down the side of the wooden shelving unit and staining the wood.

There goes the deposit on the flat, thought Cat grimly, though to be honest, the rest of the room didn't look much messier than normal. Cat was the tidy one of the pair. She did the hoovering and the dishes and the dusting and organised the bills and the rent. She never minded, though. She had found a good friend in Willow, and more than that, she was secretly fascinated by her. The life she led seemed so outrageous to Cat, with her standard middle-class upbringing, the eldest of three sisters. She had grown up with supportive parents who encouraged her in whatever she did, who made sure she always had the latest clothes and toys, who would drive her to hockey practice, to Guides, even to a short-lived spell in karate class.

And then there was Willow, orphaned at seven, sleeping rough at fourteen, stripping at sixteen, experimenting with drink and drugs and sex while Cat was at home studying for her exams. She knew there was much more to tell, but Willow was strangely guarded about her life until she had a good few drinks in her.

Now Cat wondered what secrets were locked up inside Willow's head. Could she have killed someone? She had spent a lot of time obsessing over that video, watching it repeatedly, along with those other sick films she found online, but Cat didn't believe any of that bullshit about how watching violent videos makes you a violent person.

No, Willow did not have it in her to kill. Not for fun, anyway. Self-defence? Now that was a different matter. She had seen Willow stand up to men and women alike. Cat had always envied her fearlessness.

She cautiously pushed the door wider and entered the chaotic room, which smelled of cigarettes and incense. She picked up Willow's belongings and placed them — neatly folded — back in the drawers, remembering the gleeful sound one of the officers had made when he found Willow's green dress drying on the radiator, Jessica's blood stains still visible from that awful night.

How quickly a life can unravel, thought Cat. She didn't recognise Willow anymore. She had tried to understand, to *help*, but she knew she could have tried harder.

You already lied to the police about her.

True. They could — and undoubtedly *would* — check the calls, and see that Willow had phoned her while the police were there. She was guilty of obstructing justice.

Guilty of being a good friend, more like.

Willow might be impulsive, and sometimes a little crazy, but she wouldn't get involved in murder, no matter what. It was a mistake, a big misunderstanding. If only there was some way she could help. She felt useless, pottering around the flat while her friend was hunted for a murder she didn't commit.

When Willow's room was tidy — the tidiest it had ever been, no less — Cat went to her own bedroom and lay down. She tried to nap but couldn't, her mind restless. She needed to speak to someone. Anyone. Willow had few friends, so Cat decided to call the only person she could think of.

'Cannonball Joe's,' said the gruff voice on the other end of the line.

'Hello,' said Cat tentatively. 'Is that Joe?'

'Aye. Who's this?'

'My name's Cat, we've met a couple of times. I'm Willow's flatmate.'

There was a moment of silence. 'I remember,' he sighed. 'Sorry, Willow doesn't work here anymore.'

'Since when?'

'Since she quit. Don't suppose you're good at stripping, are you? I need a new act.' It was a joke, but he was going through the motions, and neither of them laughed.

'When did you last see her?'

'Listen, I can't help you. I told you, she quit.'

'But she's in trouble,' said Cat.

'Trouble has a way of finding that one. I warned her, but

she didn't listen. Now, if you'll excuse me, I've got a beer here that isn't going to drink itself.'

'The police think she killed someone,' said Cat, afraid he would hang up on her. She wouldn't let him off that easily.

'Killed who?' he said. Cat thought it strange that his instinct was to ask *who* she had killed, the same response Willow had given.

'I don't know,' said Cat. 'A girl. They wouldn't tell me anymore.' CB said nothing. 'I spoke to her, and she said she knew where to get proof. Something about The Sunrise Palace.'

'Sunset,' corrected CB. 'The Sunset Palace.'

'What do you know?' urged Cat. 'Please, I need your help.'

CB was quiet for a long time, then said, 'I'll tell you what I told her. I don't know anything, and it's best to keep it that way.'

'What are you not telling me?' Cat shouted down the phone. 'Don't you care?'

'I care too much,' said CB. 'That's the problem.'

A noise in the hallway drew Cat's attention. She held the phone away from her and listened, CB's voice fading to a tinny crackle.

It was coming from the front door, a key in the lock.

'Willow?' she said, though she already knew it wasn't. Why would Willow have such trouble getting the door open?

Maybe she's hurt, or needs help, pleaded the rational part of her brain.

CB was saying something, but she wasn't listening.

'Who's there?'

'What's happening?' demanded CB.

Only half-listening, Cat said, 'There's someone at the door. It might be Willow. Hang on.'

She placed the phone in her jeans pocket.

'Just stay put,' said CB. 'I'll come round. Lock the door and don't answer it for anyone!'

But Cat couldn't hear him. She crept from the room and edged into the hall, afraid to call out.

It's not Willow, said the infuriatingly calm voice in her head. By then, it was too late. The lock gave, the door creaking open, a shaft of light spilling into the darkened hallway. Cat wanted to do something, but she was rooted to the spot.

'Willow?' she said, the only thing she could think to do, before the light was obscured by a presence, a dark figure entering her flat, her *home*. He wore a black raincoat and hat, the soft glow from her bedroom reflecting off beads of rain that clung to the slick material like thousands of gawking eyeballs.

'Who are you?' said Cat.

The man didn't answer. He pulled a knife from his coat and Cat ran, her phone tumbling from her pocket and hitting the ground. There was no time to pick it up. She burst into her room and slammed the door, pressing her body against it. The door juddered as the man threw himself into it, opening an inch or two before Cat pressed it shut again, her foot planted firmly on the radiator for leverage.

The door shuddered again, Cat's other foot slipping out from under her. She stretched her fingers out, finding the edge of her bedside table, and dragged it over. The man hit the door again and this time it almost flew open. She manoeuvred the table up to the wall and wedged it between the door and the radiator, then stood back, letting the man barge into the door at full force. It opened slightly, then met with firm resistance in the form of the bedside table.

She had time, but not much. How long would the door hold?

She ran for the window, skidding on a rug and almost falling. She grabbed the window frame and tried to haul it up, but it was stuck. Of course it was — that was why she and Willow had swapped rooms two years ago. The window didn't open, so Willow couldn't smoke out of it. Cat had complained to her landlord about the fire risk it posed, and he had brushed her off. She remembered the conversation well.

'I have eleven properties to maintain, Miss Howards. You can't call me for every little mishap and inconvenience. If there's a fire, you're hardly likely to leap from the third-floor window, are you?'

'Wanna bet?' snarled Cat. She slammed her fists off the glass, which wobbled from the impact. 'Help! Please, call the police!' she shouted. 'Someone's trying to kill me!'

There were several people on the street. An elderly couple, a young woman, a grown man on a scooter. Below her, a car waited, its engine revving, music blaring thunderously from inside.

She hammered on the window, screaming for help, and thought she saw the young woman look up in confusion. Then the car revved again, pumping black fumes from its oversized exhaust, drowning her out. She saw the old man reach up to his ear and remove his hearing aid, then shake his fist and shout something at the occupants of the car.

'Help!' screamed Cat, 'I'm up here!'

She turned and saw the man's head poking round the door, trying to shove the table out of the way. Cat thought her heart might leap out of her chest. Could she smash the window?

And then what? Jump? She looked out again, horror building in her mind. The door cracked behind her, a chunk of wood splintering off. She didn't have long now. Pressing her forehead to the glass in resignation, she saw movement across the street, a light in one of the flats. A man stood, gawking through a pair of binoculars.

Willow's voyeur.

'Hey! Over here!' screamed Cat, but he didn't look her way, didn't seem to notice. 'Here! Look at me!' She jumped, waving her arms over her head. He turned in her direction and watched for a moment as she frenziedly gesticulated at him. He put the binoculars down and watched from afar, unmoving. Why wasn't he doing anything?

The door smashed again, the hinges shrieking as they were wrenched loose from the wall. The old pervert went back to staring at Willow's room.

'No! Over here!' She took the hem of her baggy pyjama shirt and rolled it up over her breasts. 'Hey! Look!' she screamed. 'I'm right here!'

The voyeur turned to her. She had his attention. Leaving her top up around her neck, she grabbed a lipstick and began scrawling on the window. She wrote a large H, then a backwards E, a backwards L...

Still he stared. She finished the P and gestured at the word, tears in her eyes, ready to give up.

The man lowered his binoculars. Had he finally realised what he needed to do? Had she gotten through? They looked at each other, and then the man slowly raised his hand and pointed at her, shaking his head. He stepped back and drew the curtains shut.

Too late, Cat discovered what he was pointing at.

She felt a leather-gloved hand close over her mouth and then she was dragged backwards, away from the window. The man spun her and threw her towards where the door should be, except it lay askew across the floor and she tripped over it, sprawling into the hall.

At that moment, she knew it was all over.

It was inevitable. It was fate. She tugged her pyjama top down over her chest, figuring that if she was going to die, at least she could die with a semblance of dignity. As last thoughts went, she supposed it was pretty ridiculous, but it would mean a lot to her mother.

'Always wear matching underwear in case you get hit by a car,' her mum used to say. She thought of her now, her kind, plump face, surrounded by cats in front of a roaring fire, her father's nose buried in a book in the same room, not talking, content in each other's company.

Cat, her cheeks wet with tears, managed a rueful smile as she gazed up at the face of her killer. She got to her feet as he stood watching, waiting.

'Why?' she asked.

'Business,' he said. 'Nothing personal.' Then he lunged towards her, covering her face, pressing her up against the wall.

The blade slid effortlessly into her belly. It was an agony unlike anything Cat had ever experienced. She felt the cold steel press against her, scraping at her kidneys, an unscratchable itch deep inside.

The man drew the knife up, sawing through the soft skin of her stomach, hot blood spilling out and pouring down her legs into a shallow puddle. Something slid out of the wound and plopped onto the floor. They both looked down, murderer and victim as surprised as each other. As Cat saw part of her intestine lying at her feet, she started to scream.

The man pocketed the knife and reached inside the wound, forcing his hand through, the skin tearing further, until he grasped something. As he pulled, Cat experienced the extraordinary sensation of her insides becoming outsides, as the man tugged on her small intestine, the organs slipping through the gap.

She saw her phone on the hallway floor, out of reach, and wondered if CB was still on the line.

It was her final thought.

32

DO NOT RING, READ THE LAMINATED SIGN.

Willow — never good at following orders — jabbed impatiently at the button. A buzzer sounded somewhere above her. The sign had been nailed beside the bell, next to a faded black door badly in need of a paint job. Above, a CCTV camera behind a mesh cage pointed at her with its blinking robotic eye, roaming disinterestedly back and forth. The door had nothing on it but the number four. No sign, no mention of The Sunset Palace, yet according to the business card, this should be the place. Door four, nestled down a narrow alley off the main street.

She looked up at the camera, wondering who was watching her. She found herself thinking that a lot these days.

It's fine, I'm used to being watched. It's what I do best.

The door unlocked with an insistent tone. She took a deep breath, pushed it open, and entered. The stairwell was dark, lit — with grim inevitability — by a dying neon strip-light. Random scrawled initials, phone numbers, and genitalia were painted from floor to ceiling. It didn't bother her.

She had seen worse in some of the dive bars she had stripped in over the years, graphics and slogans that would make a sailor blush. It wasn't what was on the walls that bothered her...it was who might lurk around the corner. She remembered Eve asking if she carried a knife and wished she had one right now.

Didn't do Eve much good though, did it?

She climbed the stairs, the jittery light strobing her shadow across the wall. Water dribbled from a hole in the ceiling, and her thoughts travelled back to that fateful night in the alleyway, the momentary flash of lightning revealing the knife poised above her head, ready to strike.

Maybe it would have been better if you'd just let him stab you, she thought. *Life has been pretty shitty since then, hasn't it?*

She brushed the thought aside, angry at how truthful it was.

At the top of the stairs she could make out another door, navy blue but flecked with specks of grey. The door was ajar, bright light spilling out invitingly. Willow reached the entrance and went inside.

It was a hallway with three more doors, one on each wall. She hesitated in front of one of them. A stench caught in her nostrils, vague yet pungent, and against her better judgement she reached for the handle, glancing left and right to make sure no one was watching. The door knob was cold to the touch and she swivelled it anti-clockwise.

It was locked.

'Can I help you?'

She spun towards the sound. A man regarded her through sleep-encrusted eyes, his body filling the door-frame. She saw the knife in his hand and stepped back, bumping into the door.

'I'm sorry,' she said, groping for the handle. She found it, twisted it, discovered that it too was now locked. She pressed herself up against the door, looking at the man's bemused face.

He laughed out loud, a gregarious belly laugh that reminded her of CB.

'First time?'

He held the knife up and sliced a chunk out of an apple, popping it in his mouth and loudly crunching. He motioned with his head.

'Come on in,' he said, turning his back on her and limping inside.

33

Willow waited until he was out of sight. She had seen that limp before. Once outside her building, and once on the YouTube video uploaded by that musician. The voice, too, was familiar. She recognised it from the phone call that had woken her the night of Jessica's murder. This was the one and only Vinnie Sunset, in the flesh.

She followed, wandering into what appeared to be a conventional sex shop, if you could call a sex shop conventional. On one side were toys and paraphernalia; cuffs, clamps, gags, dildos — your standard fare. The opposite wall was lined with shelves of DVDs. At the far end of the room was a counter, Vinnie leaning on it and slicing into his apple. All the while, his dark eyes never left her. His black hair was short, almost military, which matched the loose green army jacket draped over his muscular frame.

Willow browsed the merchandise, unsure of what she was doing, or why she was here. Things were moving too damn fast, her life a juggernaut careening out of control. Aware of Vinnie, she crossed to the DVD wall and trailed her fingers along the row of discs before grabbing a box, any box, and pretending to read the blurb. She watched him out the corner of her eye as he methodically ate his apple, peeling the skin and cutting out little crescents. He dropped the core into a metal bin and the sound made her jump. She cursed herself for doing so.

A buzz reverberated around the shop, so loud that at first Willow thought it was a fire alarm. Vinnie checked the grainy black-and-white screen of a small monitor behind him. She glimpsed a face, but couldn't quite make it out. He switched the monitor off and glanced at Willow.

'You buying that?'

'What?' She realised she was at the counter, a random DVD case clutched in her hands. 'Uh, yeah, I guess.'

He took it and squinted at the title. 'Cunt Destroyer?'

Willow coloured. 'Umm, sure.'

Smooth, Will. Real smooth.

'There's no disc in there,' he smiled, sliding it back towards her. 'We're not actually a shop, but you already knew that, didn't you.' It was a statement, not a question.

'I'm looking for Vinnie,' she managed.

The man looked her in the eyes. 'Is that so?'

'Yeah. CB sent me. Said he might have some work for me.'

'Is that so?' he repeated. He held out his hand, and Willow shook it. 'Then I'm Vincenzo Dellamore, but all my friends call me Vinnie,' he said. 'My enemies too. And you are?'

His grip was tight, her bones grinding together like a bag of marbles. She squeezed back and he scowled.

'You don't need to know my name,' she said with all the confidence she could muster.

Vinnie broke the handshake. 'You're right. Names are for

front doors and gravestones,' he laughed. 'What do you want me to call you?'

'I'm here on business. You don't have to call me anything. Got a cigarette?'

He pointed to a yellowing No Smoking sign. It was her turn to sneer insouciantly. Vinnie grinned from ear to ear and fished a pack from his pocket. She took one and brought out Stone's engraved lighter, watching Vinnie carefully.

'I'll come up with a name for you,' he said, as she lit the cigarette. 'I'm good at that. Some would say it's a gift I have.'

'What about talking too much?'

'That's a curse,' he said, picking at his fingernails with the knife, his silver watch sparkling under the lights.

'Rolex?' asked Willow.

'Do you think it is?'

She shrugged, warming to her new role. 'This place was hard to find.'

'Advertising's expensive,' smiled Vinnie.

'So are Rolexes. It's only life that's cheap these days.'

Vinnie gave a hearty laugh. 'Life and sex, my friend. Life and sex. I used to make good money selling this shit until the internet came along and made pornography available to everyone. Sex doesn't sell anymore, I'm afraid. Even porn is a, uh, *affari morenti*.'

'I don't speak French.'

'Ha!' bellowed Vinnie. 'You're playing with me. I like it. I mean to say, porn is a dying business.'

'How's a man to make an honest living in such...*trying* times?' sneered Willow.

'Oh, we find a way. But again, you already knew that. You know more than you're letting on.' His smile faded. 'That's why you're here. What are you offering? I mean, what are you willing to do?' He stabbed the knife into the countertop. 'How far are you willing to go?'

Willow held her ground as Vinnie moved towards her. If he expected her to shrink in fear, he was dead wrong. She looked up at him, at least a foot shorter than the Italian, and said, 'I can do anything you want. Male or female, doesn't matter to me.'

'Yes, I heard about last night. You made quite an entrance. Cost me some money, broke a mirror. I have to go out there and fix it myself, you know.'

'And why's that?'

'People snooping around my properties makes me uneasy. I'm a very private person.'

'I'm sure you are,' said Willow. 'Well, I think we put on a good show.'

'Ah, *sì*. Two girls, hot stuff, no?'

'I thought so.'

Vinnie stared Willow down. 'You know where my clients can see a lesbian fuck?' His voice dropped to a whisper. 'The fucking internet. *Gratuito*.'

The cigarette fell from Willow's hand onto the bare floor and she ground it beneath her heel.

'You were right,' she said. 'You talk too much.'

'The cross I have to bear.'

'So what were you hoping for?'

'My clients like things...a little rougher.' He punctuated the sentence by pulling the knife from the desk.

'I can do rough.'

What the fuck are you doing? What are you saying?

She wasn't sure anymore. She was losing control. Was the tough-girl act convincing? She pictured herself as a hardboiled femme fatale, but in reality, could Vinnie see she was in way over her head?

'Rough?' said Vinnie. 'I bet you can. Ah! But I have a name for you already. Rough Stuff. It's perfect, no?'

'If you say so.'

'Why don't we go down below and you can show me how rough you like it? Ah, I don't mean like that! *Non essere ridiculo*. Just to watch a video. To check we're on the same page.'

'Down where?' said Willow, her throat dry. Vinnie motioned for her to move away, then shoved the desk forward, revealing a concealed trapdoor cut into the floorboards.

'Down here. Don't worry, it's safe, I promise. Sometimes you need...*un po 'di privacy*.' He grasped a metal ring and lifted the trapdoor, inviting Willow to look. All she could see was a staircase leading into the unknown.

Get out. People are dead, Willow. Girls are dead. You really gonna go into that fucking basement with this degenerate?

But wasn't that why she was here in the first place? Someone had to do something, and it sure as hell wasn't going to be the police. She had to see, she had to know. She had gone too far to back out now.

'Don't be nervous,' cooed Vinnie. 'Here, I'll go first.' With that, he started down the stairs. Willow waited until he was out of sight, plucked the knife from the counter, and followed him.

At the foot of the stairs was another door. Vinnie stood inside, holding it open for her and smiling.

The basement was freezing, the walls lined with unmarked VHS tapes, relics of a bygone age. Perhaps this was the crypt where archaic technology crawled to die? Maybe there were some fax machines and calculators around here somewhere...

'Sit,' barked Vinnie, gesturing to a solitary wooden chair

in the middle of the room. It faced a television, the screen blank and lifeless. He stood in the corner, watching her. 'And you won't need that knife. I'm not going to hurt you. Put it on one of the shelves, *per favore*.'

Willow started to lie, then thought better of it. She took the knife from her pocket and placed it on a dusty shelf. Vinnie grabbed a tape, seemingly at random, and shoved it into a VCR as she took her seat. Crackling static filled the screen, a chunky white PLAY symbol in the top left corner. Vinnie flicked the lights off, the room lit solely by the cathode glare of the TV. He moved into the shadows and a cold shiver slithered the length of Willow's body.

GETOUTGETOUTGETOUT

No. She was here now. She would see it through. This was all a game, and though Vinnie held all the cards, he had no idea how good a bluffer she could be. Or hoped she was, at least.

The static disappeared, replaced by an image that Willow knew all too well. It was that same damn room, though this was her best view yet, the camera far back enough to reveal hitherto undisclosed details.

Faded industrial machinery perched atop great slabs of concrete, while wide steel piping that looked like an air-conditioning unit lurked along the ceiling, the metal rusted and discoloured. Several decrepit-looking beams held up the sagging ceiling, chunks of wood and glass and plaster coating the ground. Black liquid dribbled from the crooked pipes and down the walls over an ancient EXIT sign. There were no windows.

The image held like this for several minutes. Willow wanted to ask if something was supposed to be happening, but she had no voice. She tried to clear her throat as her chest tightened. This was it. This was proof. She just needed to take one of these videos. Surely Vinnie would never notice if one went missing? There were hundreds.

Hundreds...

She felt sick. They couldn't all be—

'Hello?'

A woman's voice, coming from the TV. It sounded like her own.

It's not though.

A door in the corner of the frame groaned open, and a gaunt, spectral figure emerged. 'I need help,' the girl said as she stumbled into the derelict room. She was nude — weren't they always — and walked gingerly, the rubble on the floor causing her immense discomfort, her arms wrapped around her chest in a protective gesture. 'Please, somebody help me.'

'Great performance, huh?' asked Vinnie.

'Yeah,' said Willow.

'Think you could do that?'

Willow nodded, unsure where Vinnie was but all-too-aware he was watching. She couldn't take her eyes from the screen, trying to store every little detail for future reference. She had to find this place. The girl on the video tripped and fell, her knees landing on broken glass. Her hair was cropped short, similar to how Willow wore hers. Behind her, the door opened.

'So you take cock?' said Vinnie.

Willow nodded again. 'Sure,' she breathed. The girl didn't notice the enormous naked man until he grabbed her, and then she screamed. Willow dug her nails into her palms as she flashed back to that first night looking at Jessica's phone. The scream was different, but also somehow the same.

It didn't sound like acting.

The man wore a leather mask, covered in zippers, all of them done up so that he was surely unable to see. The girl squirmed and fought, kicking him viciously between his legs and in his stomach. He responded by throwing her backwards, her body sailing through the air and landing on the trash-strewn floor. He followed her, manhandling her up and onto a table.

The camera suddenly moved, carried in a jerky motion towards the two "actors". The man thumped the girl across the face, the cameraman capturing it in close-up, zooming in to see the blood running from her nose. Willow could hear the crunch of the cameraman's footsteps. Vinnie chuckled, but she couldn't tell if it was from the video or somewhere in the room with her. The camera jostled back and forth, and her stomach churned. It was like some immersive virtual reality experience, one she desperately wished she could unplug from, but her eyes were glued to the screen, afraid that if she looked away she would find herself in there with them, privy to the revolting degradations the helpless girl was being subjected to.

'You enjoying this?' whispered Vinnie. He was so close she could smell his sweat.

'Yeah,' lied Willow. She wanted out. Needed air.

'Show me.'

The girl's face in close-up, her eyes white and vacant.

'What?'

'Show me you're enjoying it.' He said, his breath hot in her ear. 'Show me you get off on this.'

Willow forced a smile. Did she look as deranged as she felt?

Show me.

Was this real? Her hands moved automatically to her

jeans, unzipping her fly. She thought she was going to vomit.

Think of something else.

Show me.

Her hand crept into her jeans, resting over her crotch. The girl screamed for help, gargling blood in her mouth.

If he kills her, I'm going to be sick.

Think of something else!

Show me.

She touched the thin cotton of her underwear.

The man in the video placed his hand over the girl's mouth and nose. Her eyes widened as she panicked, struggling to wrestle her head free, unable to breathe.

'How's it feel?' purred a voice in Willow's ear. Vinnie, so close.

'Good,' choked Willow, her own breath difficult to come by, her chest constricting. A tear ran down her cheek.

She closed her eyes and imagined herself as the girl, chains tinkling overhead, a low industrial hum in the background, the throbbing agony between her legs, and all the while being watched, hundreds of eyes blinking in the shadows, waiting for the grand denouement, the money shot, the killing blow.

Show me.

On the table next to her, a knife. Next to it, a hacksaw. A scalpel. A corkscrew. A nail file. A crowbar. A baseball bat. The man searched the table, fingers finding the crowbar and wrapping around the cold metal like vines.

'You see now,' whispered Vinnie. 'You understand.' He ran his tongue over her ear, hot and wet.

'Yes,' said Willow. Terror wracked her body, and she wanted to cry out, but no sound would come. Hands closed over hers, pulling them free from her jeans and placing them roughly on the arms of the chair. Was it over?

She opened her eyes and still the video played. In it, the man held the crowbar high, bringing it down on the girl's face. It shattered like a doll's, the left side caving in. Nothing happened for a second, and then blood jetted out, thick and oozing.

She looked away, sickness rising in her throat, and felt a tautness over one of her wrists as Vinnie tightened a restraint.

'You know I can't let you leave,' he said. She nodded. Vinnie kissed her on the cheek. 'I can't *ever* let you leave.'

The man smashed the crowbar across the girl's face again, continuing to fuck her. She was unrecognisable from the neck up, her head a pulped mass that ran and dribbled off the sides of the table, pooling on the floor. Somehow, the noise of the blood dripping was the worst part.

Vinnie tied a knot above her other hand, fixing her to the chair. It wouldn't have mattered. She was numb, disassociated, desperate to leave this waking nightmare behind, yet unable to move, unable to scream.

A sharp sound blasted through the room, snapping Willow from her fugue-state.

'Shit,' said Vinnie. It was the doorbell again. He smiled. 'So persistent.'

It wasn't much, but it was a lifeline, and Willow seized on it. She found her voice. 'Help me!' she screamed. 'Help!'

Vinnie balled up a fist and smacked her in the side of the head. Everything went white, and when the brightness faded she saw double. Vinnie knelt by her, and she thought for a moment he was praying. She felt him fiddling with her shoelaces and tried to kick him, but he held her leg tight and worked one shoe and sock off. He stood, forcing her mouth open, and shoved the sock in.

'Stay here and shut up,' he said. *'Pretty please.'*

He left her there in front of the screen, the video playing on and on, unending in its horrors.

Then the door banged shut and she was alone once more.

34

The ropes cut into Willow's wrists as she struggled, clenching her fists, trying to break free. She craned her neck to bite at the knots, feeling the strain in her spine, but they were out of reach. The best thing to do would be to relax, she knew, but that was easier said than done. Whoever came up with that idea probably didn't have their eureka moment while tied up in a basement by a maniac. Fear mounted, her heart thumping crazily as she used her tongue try to force the sock from her mouth, fearful that if she vomited, she would choke.

On the television screen, the man had finished. He sat on the edge of the table, feet on the floor, penis limp between his thighs, and looked at the camera.

'How was it?'

'Real good,' said Vinnie, and for a second Willow thought he was in the room with her. No, it was coming from the video. That was all. She was by herself, waiting for him to come back and kill her. She wondered if she was being filmed right now, and searched for the blinking red light of a camera.

She had to escape.

Her hands were useless, the circulation stopping. She imagined them lying there blue and ineffectual, two blocks of ice, then remembered a film she had watched as part of her research, a Chinese one called *Men Behind the Sun*, in which a woman was tortured by having her hands frozen in ice, and then thawed with boiling water. The skin had peeled right off them like a fleshy glove.

'When do I get paid?' asked the man on the video, as he unzipped his black mask and yanked it off over his head, revealing a thin face with flattened hair and a vain attempt at a moustache.

'It was too quick,' said Vinnie from behind the camera. He zoomed in on the man's face.

'Jesus, are you still filming?' The man held a hand up to hide his features like a celebrity escaping the attention of the paparazzi.

Vinnie chuckled. 'Value for money, my young friend. Some people *work* for a living. When they spend their hard-earned cash, they expect a little more, no?'

The man squirmed under the gaze of the camera.

'Please stop, I've taken the mask off,' he pleaded. 'Someone might recognise me.'

'Who?' said Vinnie. 'Your family? Your *friends*?' He laughed.

'Where's my money?'

'Over there,' said Vinnie, panning over to a metal locker.

Willow's eyes widened.

My god.

The man walked sluggishly to the locker, his bare feet shuffling along the ground, his bony arse moving like pistons.

Willow scrutinised the image. She had seen it before,

and not in one of the videos. Those were indelibly etched in her mind, and would never leave her, but this was something different. It was half-glimpsed picture, a hazy dream. Where had she seen it?

Think think think!

The man opened the locker and took out his clothes, slipping into his baggy boxer shorts. Vinnie's video followed, floating peacefully, capturing the man dressing.

'Stop filming me,' he said.

'You liked it before,' said Vinnie.

'That was different. You couldn't see my face.'

'You were too fast.'

'I'm sorry. I didn't know it would be so...easy.' He stopped and stared at the camera, his eyes damp with confusion. 'She...she just fell apart.'

'Killing is easier than fucking,' said Vinnie. 'And it pays better.'

The man pulled his combat trousers over his waist and fiddled with the button with shaking hands. 'You're going to kill me too, aren't you?'

And then Willow remembered. She remembered *exactly* where she'd seen this place before. It was this new angle that had jogged her memory.

Oh well done, dipshit. You couldn't have remembered a week ago? No, you had to wait until you were trussed up in a sex dungeon waiting to be slaughtered.

'Yes,' said Vinnie. He held up a gun, his hand appearing from the corner of the screen like a shoot-em-up video game. The man backed away, holding his hands up in submission and letting his trousers droop to his ankles, a dark patch of urine spreading across the crotch of his shorts.

Vinnie pulled the trigger.

The chamber was empty.

Vinnie laughed at the cowering man, but Willow wasn't paying attention anymore. She knew now where she should be, where she should have gone, if only CB hadn't sent her to The Sunset Palace instead.

If only she'd realised sooner, the moment she saw the photo hanging in the upstairs hallway of Jessica Chalmers' parents' house.

It had been nestled amongst several photos of urban buildings and landscapes, and if the video on Jessica's phone hadn't been so goddam hard to see, she might have made the connection instantly.

Jessica's *parents*. Could it be possible?

A loud noise caught her attention, and when she looked at the screen, the half-dressed man had a fire-axe in his back and was screaming bloody murder.

How long has this been going on? And more importantly, where the fuck is Vinnie?

She glanced over towards the door, checking for him, and spotted Vinnie's knife resting on the shelf where she had left it. An idea came to her. It was her only chance. How much time did she have?

To the soundtrack of a man being hacked apart by an axe, Willow shuffled the chair along the floor, pushing with her feet, which thankfully remained untied. The wooden legs scraped noisily over the rough stone ground, but speed was of the essence, not stealth. By the time she made it to the shelves, the video had ended, leaving a screen of wild snowy static and white noise. The knife sat on a shelf in front of a row of VHS tapes, but it was too high to reach with her hands. She rocked forwards until she could stand, hunched over at the waist by the chair, and rested her chin on the shelf. Despite the continued presence of a sock in her mouth, she placed her lips around the handle of the knife.

Sounds drifted down from upstairs. It sounded like Vinnie was arguing with someone. Willow slid the knife from the shelf, gripping it with her teeth. It was heavy, and she felt it slipping. She manoeuvred it over the shelf beneath, and laid it within reach.

Above, the men's voices were raised, someone bellowing at Vinnie, and that was fine with Willow. The longer and louder they argued, the better.

She wiggled the fingers of her right hand to get the blood flowing, before reaching for the knife. If she dropped it now, it was all over. Bending her wrist as far as possible, she closed her fingers over the handle. It wasn't a powerful grip, but it would have to do. She held the knife with the blade facing down and started to saw through the ropes.

As she worked, she formulated a plan. She'd have to get past Vinnie. Should she wait down here and surprise him when he returned? Once he was dealt with, she would have to go to the police...no, she was wanted for murder, wasn't she? Maybe she should go straight to the Chalmers residence and leave the police out altogether, or call on Cat, ask for her help. Her mind reeled, a tornado of indecision.

Don't think about it yet. Escape first, and hurry.

The razor-sharp blade made short work of the bindings, Willow wincing as it sliced her skin. A trickle of blood seeped from the wound, but soon her hand was free. The first thing she did was place the knife on her lap and remove the sock from her mouth. She hurled it across the room and began work on the other rope.

Things had gone quiet upstairs, and that was a serious concern. Willow doubled her efforts, sawing rapidly, not caring if she cut herself. The ropes fell to the floor and she stood, crossing her arms and flexing her fingers. She felt manic, adrenalised, energy surging through her limbs.

Gripping the knife, she buttoned up her jeans and crept towards the door. Her discarded shoe lay in the centre of the room like a forgotten toy, and she ignored it. There was no time to spare. Not now, when she was so close. She turned the handle, throwing the door open.

When she came face-to-face with Detective Stone, she screamed.

He looked tired, deep purple bags weighing down his eyes, his face more creased than usual. Willow clutched the knife, ready to use it.

Stone's mouth drooped open and he let out a long, ragged sigh. He looked down at his stomach, where his hand was clamped, blood seeping between his fingers.

Willow raised the knife as he staggered towards her, tripping over his own feet.

'What the fuck are you doing?' he said, his face screwed-up in agony. 'I'm here to help!'

'You're part of it,' she said, eyes wide. 'You were there last night.'

Stone grimaced at her. 'Aye, I've been following you for days, ya daft wee bint. You fair get around.'

Willow lowered the knife, but kept her distance. 'Then you know it's not me,' she said. 'You know I'm innocent.'

He managed a miserable smile. 'Aye. I can't be right *all* the time.'

Detective Stone never even registered the gunshot before the bullet tore through his skull and exploded out the other side, popping his eyeball as it went. The projectile carried on its journey, smashing into several videotapes on a lower shelf as his body hit the cold floor with a sickening splat.

His hands jittered a moment and then were still.

A puff of smoke casually unfurled from the top of the stairs, drawing Willow's attention.

'Fucking police,' said Vinnie. He pointed the gun at Willow and spat out a glob of blood-flecked phlegm. 'Now, *they* talk too much.'

35

VINNIE TRUDGED DOWN THE STEPS, THE GUN DIRECTED AT Willow. Neither of them spoke. What was left to say? It was over. She had lost. She looked at Stone, his ruined face sinking into the floor as if the pool of blood surrounding it was acid, rapidly eating away at skin and bone.

'You have caused me so much trouble,' said Vinnie as he entered the basement. He lowered the gun slightly, the barrel still aimed at her, and walked towards Stone's prone, lifeless body. He gave it a kick. '*Disgustoso*.'

'I thought you'd be used to that sort of thing,' said Willow in a dry, throaty voice.

'Not in my place of business.' He looked at her as though she were being naïve. 'Not in my *home*. Who's going to clean this up? Perhaps I should make you do it.' He scowled. 'There are a *lot* of things I'd like to make you do before I kill you. I have a *very* open mind.'

'Fuck you.'

'That's just *one* of the things.'

'I'd rather die.'

'Be patient, Rough Stuff. You will.' He kicked Stone's

corpse again. 'Shame. You could have been a big star. You're not like the rest, those skinny junkie bitches. No, we could have made good money from you. But not as the victim, no.' He pointed a nicotine-stained finger at her. 'You would have been the killer.'

'Never,' she said with a look of revulsion. 'I'm not like you. I couldn't kill.'

'I wonder if you know yourself as well as you think you do?'

'I know I'm not a murderer.'

'We must agree to disagree.' He aimed the gun at her chest and smiled.

'Who's this *we* you keep talking about? The Chalmers?'

Vinnie raised an eyebrow.

'*Percettiva*, my dear, sweet Rough Stuff. Perhaps I never gave you enough credit. Maybe, with more time, and against a weaker, more simple opponent, you might have brought the whole operation down. But not me. I'm too smart, and my friends are too powerful. They mix in circles that neither of us will ever access. It's a different world, you know?'

Willow nodded. 'I guessed there'd be someone else in charge. A cockweasel like you could never pull this off on his own. You make me sick.'

'But I also make money. I used to make it from sex, then the internet ruined everything. Soon, I may not even be allowed to live in this country. Times are tough, baby.'

'So you kill innocent girls for money?'

'Life is cheap, Rough Stuff. But Rolexes are expensive.'

Willow almost laughed at the mundanity. Money. It was all for money. She stared ahead, looking down the barrel of the gun, a peculiar zen-like calm descending.

'Are you smiling?' said Vinnie.

'Life is cheap, but Rolexes are expensive. You should get that on a fucking t-shirt.'

Vinnie's smile wavered. 'You disrespect me? You realise I'm about to kill you?'

'So you keep promising.'

He watched her through unblinking eyes. 'You don't fear death,' he said. 'Why not?'

'Oh, I fear death,' said Willow. 'But I don't fear you. Death has earned my respect, whereas you will forever be nothing more than a worthless piece of shit.'

'I'm an artist, you fucking peasant,' he snapped. She was getting to him, his demeanour altering before her.

'You're a murderer,' said Willow.

'Murder *is* art, in the right hands,' said Vinnie. 'Tell me... since you saw my work, have you been able to stop thinking about it? Have you been able to get it out of your head?'

'No,' she admitted. 'But that doesn't make it art. Anyone could do this, but most people aren't sick enough.'

'No, no,' he said, the annoyance in his voice obvious. '*Not* anybody. I make death beautiful. Erotic. Anybody can point a camera, and anybody can kill. But not like me. It's like the blues. You know the blues, Rough Stuff? Anybody can play the blues. It's all the same. But it's now about *what* you play, it's *how* you play it.' His mouth widened into an obscene grin. 'This is the dead girl blues, Rough Stuff. Won't you sing it with me?'

'You're fucking mental.'

'I'm an artist. But even great artists need inspiration.' He smiled like a smitten lover. '*You* inspire me, dear Rough Stuff. You've awakened something inside of me, a *passion*. Do you not feel it too? A connection between us, stronger than family, thicker than blood.'

'I feel nothing,' said Willow.

'And that is why I think I love you, Rough Stuff. I see it now, it's all clear. You're my muse.' He shook his head in disbelief. 'My beautiful, fearless muse. I will make you a star, a beautiful shining star that lights up the whole galaxy. You will perform in my masterpiece, my greatest work. Are you ready, Rough Stuff? Think you got what it takes?'

'I won't kill for you,' said Willow.

Vinnie grinned, displaying a mouthful of red teeth. 'Let's take a drive,' he said. 'I'd like you to meet my friends.'

36

THEY DROVE THROUGH THE NIGHT, VINNIE BEHIND THE WHEEL, Willow in the passenger seat, her hands cuffed to the door. The gun rested on Vinnie's lap like a dozing feline, the rain pounding off the windows and drizzling down the glass as he negotiated the streets at the requisite twenty miles per hour, a model citizen, law-abiding and considerate. She supposed it wouldn't do to be stopped by the police right now.

Rows of expensive-looking houses rolled by, and Willow knew where they were headed. Morningside, where Jessica Chalmers' parents lived. Sure enough, Vinnie pulled into a driveway behind a red Mercedes and waited, the engine idling.

The roof of the vehicle was alive with the thrum of rain, the wipers working overtime to clear the windscreen. Vinnie switched the radio on and searched the stations. He paused at an Al Green song, nodded, and hummed along, drumming his fingers on the wheel in time to the beat.

Willow stretched, wincing as the metal handcuffs rubbed against her exposed skin. She still only had one shoe on, the other lying in the basement of The Sunset Palace.

And I never even got a chance to say goodbye.

'Can you put the heating on?' she asked.

'Fuck off,' said Vinnie. Then, after a while, he said, 'I love this song. You like Al Green?'

She glared at him. 'Are you making small talk?'

'We could be here a while. They never hurry.'

She looked away from him, out the window at the puddles dancing with exaggerated splashes. A light in the house went off, and minutes later Jessica's parents stepped out under the safety of an enormous blue and white golfing umbrella.

Mr Chalmers opened the back door and held it for his wife, then walked unhurriedly round to the other side and let himself in.

'Bloody awful weather, isn't it?' he said as he buckled his seatbelt, before helping his wife do the same.

'Jeremy, please,' said Mrs Chalmers. 'Mind your language.'

Willow could see her in the wing-mirror. The woman looked vastly different to the ghoul that had wept through the funeral. Her face glowed, hair loose around her shoulders.

'Apologies, Judith,' said Jeremy, lightly patting her knee. 'Ready when you are, Vincent.'

Without a word, Vinnie reversed out, and drove slowly down the quiet street.

'Miss Zulawski, I presume?' said Jeremy Chalmers.

Willow didn't respond, and Vinnie punched her hard on the arm. She yelped in pain.

'Answer the man,' said Vinnie.

'Now, now, Vincent,' said Jeremy, 'there's no need to resort to violence.'

'We're all civilised,' said Judith, and she and Jeremy smiled at each other.

'That may surprise you, Miss Zulawski, but it's true,' said Jeremy. 'Oh, I imagine you think we're a real pair of monsters. Or perhaps insane? But no, I assure you, we are quite rational.'

'You kill people,' said Willow.

'They weren't going to be missed. They were from the streets, destined for nothing but poverty. At least we gave their lives purpose, albeit fleetingly.'

'But you *killed* them.'

'They were killing themselves. We simply expedited the situation.'

'But *why?*' It was like talking to a politician, one who had convinced himself he was correct about everything.

Judith snorted. 'You think this lifestyle is easy? You probably don't even earn enough to pay tax. But for us, life keeps getting harder. Jeremy's pension won't sustain us when he retires...how, I ask you, is a family supposed to live these days?'

'So true,' said Jeremy. 'Why is it that the more you contribute to society, the more you're penalised for it? We live in Broken Britain, that's for sure.'

'Are you fucking kidding me?' said Willow. She wanted to climb into the back seat and put her hands around his throat.

'Please dear,' muttered Judith, 'there's no need for profanity.'

'Really Judith,' said Jeremy, 'the lower classes have always had trouble expressing themselves without resorting to foul language and blasphemy. It's one of their more disagreeable traits.'

'The lower classes?' snapped Willow. 'You're murdering people to fund your fucking *dinner* parties, you cunts, so don't speak to me about good fucking manners.'

'There's more to it than that,' said Jeremy, 'but I imagine you would be too uneducated to understand. I prefer to only discuss politics with my intellectual equals.'

Willow laughed dryly and turned away, staring out the windscreen. They had left the city, Vinnie navigating the car through country lanes, swapping tenements for ancient pine trees, the tyres splashing through waterlogged potholes that dotted the single-track roads. The moon was nowhere to be seen, skulking in fear behind a bank of clouds.

'How long?' said Willow.

'Excuse me?' said Jeremy.

'How long has this been going on?'

Jeremy chuckled. 'Oh, I couldn't say. Years, that's for sure. I used to do it myself, until I brought young Vincent on board. His help has been greatly appreciated.' He leaned forwards and gripped Vinnie's shoulder. Vinnie nodded in response.

'I found it all rather distasteful at first,' said Judith, 'but it's funny how you adapt. How soon it becomes enjoyable.'

Willow shook her head in disbelief. 'And how much will you be paying *me*?'

Judith shrugged nonchalantly. 'If you had come to us sooner, perhaps we could have worked out a deal, and avoided this unpleasant turn of events.'

'I can't be bought.'

'Nonsense. For the right price, you people will do anything. Now, I suppose you'll have to work for free.'

'I'll die before being in one of your sick little films,' said Willow.

'Then so be it,' said Jeremy. 'You might change your mind when we visit the set. Won't that be exciting? Your kind dreams of fame, when you're standing in line at the dole office, or queueing up at the food bank. You think that money will make you happy, and you know what? You're right. It does. What a pity you'll never get to experience it. Fortune favours the wealthy.'

Willow snorted and glanced at Vinnie. 'Life is cheap, but a mortgage in Morningside is expensive, right?' she said.

Jeremy nodded. 'I like it. Crude, but true. You're certainly different to the other girls. You have a bit of gumption. I'm almost impressed.'

'And what about Jessica? She was your *daughter*, for fuck's sake.'

'A regrettable mishap,' said Judith, though it didn't sound like she meant it. 'Jeremy thought it wise to introduce her to our little sideline, but her heart wasn't in it. Luckily she would do anything for money. Or in her case, drugs. Once Jeremy had her addicted to the stuff, she became more open to new ways of working. Then she met that awful girl, Lina, and her whole attitude changed. She tried to ruin us.'

'Tried but failed,' said Jeremy.

'So you killed your own daughter,' said Willow, so quietly she didn't think they heard.

'Indeed,' said Jeremy. 'Now that's enough questions. I'd like to enjoy the drive.'

Willow sat back, unsure if she was dreaming. The events of the last week were catching up to her. Sheer momentum had kept her going, but now the ride was over and it was time to get off.

She was going to die.

How and where she did not know, but this was the end of the line.

She pressed her forehead to the glass and watched the world speed by. They passed a field, a lone scarecrow standing watch, wearing baggy trousers and nothing else.

She made eye contact with a cow and could have sworn it winked at her.

Willow laughed.

'Happens to them all,' said Jeremy, turning to his wife. 'The hysteria of fear.'

Judith nodded. 'Darling, if you ever write a book on the subject, that would be a *fabulous* title.'

With that, they lapsed into silence again. There was nothing left to say. The car pulled off the road and rumbled up a gravel path. The rain had stopped, and when Willow peered through the window, all she could see were rolling hills lined with the dark outlines of bony trees. She glanced in the rearview mirror and watched the twinkling lights of Edinburgh fade into the distance.

Were they going to kill her in the middle of nowhere?

Why not?

Vinnie killed the engine.

'Get out,' said Jeremy, as Vinnie unlocked Willow's handcuffs. She complied. Her feet sank into the wet grass, the mud squelching between the toes of her one bare foot. Vinnie jabbed the gun into her spine.

'Move,' he said. It was the first word he had spoken in a long time. It was clear that The Chalmers were the puppeteers, and Vinnie just danced at the end of their strings.

'Where are we going?' she said.

'Just walk.'

And walk she did. Jeremy led the way, using a torch to

guide them, and the oversized umbrella as a cane. He turned to Willow and said, 'You can scream if you want. There's no one around to hear you. No one for miles.'

'I'll be okay,' she said curtly, refusing to give him the satisfaction of her increasing terror.

There was no path to follow, just a line in the grass where the vegetation had eroded. Willow wondered how many innocent girls had made this doomed journey, girls that Judith and Jeremy Chalmers had regarded as worthless, lesser than them because they hadn't been born into money, because they hadn't attended the best private schools, because they had to work two, maybe three jobs to make a living. Girls who lived in poverty, where every day was a struggle.

And boys too, don't forget.

As if she could. The video in Jessica's flat still haunted her. It *all* haunted her.

You brought it on yourself. You couldn't let it lie. Curiosity killed the cat.

Someone had to do something.

And look where it's brought you.

'Stop,' said Jeremy. They were in a clearing, the dark shadows of the trees towering over them on all sides, blocking the wind and creating an eerie stillness, like a graveyard on Halloween Eve. Jeremy kicked away fallen leaves and branches, revealing a metal circle embedded in the earth like the gateway to Hell.

Willow shivered, the awful spectre of death breathing down her neck.

'No,' she said involuntarily, and Jeremy laughed. He removed a metal bar from his North Face rucksack and jammed it into the circle, levering it up. Willow half expected to see smoke billowing out and fire licking the sides. She felt sick, an iron fist clamped around her stomach. Jeremy deposited the cover to the side of the hole, then looked at Judith.

'After you, darling,' he said.

'You won't get away with this,' said Willow, painfully aware how lame that sounded.

'On the contrary, we already have. We've been getting away with this for years. Who would suspect a nice respectable couple like Jeremy and Judith Chalmers? We're pillars of the community. Good, God-fearing folk.' He smiled. 'And we make sure to donate very generously to charity every year.' He smiled at her, looking for all the world like the innocuous fifty-something man he was. 'It's tax deductible, you know.'

'My friend knows I'm here,' said Willow, as Judith descended the ladder. 'She'll be tracking my phone right now. She's probably called the police already.'

Jeremy cocked his head at her. 'Would this be your flatmate? Catherine, I believe?'

Willow said nothing. The wind picked up and rustled the branches of the pine trees. In the distance, a bird sang its lonely song.

'Funny thing,' continued Jeremy. 'I paid her a visit earlier this evening. I'd actually gone to find *you*, Miss Zulawski.'

'What did you do to her?' asked Willow.

Jeremy sighed. 'Come now, you already know the answer to that. I imagine the police will mop up what's left of her once the neighbours report the smell.'

The words hit Willow like a punch to the gut. She thought of Cat. Sweet, dependable Cat, who hadn't watched the video, who posed no threat to anyone.

The police will mop up what's left of her.

'Just shoot me,' mumbled Willow.

'Oh, don't be silly,' said Jeremy. 'Haven't you always wanted to be a star? Isn't that every teenage girl's dream?'

'I wanted to be an astronaut,' said Willow, staring at her feet.

One shoe on and one shoe off.

'A laudable goal,' said Jeremy, 'and a rather unlikely one at that.' He turned to Vinnie. 'I'm going to join my wife, Vincent. You make sure Miss Zulawski follows us.'

He started down the ladder and disappeared from sight, leaving Willow and Vinnie above ground. When he reached the bottom, he called up. Vinnie jabbed the barrel of the gun into her again, and Willow forced her tired legs to move towards the hole in the ground. She put her foot into the blackness, finding the top rung of the ladder. It groaned with every step, the metal bending as she placed her weight onto it. She looked up and saw Vinnie's face silhouetted against the night sky. She couldn't see the gun, but knew it was pointed at her.

Her feet met concrete.

'Turn around, take three steps forward and wait with your back to the ladder,' instructed Jeremy, his deep voice booming off the walls. There was a loud noise, something roaring into life, and then a series of lights flickered on, leading down an enormous tunnel that seemed to go on forever, the arched ceiling giving the impression of a set from an old sci-fi movie. Rusted pipes lined the corridor. A dented oil drum lay on its side.

'What is this place?' said Willow.

'A disused bunker,' said Jeremy. 'Built in the fifties, I believe, as an RAF command centre. Three storeys deep, no less. Impressive, isn't it?'

'This is where you take them,' shuddered Willow. 'This is where they come to die.' She whirled on Jeremy. 'How many?' she demanded, thinking of the videotapes in The Sunset Palace. They couldn't all be...could they? 'How fucking many?'

'My husband told you, we don't keep count,' said Judith, appearing from behind a generator and raising her voice to be heard over the petrol-fuelled racket.

'We keep the bodies on the lower floor,' said Jeremy. 'You're welcome to go down and count if you like. But be aware...the smell is quite overpowering.'

'You keep the bodies...here?'

'Well what else are we going to do with them?' said Jeremy. 'Give them a proper burial?' He laughed at that. They both did, Jeremy and Judith Chalmers, laughing at their slaughtered victims as they stood over their mass grave.

She heard Vinnie slide the metal cover shut, then moments later the gun was once more pressed into her spine.

The time for talking was over.

37

THEY PASSED THROUGH THE TUNNEL AND WOUND THEIR WAY down labyrinthian corridors that twisted and turned back on themselves, a dimly lit underground warren. The walls were green with damp moss, black scorch marks scarring the floor. Around one corner, WELCOME TO HELL was spray painted, the letters dripping like fresh blood.

'Our Jessica always had a flair for the dramatic,' said Judith, her husband snorting in acknowledgement, and on they continued, heading down a flight of buckled stairs into a tenebrous area lit only by emergency light bulbs that throbbed a deep red. Willow's head pounded. Every step felt like her last, a condemned prisoner marching towards her fate.

'Mind yourself here,' said Jeremy, taking Willow by the arm and dragging her to one side of the tunnel. 'Floor's unsafe.'

Unsafe was putting it mildly. The floor had given way, two long wooden beams forming a makeshift walkway across the chasm. They walked one after the other, clinging to the wall, the arched ceiling making them bend awkwardly, forcing Willow to stare down into the impenetrable murk.

Jump, she thought. *Step into the unknown and at least then it'll be over. You're going to die anyway.*

'No,' groaned Willow, and Jeremy turned to look at her.

'Almost there,' he said. 'Don't look down.'

She did, though. She couldn't stop herself, the inky void rushing up towards her, wind howling through the tunnels, bringing with it the dread screams of the slaughtered. Her heart beat faster, the tunnel shrinking, closing in, pushing her head down into the emptiness, forcing her to stare into the dark eyes of insanity, to face the overwhelming sense of loss, the maddening sadness that brimmed up from the depths of the bunker.

This is where they take them.

Stay calm, she told herself. *You're having a panic attack.*

'Move along,' said Judith, but Willow could go no further. A dank odour assailed her nostrils, and she found it difficult to breathe. She thought of all the other girls who had made this journey before her, none of whom had ever come back. They were all still here, piled up in a mass grave below her feet, below her feet *right now,* my god, *my god*, it was too horrifying, she couldn't breathe, she couldn't fucking *breathe*.

'I can't,' she panted, her chest tight. She could *smell* them, she was sure of it, the bodies of all those before her, and she would end up there too, another statistic, another body in this museum of unfathomable cruelty. She fell to her knees, weeping, almost toppling over the edge, and Jeremy grabbed her by the arm, hauling her across the beams and onto solid ground.

'Come on,' he said, not slowing his pace, dragging her behind him, shards of glass and metal raking along her legs, and she choked, tasting vomit in the back of her throat.

Unable to stop herself, Willow let loose a throat-shredding scream that echoed throughout the bunker, tapering off into pitiful nothingness. She kicked out and caught Jeremy on the shin, but his grip never loosened. She screamed again. It felt good to scream.

It was all she had left.

~

She didn't know how she ended up in the room. There had been a sharp pain in the side of her head, then sweet, blissful nothingness. When she opened her eyes, the pain had become a dull pulse, and there she was, cold and alone. Where had everyone gone? She looked down at the greying floor and realised she was naked. How? When? A high-pitched hum blared in her ears, the room lit by a single spotlight in the corner that blasted white incandescence across her pale body.

Willow choked back a sob and shuffled out of the glare of the beam. She looked around, blinking away the coloured lights that pulsated before her eyes.

She knew where she was. The broken exit sign, the locker, the walls that wept filthy black tears. It felt strange to finally be here, to see the grainy, pixelated image come to life in all its dour and horrifying glory.

You did it. You found the location and the killers and solved the mystery. Was it worth it? Was it worth dying for?

In the centre of the room stood the familiar steel gurney. Willow got to her feet, ignoring the pain in her cut and bruised legs. There was a body on the gurney, covered in a sheet that might once have been white. She lumbered towards it. A table had been set up to the side, various tools and implements of torture laid out neatly on top.

The room stank of blood.

'Camera's rolling,' boomed Jeremy's voice, and she turned to see a grimy window into the adjacent room. Through it stood Judith, Jeremy and Vinnie, who held a chunky camcorder in his sweaty hands, pointing it towards her.

'Kill her,' said Jeremy, 'and prove yourself worthy of a starring role.'

She looked away, searching for an exit, and something under the sheet moved.

Not something...someone...

Whoever was under there was still alive, and Willow was expected to kill them. She took small, faltering steps towards the gurney, reaching out a trembling hand. The sheet was unwashed, the dried blood forming an indecipherable pattern. It rose with each rasping breath, then sagged into place. Up...and down. Up...and down.

'Do it,' said Jeremy. 'Show me you have what it takes.'

Was it possible to feel your mind snap?

Life is cheap.

Up...and down.

'Kill her!' roared Jeremy.

Willow took the corner of the sheet and pulled. It fluttered to the floor.

'No,' she said, a tear tracing its way down her bruised cheek. She stared at the naked girl on the gurney, into the face she recognised.

'Lina,' she said. 'Oh god, *Lina*.'

The girl looked at her in confusion. She tried to say something, but her tongue had been crudely removed, the nub hiding far back in her mouth, blackened where white-hot metal had cauterised the wound. Her eyes were blank and haunted, her lower lip trembling. Her hands lay unbound by her sides, gripping the edge of the steel gurney with knuckles that burned white in terror. She gently touched Lina's hand, and the girl pulled away.

'Hey,' she said, stepping back, giving Lina space. 'It's me. Do you remember? It's Willow. I gave you the locket.'

But Lina's glazed expression never changed. What horrors had they subjected her to? The visible damage was obvious, but the mental strain was incalculable.

Willow held her hand out. 'I'm going to get us out of here, but I need your help.'

With great trepidation, Lina reached her bloodstained hand up to Willow's, cautiously taking it. No recognition flickered across her eyes, one of which was blood red, the surrounding tissue purple and green. As she helped the girl into a sitting position, Willow noticed the contusions around her neck, the fresh scars on her stomach.

'What did they do to you?'

Lina stared at her, and Willow doubted she understood what was happening, or where she was.

'It's okay, it's going to be okay,' she whispered. She put her mouth to Lina's ear and whispered, 'We have to work together. You and me, we can escape, but I need you, Lina. I can't do this alone.'

Lina stared through her, expressionless.

'For Jessica, Lina. Please, do it for *Jessica*.'

She looked into her eyes, trying to forge a connection. Slowly, the girl nodded, her arms dangling by her sides. She spoke one solitary word.

It sounded like, '*Jessica*.'

'That's right,' said Willow, brushing a strand of curly hair from Lina's face. 'They killed Je—'

A pain in Willow's stomach — a sharp, needling agony — cut her off. Something wet splattered onto her feet and for a second she thought she'd peed herself. Then the pain intensified, a burning sensation that only grew hotter.

'What,' choked Willow, looking down, down to where the scalpel protruded from her stomach, a scalpel gripped in Lina's psychotic grasp.

Lina's eyes widened, her pupils dilating. She withdrew the blade, a spurt of blood hitting the floor, and Willow realised it was too late. Lina was gone, only an empty husk remaining. It wore Lina's face and skin and eyes and body, but there was nothing inside, nothing recognisable as the grieving, desperate girl she had met only days before.

Lina jabbed with the scalpel again and Willow dodged, the blade nicking her exposed belly. She retreated, as Lina scrambled off the gurney and came at her with unbridled fury, swinging the scalpel, trying to scream but only grunting and whining instead.

'That's it!' shouted Jeremy from behind the window, as Judith clapped appreciatively. 'More blood!'

'Lina, stop!' said Willow, as the crazed girl advanced on her. 'For god's sake, stop!'

Her ass hit the table and it toppled, the tools spilling onto the floor and scattering with a tuneless metallic scrape. Lina attacked, the scalpel grazing Willow's cheek, just below her eyeball. She shoved Lina backwards and the girl fell, landing hard.

'Lina, please,' begged Willow. 'Think about Jessica!'

Lina paused, looking up at Willow, taking deep lungfuls of air. Her lips peeled back in a snarl, dead eyes glazing over. She came at her again, the blade heading for Willow's neck. She ducked out of the way, grabbing Lina's wrist and using her momentum to pull the girl forwards. Lina slammed headfirst into the wall with a loud crack. She stumbled, using her free hand for balance, and turned to face Willow, blood seeping from her nostrils, her front teeth stuck in her lower lip.

Blood trickled from the wounds on Willow's belly. She pressed her hand over them and watched as Lina opened her mouth, her teeth pulling free from her lip, coming away red and bloody. One of them didn't come out, the broken stump of enamel protruding from her lower lip like a tombstone.

It was the exact moment that Willow knew she no longer had any choice. Any idea of changing Lina's mind, of the two of them working together to escape, had gone.

It was kill or be killed.

She saw Jeremy and Judith watching through the glass, Jeremy licking his lips in anticipation, Vinnie lurking behind the camcorder.

They were all watching her, waiting for her to slip up.

Ah, fuck it.

She was used to being watched.

The hum of the generator...the shouts and cries of her audience...Lina's animal grunts...all these sounds faded, dimming like the setting sun. Willow saw herself on the side of the stage, an expectant crowd murmuring anxiously, awaiting the main attraction. Her body tingled as music drifted through her head, cloaked her, enveloped her.

Her breathing slowed.

Lina started towards her, making a vague approximation of a scream. She seemed to move in slow motion. Judith banged her fists off the glass, and Vinnie turned the dial, zooming in for the killing blow.

Willow dropped, her fingers groping for the nearest weapon, closing around the handle of a rusted machete.

You're not a killer, you're not a killer, her mind insisted, but as much as she hated to admit it, Vinnie had been right. She was *precisely* that.

Lina lunged forwards as Willow closed her eyes, swinging the machete in a wide arc, trusting her instincts.

She heard a sound akin a branch snapping, and then hot liquid gushed onto her face, getting in her eyes, her mouth. She recognised the coppery taste, and released the machete, expecting to hear it clang to the ground.

It didn't.

She looked at Lina, at the long blade embedded in her gaunt neck, her fingers groping helplessly as arterial fluid sprayed from the wound, an inferno of blood painting the walls a hideous scarlet.

For one moment, Lina seemed to recognise her. She expelled a lungful of blood and dropped, wheezing, to her knees, her eyes pleading with Willow to finish the job, to end the suffering.

There was so much blood.

So much blood.

Tears spilled down Lina's cheeks. Her head flopped to the side, and the skin tore, the large puncture wound opening wider, yawning, more blood pouring down her milky-white skin.

Lina held out a hand and mouthed two words, her head lolling at a ninety-degree angle.

Help...me...

Willow gripped the gore-drenched machete handle, tugging it free from Lina's neck, blood pumping in an endless crazed torrent. She looked her in the eyes and saw a flicker of the doomed young girl she had encountered in the alley.

'I'm sorry,' she sobbed. 'I'm so sorry.'

She forced herself to look as she raised the machete high, then brought it down, aiming at what remained of Lina's neck.

Her head hit the floor, followed seconds later by her body.

The machete slipped from Willow's hands. One thought repeated over and over, until it seemed she would never think of anything again.

What have you done? What the fuck have you just done?

'My goodness,' gasped Judith. She turned to Vinnie and asked breathlessly, 'Did you get it all?'

'Every second,' said Vinnie. 'Every last drop of blood.'

'I told you she'd be good,' said Jeremy. 'No, never mind *good*...she was exceptional.'

'What's she doing now?' said Judith, watching Willow as she sat on the floor, holding one hand in front of her face, blood dripping from her fingers.

Jeremy put his arm around his wife and squeezed her. 'My dear, I do believe she's gone over the edge.'

'I suppose sooner or later, they all do,' said Judith. 'But I expected her to last longer. It looked good though. Perhaps we should do that more often?'

'What, have them fight?'

Judith nodded. 'Yes. We could turn it into a game, take bets on who wins.'

Jeremy leaned over and kissed Judith on her forehead. 'Darling, I love the way your mind works.' He smiled, his face creasing in delight. 'Take bets on who wins...how *deliciously* twisted!'

38

Willow watched them scurry about their duties.

They paid her scant attention. She was no longer a threat — now she was little more than a mad inconvenience.

She hoped they were wrong. Or *had* she gone mad? Had she gone completely, hopelessly insane? After all she had seen, all she had done...she had *killed* a girl. Butchered her, decapitated her. That was not the action of someone who was right in the head.

It's survival, she told herself.

Isn't that what a crazy person would say?

Jeremy Chalmers unrolled a sheet of polythene, struggling to flatten it, while Vinnie lifted the headless body of Lina under the armpits and hefted her onto the sheet.

'One more for the pile,' said Jeremy. He pointed at Willow. 'What about her? Think she's got another film in her?'

Judith squinted over the rim of her glasses. 'I doubt it. She looks half-cracked.'

Oh, you don't know the half of it, thought Willow, and giggled. She looked at her hands. They were so red!

Hold it together!

'Can you be bothered cleaning another one up?'

'Oh Jeremy, it doesn't take long.'

'True, but I'd rather not get blood all over my suit. It's just back from the dry-cleaners, and you *know* how long it takes them.'

'Well, put on an apron, for crying out loud. I told you before we left the house to wear something casual. We can't leave her here. The whole place will stink of faeces by next week.'

'Fine,' he grumbled. 'But we'll shoot her. I'm tired, and we have to be up early tomorrow.'

This is normal to them. This is just their lives.

Jeremy signalled and Vinnie trotted dutifully over.

'Vincent, kindly help me dispose of our daughter's dear, deceased paramour,' he said, as they each grabbed a corner of the sheet and began to drag the corpse out the door.

'Jeremy,' shouted Judith. 'Haven't you forgotten something?'

He looked at her, his befuddlement turning to laughter when he spotted it.

'Goodness,' he said, walking towards the corner of the room where Lina's severed head lay. He kicked it across the floor, nudging the head onto the sheet alongside the rest of her. 'You always say I'd forget my head if it wasn't screwed on,' he chortled.

'Oh *Jeremy*.'

'Tell you what,' he said, gesturing towards Willow. 'Why don't *you* take care of this one?'

Judith beamed with pride. 'Really? It's been...it's been so long.'

'Make it quick, though. No torture. I want her dead by the time we return.'

'Of course.' Her face coloured, smiling as Jeremy and Vinnie left the room, dragging Lina between them, the polythene sheet screeching down the hall. Neither man paid Willow any attention. She had served her purpose, and now she would be discarded and forgotten.

'What a pity it had to end like this,' said Judith, peering at Willow the way a child with a magnifying glass watches an ant. She smiled sadly. 'You could have taken Jessica's place. You would have made a *fine* killer.' She bent and picked up a baseball bat, six nails hammered into the barrel.

Willow looked up at Judith. An unfamiliar sensation burned within her, a desire to hurt, to maim...to kill. To wrestle the bat from the woman's hands and bury it deep in her head, to smash her skull. She hated herself for it, and yet, she could think of nothing else.

'I'm going...to kill you,' said Willow, every word an effort. The blood on her face — some of it hers, some of it Lina's — was cold and sticky.

Judith's smile faltered. 'Oh,' she said, taking a step backwards, suddenly unsure of herself. 'You're awake.'

Willow struggled to her feet. She knew that if Judith came for her now, weak and unprotected, it would be all over. Instead, she read fear in the older woman's eyes.

'What's the matter? Scared?'

'Don't be absurd,' Judith whispered as she nervously retreated. She held the bat aloft, and Willow noticed the tremor in her hands. 'What'll you do...kill me, then go back to your miserable life?'

'That's the plan, yeah,' grunted Willow, the taste of blood coating her tongue.

'You think that's living? Your whole existence is worthless. It's *less* than nothing.'

Willow advanced, every move agonising, bleeding out

from the small puncture wounds in her stomach, one eye swollen shut. She stood as best she could, advancing on Judith Chalmers like Quasimodo.

'Accept your fate!' spat Judith. 'You have no money, no prospects, no hope. What are you *doing* with your life? You're *nothing* out there. You're a pawn.' She screwed up her face in fury. 'You're *shit*.'

'Sticks and stones will break my bones,' said Willow, picking up a cordless power drill from the floor, pulling the trigger and watching the tool whir into life with ruthless speed, 'but names will never hurt me.'

'You're insane,' said Judith. Her back hit the wall and she almost dropped the baseball bat. Willow pulled the trigger again, and Judith squirmed.

'Don't come any closer,' she said. 'I can pay you.' She tried to smile. 'We're rich beyond your *wildest* dreams.'

'You know, I never really knew my parents,' said Willow.

'What?'

'They died when I was seven. I don't have many memories of them, but I do remember something my dad once told me.'

'One hundred thousand,' sputtered Judith. 'In cash.'

Willow ignored her. 'You see, they didn't have much money. My dad was just a poor immigrant. My mum was from a rich family though. You would've liked them, they sounded like real arseholes.'

'Tonight. I can get you the money *tonight*.'

The drill roared into life again in Willow's hands.

'My mum's parents threatened to cut her out of the will. Couldn't have her marrying a penniless Polish immigrant.'

'We have a safe in the house, I can—'

'But she didn't care. They married anyway, and she lost out on *all...that...money*.'

Willow squeezed the trigger again, the high-pitched whine impossibly loud in the hushed bunker. Judith gripped the baseball bat in both hands and swung it, telegraphing the move way in advance. It was a rookie mistake, one that Willow saw often from the young dancers at CB's, their moves calculated and obvious. She stepped back, easily dodging the blow, and stole the bat from Judith, hurling it across the room.

'*Five* hundred thousand,' stammered the woman. '*One million!*'

The drill roared again.

'Neither of them cared, though. They had the one thing money couldn't buy,' said Willow. She paused. 'They had *love*.'

Judith looked at her for a long time. The room fell silent. Judith's face crumpled, and Willow thought she was about to cry.

'Love?' said Judith. She started to laugh. '*Love?*' Her laughter grew louder and louder until her whole body shook, her shoulders bouncing with hilarity. She stopped abruptly, her eyes glancing at the power drill.

'I'd rather be rich,' she said coldly.

'Fuck your money,' said Willow. She thrust the drill into Judith's face. The woman screamed as the drill bit tore through her cheek, twisting the skin like a whirlpool, tightening until the flesh ripped and tiny strips spun off in all directions. Willow, grimacing like a lunatic, wrenched the drill from Judith's face, blood spiralling across the walls, then plunged it back in, penetrating the side of her skull. Judith screamed, but Willow kept pushing, the metal grinding against bone. There was a hideous splitting sound as smoke rose from Judith's mutilated face. Something cracked, and the drill shot forwards. Willow kept her finger on the trigger, driving the power tool on until she met resistance from the brick wall.

Judith's jaw dropped open and hung there, slack and hopeless, hot blood gushing down her chin. Her eyes rolled up into their sockets until only the bloodshot whites were visible.

When Willow finally let go, Judith Chalmers remained slumped against the wall, the drill pinning her there, most of it hidden by the sagging remains of her face.

'I'm not a killer,' she said, but she knew it wasn't true.

She had killed, and would kill again.

39

HEAVY FOOTSTEPS RESOUNDED THROUGHOUT THE CORRIDORS that honeycombed the bunker.

They had heard her.

Whether it had been Judith's screams or the screeching buzz of the drill, Willow would never know, but now they came for her. How far had they gotten, dragging that mutilated corpse? How long until they entered the room and caught her staring dumbly at the door?

The footsteps grew louder. She moved to run, but what if they were just outside? She was tired and sore and bleeding and maybe a little mad. If they gave chase, they would surely catch her.

No, she needed to be the one stalking *them.*

The element of surprise.

She hastened towards the locker and threw open the door. Taking a deep breath, she stuffed herself inside, the metal raw against her skin. It was a tight squeeze, but a risk she had to take. They would expect her to run, and she was through running.

She closed the door behind her, encasing herself in the

cold, metal coffin. Seconds later, the men thudded into the room. Willow could hear them through the thin slats on the locker door.

'Judith!' cried Jeremy.

'*Fanculo*,' murmured Vinnie. They took slow steps towards the ruin of Judith, displayed on the wall like a poorly hung painting.

'That little *bitch*,' said Jeremy.

'Where is she?' said Vinnie, a trace of fear in his usually placid tone. 'She's gone.'

'She'll never find her way out,' said Jeremy. 'She's badly injured.' He didn't sound angry. In fact, Willow thought he was crying.

'Come on,' shouted Vinnie, 'If she escapes we're fucked!'

'She won't escape. She's just a foolish girl.'

'She's dangerous.'

'And so are we,' said Jeremy, composing himself. 'You ever go fox hunting, Vincent?'

'No sir.'

'Well, first time for everything,' he sighed. 'Grab a crossbow from the locker and let's kill ourselves a wild animal.'

Willow's heart stopped. The locker.

The fucking locker.

Her fingers found the latch on the inside of the door and pressed down on it. She heard Vinnie walking closer, his shape blocking the light that forced its way in through the slats. The lock rattled as he turned the handle. The latch raised, and Willow pushed back.

'Fucking thing's stuck,' said Vinnie. He tried again, harder this time, and Willow jabbed a finger in between the latch and the door, the metal squashing her digit like a vice. She closed her eyes, tears running down her cheeks, as unmentionable agony seared up her arm. She wanted to scream in pain as Vinnie again turned the handle, the metal bar raising and catching on her finger. Her fingernail cracked and she bit down hard, grinding her teeth. The nail splintered, and now the only thing preventing the door from opening was the soft pink skin of her fingertip wedged in between the two metal pieces.

'What's taking you so long?' said Jeremy.

'I can't get it open!'

'So leave it then! Use your bare hands, Vincent. We'll make a man of you yet.'

The pressure on Willow's finger abated as Vinnie released the handle and turned his back to the locker.

'If I catch her,' he said obsequiously, 'may I have her?'

'You can do whatever you want to her, Vincent, as long as it's slow and painful and you clean up after yourself. Now hurry along.'

They left the room.

Willow pulled her finger from the lock, clenching her fist tight, nursing the throbbing digit. She thought for sure she would pass out. How much more could she take? She was no stranger to pain — the owner of Le Boudoir had once made her dance six nights in a row with a broken ankle — but the human body had its limits.

So does the mind, she thought, but it was too late to do anything about *that*.

She peered through the slats at the empty room, then opened the door and abandoned her hiding place. The gurney lay overturned, the weapons and tools littering the floor. Judith remained pinned to the wall. Willow turned and looked at her, expecting to feel remorse, or horror, or even joy.

She felt nothing.

Life is cheap, but Rolexes are expensive.

Only the industrial vibration of the generator filled the silence as Willow crept towards the door. She peered out at the empty corridor, dotted with anonymous doorways, the lightbulbs concealed behind metal bars.

A light flashed, and Willow tensed. It was one of them. She lifted the blood-smeared machete from the floor — it had served her well — and held it close to her chest as she left the murder room behind. An odd feeling of regret filtered through her, as if she were abandoning her destiny, or life as she knew it was coming to an end. She supposed in a way it already had, from the moment Jessica Chalmers had appeared ghost-like from that alleyway and destroyed Willow's life. But she also knew it had given her purpose, and she would not rest until those responsible joined the legion of corpses that festered beneath their feet.

She clung to the walls of the tunnel, glancing nervously around. Had the two men split up? She hoped so. It was her only chance.

Out of nowhere she thought of Cat, poor, innocent Cat, in the wrong place at the wrong time.

It should have been me.

She blinked away tears. There was no time to cry. Perhaps there never would be again. Light shone from a tunnel that forked off to the right, and a nearby door slid open. She froze as a rat scampered past her, its pink tail trailing. The light grew brighter, someone getting closer. She slipped into a doorway, concealing herself in the shadows as the torchlight flared by the door, briefly illuminating the contents of the room, several desks and cobweb-strewn chairs in neglected disarray. Then the beam passed by, stealthy footsteps echoing away from her. She poked her head round and saw a shadowy figure lurching down the corridor, guided by the flashlight.

Jeremy Chalmers. He was alone. Her fingers closed around the handle of the machete.

This was it. This was her chance.

She edged forwards, and then a coarse hand closed over her mouth, clamping it shut, dragging her backwards into the gloom. She squirmed violently, but her attacker locked her in a death-grip, their arm snaking around her neck.

'Got you,' said Vinnie.

He loosened his grip, and thrust her headfirst into the wall. Willow's vision exploded in a brilliant white light, the machete dropping from her stunned hand. She balanced precariously, desperate to maintain her balance, until Vinnie kicked her legs out from under her and she slammed to the floor, jolting her shoulder.

'I told you,' whispered Vinnie, 'I'm too smart for you.'

She tried to get up, but he booted her in the ribs. Moaning, she rolled onto her back, dragging herself away from him, but she was too slow, and he lashed out with a wicked kick to her thigh.

'Damn women,' he said. 'Always sticking your nose in where it doesn't belong.'

He knelt by Willow and lifted her by the jaw.

'Can't just do what you're told.'

He threw her head back and it smacked off the hard floor. Willow ebbed in and out of consciousness. She felt Vinnie climb on top of her, sitting across her belly, reopening the scalpel wounds. The pain brought her round again, snapping her back to reality from the brink of blessed, merciful concussion. A dazzling light blazed into her eyes, and she turned away from the intensity.

'Now it's finally time for the climax,' said Vinnie, as he

pointed the clunky digital camcorder at Willow's bruised, swollen face, using his knees to pin her arms. 'You're not so beautiful now, you whore,' he chuckled. 'That's the thing with pretty girls...they all look the same after a beating.'

She tried to spit at him, but her strength abandoned her, and the bloody spittle dribbled down her chin instead.

'I'm going to kill you,' she managed to say, forcing a smile.

'That's it,' said Vinnie. 'Smile for the camera.' He reached up onto the filthy desk and grabbed a pair of rusted hand-scissors. Willow could see nothing, the gleaming light on top of the camera blinding her. She first became aware of the scissors when Vinnie opened them wide and touched one of the blades to her cheek.

'Don't move, Rough Stuff,' he said with undisguised glee. 'Or my hand might slip.'

He ran the blade in ever-decreasing circles around her eye socket, scratching at her skin until the blade ended up pressing into the corner of her eye.

'Try not to blink,' he laughed, running the sharp metal along her lower eyelid. Willow lay rigid, the sensation of the scissors scraping her eyes causing her stomach to spasm grotesquely. Vinnie laughed again, a rancid coughing sound.

Guided by Vinnie's steady hand, the tip of the blade rasped down her face, past her nose and down to her mouth. He paused there a moment, using the scissors to pull her lips open, forcing the revolting blade between her teeth. The metal jarred against them and she reluctantly opened her mouth, tasting the corroded metal on her tongue. All the while the camera rolled, recording to old-fashioned tape in what probably amounted to some twisted aesthetic decision.

'Should I cut out your tongue like I did to Lina?' sneered Vinnie. 'No. I want to hear you beg for your life. It's more fun that way.'

He shuffled uncomfortably, moving further down her body so that he sat across her hips. The camera moved down to her chest, the glaring light no longer in her eyes. The scissors followed.

Down they went, tracing a shallow line over Willow's chin, her neck, then onto the swell of her breast.

'How about I start with these?' said Vinnie, and Willow felt the blade nudge the soft bud of her nipple. Her eyes widened in horror. 'Ah, that got a reaction! That's what I want to see. The fear!'

She raised her head as best she could and saw Vinnie holding the scissors in one hand, the camera in the other, his eye pressed to the chunky viewfinder, his grin spreading like the plague. She imagined herself as Vinnie saw her, black and white like a silent movie, a single red dot flashing in the corner, just another part of the rich tapestry of Vinnie's art.

Murder is art.

Show me.

Play those dead girl blues, Rough Stuff.

She looked past the lens — that cyclopean metal eye — and saw the heavy construction of the camera, the chunky metal body.

They don't make 'em like that anymore, she thought.

'Hey Vinnie,' she croaked. He pulled the scissors away and looked at her through the camera. 'Ready for your close-up?'

'Huh?' he said, but he didn't have time to finish the thought. Willow pulled her arm back, then thrust it into the lens.

Vinnie screamed as the viewfinder pierced his eye. He sat for one dreadful second, the viewfinder inserted halfway into the socket, bilious white goo dribbling down the black metal. Then he rolled off Willow, holding the camera steady, whimpering in pain. In a burst of maniac strength she followed him, grabbing the camera with both hands and hauling the device free, leaving a gaping red hole in Vinnie's wretched face. Unidentifiable stringy goop hung soggily down his cheek, and he stared at her with his one good eye, his face contorted with rage.

Willow raised the camera above her head — these old things were surprisingly heavy — and brought it down on his skull. One of the two cracked, but she wasn't sure which. She slammed it down again, clubbing the Italian across the face.

'Beg me, motherfucker,' roared Willow, the camera soaked with blood that ran down her hands and arms. Vinnie tried to crawl away, but Willow smashed the camera on the back of his head. 'Fucking beg me to make it quick!'

She rolled him onto his back and took a long look at the gruesome shambles of his face, his remaining eye swamped with thick brown blood.

'Please,' he whispered, as Willow raised the camera above her head. He looked pathetic, like the snivelling, rancid piece of shit he was.

'This is for Jessica,' she said.

She closed her eyes, listening to the violent impact as metal met skull for the last time. It sounded like that time she had dropped one of Cat's fancy china plates on the kitchen floor, only muted by soft, torn flesh. She let go of the camera and it fell to the side with a dull clang.

After a while, she opened her eyes and looked at the soggy, grisly mess of Vinnie's face. It reminded her of the flattened, screaming horror from the video, broken shards of bone piercing through skin, grey matter leaking onto the floor.

His mouth opened but emitted no scream, just an exhausted, feeble rattle.

His chest rose, and then fell, rose, and then fell...and then rose no more.

40

SHE HAD NO TIME TO THINK. THE FLASHLIGHT BEAM DANCED across the corridor walls, heading in her direction. Jeremy must have heard the struggle. She grabbed the discarded scissors and dashed from the room.

'Hey!'

She turned. Jeremy stood a hundred feet away, the torchlight trained on her. She froze, clutching the scissors, neither of them moving. Slowly, Jeremy raised his hand and pointed it at her, and Willow instantly understood. The gunshot rang out, and she started to run, the noise deafening in the enclosed space. The bullet ricocheted off the wall, showering sparks over her blood-caked body, her bare feet slapping off the ground, stones and shrapnel jabbing at her unprotected soles like thousands of tiny needles.

She tried a random door, but it wouldn't open. Jeremy fired again, the whole corridor lighting up. The shot was way off-target, and she saw he was running towards her as he fired. Her only chance was to keep ahead of him. Normally, that wouldn't be a problem. She was young, fit and reasonably healthy — apart from the cigarettes — and

Jeremy was in his fifties or sixties. But she bled as she ran, from her feet to her stomach to her nose, and a harsh ache drummed in her head. How far did the tunnel go, and where was the exit? She didn't even know what floor she was on.

Another shot thundered through the corridor and Willow roared as the bullet grazed her thigh, shearing skin off her leg, blood flowing from the ruptured area. She dropped to one knee for a moment, and Jeremy took aim. This time the projectile rippled past her face. She couldn't stop, not for a second. How many shots had he fired?

Ignoring the agony in her thigh, Willow powered through the pain and hobbled on. She rounded a corner, her hand pressed to the wound, the blood hot on her skin. The lights were out in this section, and a chilling void loomed before her. She kept running, every step flaring painful twinges through her limbs.

Ahead of her was a door, cool blue light pouring through the crack in the frame. She headed for it, Jeremy's heavy steps pounding after her. She saw Lina's corpse lying neglected on the polythene sheet like a slumbering ghost, and leapt over it.

'You can't run forever,' he called after her, though he sounded out-of-breath. Was it her imagination, or were his steps slowing? The gun went off again, the crack of the shot splitting Willow's eardrums, and she pushed on, nearing the door, reaching it, seizing the handle and throwing it open. She carried on through, her feet finding nothing, no floor, no stairs, just a great yawning abyss that her momentum propelled her into.

Her grip tightened on the handle as she tumbled into the dark, grasping for dear life, swinging out over the emptiness beneath her. The scissors fell from her hand as she threw her arm up in a last-ditch attempt to hang on. She found the handle and hung there, the door opening and slamming her into the wall, her feet dangling. Her sweat-coated hands slipped, losing purchase on the thin metal cylinder. She tried to kick off from the wall, to swing the door back, but it was heavy, her legs too weak from the exertion. Slipping another inch, she hooked the fingers of her left hand over the handle, her right hand clinging on. It was only then, when she knew she could not get back towards the corridor — that she was stuck here — that the smell hit her, the acrid, pungent stench of age-old death, of rotting, fetid carcasses piled high.

She had found the area where they dumped the bodies.

She didn't want to look, but she did. There, fifty feet below her, were the corpses of all those who had lost their lives in this evil place. There were untold numbers of cadavers in various stages of decomposition, the flesh green and purple, limbs entangled or unattached. The damage to their bodies rendered many of them almost inhuman, a savage mass grave of horror and despair. Willow screamed, and screamed, and screamed. She could swear the heads were turning to watch her, the blank, dead eyes beckoning her down to join them.

She tore her gaze away, looking instead at the collapsed staircase that had once led down to the lower level, this stinking abattoir where the dead slept their fitful and restless sleep.

'Looks like you found it,' said Jeremy Chalmers, standing in the doorway, hands on his knees, drawing in long breaths. He smiled at her. 'How many can you count?'

'Help me,' shrieked Willow. 'Please, help me up! Please! Dear god, please help me!' She was unaware of how manic she sounded, or of the frenzied expression on her face, or of the way her legs kicked feverishly as her hands slid further down the handle towards hysterical oblivion.

Jeremy leaned against the doorframe, pretending to mull over the idea of helping her. He pulled the gun from his pocket.

'No,' he said. 'I don't think I will.'

'Please,' sobbed Willow, the anger leaving her, replaced by a terrifying resignation.

'You killed my wife,' said Jeremy. He was devoid of emotion, a mannequin, a devil. His eyes narrowed to slits like cuts from a razor blade.

'You made me do it!'

'We all have the capacity to kill,' said Jeremy in a flat tone. 'Some are just better at it than others.' He looked at Willow. His voice cracked. '*You* are better than most.'

One of Willow's hands slipped. Three fingers wrapped claw-like over the handle were all that remained between her and the pit. She was strong — her years working the pole had seen to that — but she couldn't hold on forever. She kicked out again, and the door swung away from the wall, creaking menacingly as it did so, before stopping half-way. Jeremy now had a clear view of her, the easiest shot of his life. He pointed the gun and hesitated, perhaps debating whether it would be more entertaining to see how long she lasted. Behind him a searing bright light glowed, strange and unearthly. Jeremy didn't seem to notice, even though the lustrous radiance dwarfed the shadows, casting them out.

He cocked his head and looked at her, puzzled, as Willow stared beyond him into the celestial glow. It was as bright as the sun, yet it didn't hurt her eyes. If anything, the light soothed her, imbued her with strength. Within the light, a dark shape flitted in and out of existence in the blink of an eye, gaining in size, forming into something resembling a human.

'No one's coming to help you,' said Jeremy.

The shadowy figure was close now, closer, then suddenly there, right *there* behind Jeremy, one long arm outstretched, a finger pointing at Jeremy Chalmers.

Willow smiled. She knew who the shadow man was. She recognised him from dreams and faded memories, and though she hadn't seen him in about fifteen years, he was exactly as she remembered.

'What are you looking at?' asked Jeremy, but Willow couldn't hear him. Time had stopped.

'Dad,' she said, and Jakub Zulawski looked at his daughter and smiled. He pressed his fingers to the back of Jeremy's head.

'I love you,' she thought he said.

Jeremy started to turn, and then his head burst like a ripe tomato, splattering across the walls with a deafening report. His body remained standing for what felt like forever, swaying on stiff legs, arms dangling by its sides, before toppling backwards into the charnel pit without making a sound, the landing cushioned by hundreds of soft, decaying corpses.

Jakub Zulawski leaned out and offered a hand, and Willow gratefully took it.

She looked at her father and smiled.

'I love you too, dad.'

She closed her eyes.

41

'JESUS CHRIST, WILLOW,' SAID CB.

She sat at his feet, naked and drenched in blood, looking up at him with her piercing blue eyes. CB clumsily removed his jacket and draped it over her shoulders.

'Are you okay?' he asked. 'Do you know where you are?' He sounded out of breath, panicked.

'Dad,' she said, a beatific expression on her face.

'No, love, it's Joe. It's CB Joe.'

She stared at him as if at an angel. 'Oh yeah,' she said vacantly. 'It's CB Joe.'

'That's right, love. That's right.' He put his hand on her shoulder. 'You're safe now.' He got to his feet and took a cautious step towards the doorway, surveying the mass of bodies, recoiling from the smell. 'My god,' he said, shaking his head.

'My father was here,' said Willow dreamily. 'He saved me.'

CB nodded, backing away from the edge. 'You're going to be okay, Will. I promise.'

She looked at the gun clutched in his hand. 'Are you going to kill me?'

He seemed surprised to find he was still holding it, and tucked it away in his pocket. 'No. I'm gonna get you out of here.'

He sat beside her and Willow reached up and wiped a tear from his bristly cheek.

'Don't cry,' she said. It was odd, like seeing your father cry.

Your father.

She supposed CB was as close to a dad as she'd ever have.

'You can't choose your family,' she said idly.

CB wasn't listening. 'I had no choice,' he mumbled. 'I couldn't say anything.'

'It's okay, I understand.' She rested against his burly arm.

'No, you don't, Willow,' he said. 'I wanted to help you, I really did. I tried to warn you, but it was too late. They took my daughter.'

'Your daughter?' Willow felt an absurd pang of jealousy.

'Aye. They kidnapped her and made me string you along. It was all a game to them...all a fucking *game*. They said they'd kill her if I helped you.' He put his head in his hands. 'I'm so sorry.'

'How did you know I was here?' said Willow.

'I didn't.' He cleared his throat. 'Listen, Willow, I dunno how to say this. You know I'm not good at this sort of thing. Your, uh, flatmate is dead.'

'They told me,' she said simply.

CB nodded. 'I was on the phone to her when it happened. I heard her die. Now, I don't have much, Will. No money, no wife, a failing business. But I have two things. A daughter that I love, and integrity. Not much, granted, but a little. Enough that I can sleep at night. After they murdered your flatmate, I drove to The Sunset with a loaded gun. I was going to find my wee girl, and then, I think, I was going to kill Vinnie. I was out of my mind.'

'He's dead.'

'What?'

Tears sprang to her eyes, and she buried her face in CB's shoulder, soaking his shirt.

'I killed him.'

He put his arm around her. 'You did what you had to do.'

'I'm a murderer.'

'Bollocks,' said CB. 'You're a survivor. I'm just glad you're alive. When I arrived at The Sunset, the police were there. I saw them removing a body.' He paused, swallowed hard. 'I figured it was you, after I sent you there.' He looked down at his feet. 'I thought you were dead, Willow.'

She regarded him blankly. 'I wish I was.'

'Don't say that. Don't *ever* say that.'

'They made me kill a girl,' she said, pointing over to the decapitated body, the head turned towards the wall. 'They made me do *that*.'

She wept, and CB held her for a long time. She felt safe in his arms.

'It's over now,' he said. 'They can't hurt you anymore.' He stroked her matted hair, and when she raised her head to look at him she left a bloody faceprint on his shirt-sleeve.

'I want to go home,' she said.

CB forced a smile. 'Me too.' He forced himself up, using a pipe for leverage. 'If we follow the sound of the generator, we'll find the way out.'

He extended a hand and Willow took it, almost collapsing into him as he helped her up. Blood dripped from her nose and belly, and she could only see out of one eye. She thought of the scissors pressing into her eyeball and retched, falling to her knees. CB held her as she vomited. She tried to stand and shuddered in pain.

'Take it slow,' said CB. 'My car's outside.'

Willow crouched, staring into a pool of vomit that was mostly blood, the smell an improvement over the pit of corpses.

'How did you know?' she whispered, staggering to her feet.

'Know what, love?'

She let out an exhausted sigh. 'How did you know to come here?'

'Vinnie,' he said. 'He used to shoot here. Years back, before all this business began, he made pornos and sold them through his shop. Quite good ones, actually. One time I asked where he shot them, and he invited me on set for a day, simple as that.' He noticed her startled expression. 'Christ, I don't mean I was *in* one. Nae fucker would want to see *that*.'

Willow almost smiled. 'So you came here to kill Vinnie?'

CB shook his head. 'Aye, but not just that. I came here to look for my daughter.' His voice quivered. 'I came here to look for Lina.'

Lina.

Willow's blood ran cold. She stumbled woozily into the wall, trying to speak but finding words difficult to summon.

'You okay?' asked CB, and the concern in his voice broke Willow's heart.

She swallowed hard, the room spinning.

'What was her name? Your daughter...what was her name?'

He looked at her a moment, puzzled. 'It's Lina. Listen,

I'm going to take you back to the car, then I'm coming back in to search the place. She has to be—'

He stopped. His face fell, darkening. Neither of them spoke, silence chilling the air. She stared at the body, and CB turned to look. He let go of Willow, and she collapsed against the wall, sliding down it.

'No,' he said, shuffling zombie-like down the corridor. 'No...' He no longer sounded like CB. Gone was the brusque manner, the matter-of-fact, sarcastic tone. It was the voice of a man who has lost everything. His joints popped as he knelt by the corpse, reaching for the head, turning it towards him.

Willow drew her knees up and hugged them.

'They made me do it,' she said, unsure if he was listening.

CB sat heavily, making a low moan like an injured creature dying alone in a forest.

'They made me do it,' she said again, but this time she was definitely talking to herself.

CB lifted his daughter's head and cradled it in his arms.

'Lina,' he said.

Willow stared blankly at the wall.

'They made me do it,' she whispered.

42

At four in the morning, CB emerged from the bunker. If anyone had seem him, they would have thought it a ghoulish sight. His movements were slow and painful, and he carried something under his arm.

A severed human head.

Laying it carefully on the grass, he dragged the metal cylinder back into place, covering the hole. The act exhausted him, but he didn't stop. He wiped sweat from his brow, and gathered sticks and leaves in his aching arms, placing them ceremonially on the entrance.

Once it was hidden, he picked up Lina and walked somnambulantly to his car. He put his daughter in the passenger seat, ran his hand through her hair, then popped the trunk.

The can of gasoline was almost full, the liquid sloshing around as he carried it to Vinnie's car. There, he doused the interior of the vehicle, leaving a trail of the flammable liquid all the way to his own car. He climbed in, leaving the door open.

Tired — so very, very tired — CB fumbled in his pocket

for a smoke. He lit up, inhaled, and dropped the lighter onto the gasoline. The trail caught fire immediately. CB slammed his door and gunned the engine. He saw a bright flash in the rearview mirror, but didn't turn round. There was nothing to see there.

He didn't know where he was going, but it didn't matter.

He had no place to go.

Around seven, the sun started to rise, golden rays bursting from behind the treetops, dispersing the early morning mist.

It was going to be a beautiful, brisk autumn day. He could see the bloodstains on his hands, and wished he could wash them away. Every so often, he would glance at the passenger seat, where Lina's head rolled back and forth, and imagine himself being stopped by the police. He laughed softly to himself, picturing the officer's face when he pulled them over and found Lina beside him in the car.

'Call off the search,' said CB with the faint trace of a smile. 'I found her.'

He had wanted to bring her body, but when he tried to lift it his strength abandoned him. Cannonball Joe had never felt so old and weak.

It was fine. He had her head, and that was enough.

Together again, they drove through fields and forests, until they arrived at the coast. CB pulled into an empty parking area and sat a moment, thinking. He slipped his shoes off, picked up Lina, and got out of the car.

The sand felt glorious between his toes. When was the last time he had set foot on a beach? Probably when Lina was a toddler. She always loved the beach.

He carried her into the sea, the freezing water lapping at his waist, and cleaned the blood from her face, her hair, even the section of spinal column that protruded so unattractively from her neck. He washed *that* until the bone gleamed white.

Afterwards, they sat drying on the sand together, watching the sun rise and shimmer across the waves. He stroked Lina's hair and told her he loved her, and that he was sorry he had been too late.

She told him she forgave him.

Then, when the sun was up and the time felt right, he took out his gun, placed the barrel in his mouth, and pulled the trigger.

43

In her dream, her parents were alive. They had been walking along a rocky beach, the three of them, the sun bursting over the horizon.

She had stopped to look, gripped by the awesome beauty of nature, but her parents kept strolling, hand-in-hand, not waiting. When she tried to catch up, she couldn't seem to close the distance. They got further and further away, until they were little more than specks, the sand turning to wet cement, impeding her progress. She passed an old man sitting on the beach. He waved at her as she ran, but she didn't recognise him. His face was covered in wrinkles, the sand piled up around him like he had been sitting there forever.

She didn't wave back.

~

One eye flickered open. Willow lay still, unable to move.

'Dad?'

No...not her father. He was dead, had been for years. She

tried to recall her dream, but already it was fading from her subconscious, elusive and forgotten.

'CB?'

Yes. That was it. CB had saved her, had lifted her to safety. So where was he now? She wanted to shout his name, but her voice was nearly gone, and she choked, the motion sending vibrations of pain shooting through her body.

At least one thing was certain. She was alive. My god, she was still alive.

With aching slowness, she raised one arm, touching her fingertips gently to her face, not recognising herself. Everywhere she pressed was sore, one cheek so inflamed it covered her eye. She slid her hand down her body, coming to rest on her stomach, finding the nasty cuts from the scalpel. The blood was dry and crispy, but the damage could have been worse. A lot worse.

She lay awhile, eyes closed, a blinding pain in her head. Breathing was difficult, her nostrils choked with dried blood, and something jabbed into her back, a loose bedspring in a lumpy mattress. Where was CB? He must be coming back for her...she needed him.

And then she remembered Lina.

'Oh god,' she spluttered, forcing her decrepit limbs to move. She attempted to sit, screaming internally from the pain, but her hand slipped through a soft crack in the ground, or whatever she was lying on.

Something was very, very wrong.

She forced her eyes open, averting them from the fluorescent strip-light far above, and saw the broken staircase that once led to the upper floor, the door now firmly closed.

She spread her fingers, investigating her surroundings, though deep down, she already knew where she was...and what she was lying on.

'No, no, no, no, no,' she said, each time her voice gaining in pitch, her heart pounding, her stomach tightening, the panic rising, rising, *rising*, her hands shaking, adrenaline or terror alive in her body like thousands of insects crawling through her veins, the throbbing headache reverberating throughout her entire being.

She touched a human face, turned and looked at it, the flesh discoloured, the jaw missing, the eyes just hollow sockets. She screamed and tried to shuffle away and a mad thought flashed through her mind, an old woman's voice saying, 'It's corpses all the way down,' and then she found herself sinking into them, *between* them, the putrefying bodies washing over her like giant maggots, feeding on her, *crushing* her with their revolting wet bodies. The more she struggled, the deeper she went, until she could no longer see the light. She tried to scream but her tongue brushed something old and dead and rotten and she gagged and sank further into the mass, thrusting her hands out, digging her nails into dead flesh and dragging herself up, her head emerging between the decomposing bodies.

She looked to the doorway floating above her, impossibly out of reach, and stretched a hand out towards it.

'They made me do it!' she screamed, and then the bodies tumbled over her again and everything went dark.

So very, very dark.

AFTERWORD

Dead Girl Blues was conceived as a *giallo*. For those unfamiliar with the term, it refers to a series of Italian murder mystery films that combined sex, fashion, and violence with a typical Agatha Christie-style *whodunnit* plot. The golden age of the *giallo* was in the early 70s, spearheaded by directors such as Dario Argento, Mario Bava and Sergio Martino. The term is derived from a series of thrillers published in Italy since the 1930s, easily recognisable thanks to their striking yellow covers, much like the one you're holding in your hands right now. *Giallo* is the Italian word for yellow, which explains why the term has also come to mean *thriller*.

The finished book deviates a lot from your typical *giallo*. The films are often notable for their stylish, fashionable aesthetic, something Scotland is not exactly world-renowned for, unless your idea of high fashion is a grey tracksuit tucked into white socks.

It also created the challenge of promoting a book written in a genre most people haven't heard of, which is why I'm coining the term Slasher Noir.

You read it here first, people.

As usual, a big thanks to my lovely wife Heather for her support and design skills. I'll write a nice book you can enjoy reading one of these days, I promise!

Cheers to Boris the pug for keeping me sane during long evenings of writing.

Thank you to Connor for his incredible cover art. He absolutely nailed the painting, and I still can't stop staring at it.

Big shout out to Bradley, Mike and Steve for their invaluable feedback. My books would not be what they are without the help of my beta readers.

And lastly, thanks once again to you, dear reader. Without you, I'm just a weirdo writing a lot of nonsense while a pug stares at me, yawning, his eyes judging me, demanding to know if it's time for dinner yet.

Thank you for reading. You make it all worthwhile.

This book was written while listening to the following soundtracks.

Berto Pisano — *Interrabang*
Bruno Nicolai — *All The Colours of the Dark*
Bruno Nicolai — *...And Then There Were None*
Bruno Nicolai — *The Case of the Bloody Iris*
Bruno Nicolai — *The Case of the Scorpion's Tail*
Bruno Nicolai — *Eyeball*
Bruno Nicolai — *The Night Evelyn Came Out of the Grave*
Bruno Nicolai — *The Red Queen Kills Seven Times*
Daniele Patucchi — *Sex of the Witch*
Ennio Morricone — *The Cold Eyes of Fear*
Ennio Morricone — *The Fifth Cord*

Ennio Morricone — *Forbidden Photos of a Lady Above Suspicion*
Ennio Morricone — *A Lizard in a Woman's Skin*
Ennio Morricone — *My Dear Killer*
Ennio Morricone — *Short Night of the Glass Dolls*
Ennio Morricone — *Spasmo*
Ennio Morricone — *What Have You Done to Solange?*
Francis Lai — *Anima Persa*
Gianfranco Plenizio — *The Cat in Heat*
Guido and Maurizio De Angelis — *Torso*
Nora Orlandi — *The Sweet Body of Deborah*
Nora Orlandi — *The Strange Vice of Mrs Wardh*
Stelvio Cipriani — *Death Walks on High Heels*
Stelvio Cipriani — *The Iguana With the Tongue of Fire*
Stelvio Cipriani — *The Killer is on the Phone*
Teo Usuelli — *Amuck!*

ABOUT THE AUTHOR

David Sodergren lives in Scotland with his wife Heather and his best friend, Boris the Pug. Growing up, he was the kind of kid who collected rubber skeletons and lived for horror movies.

Not much has changed since then.

His first novel, The Forgotten Island, was published in 2018. This was followed by Night Shoot, a brutal throwback to the early 80s slasher movie cycle, in 2019.

2020 will be Sodergren's biggest year yet, with two new horror novels being published. Dead Girl Blues is a slasher-noir mystery, and it will be followed by a return to full-blown supernatural horror before the end of the year.

Find David at the following locations —

twitter.com/paperbacksnpugs

instagram.com/paperbacksandpugs

COMING SOON

Maggie's Grave

Printed in Great Britain
by Amazon

81426276R00160